The Life of Jo

THE LIFE OF JO

A Harrington Friends Story

Tamara Martin

The Henry Mayberry Group
Adelaide

First published in Australia 2019 by The Henry Mayberry Group

www.tamaramartinauthor.com

National Library of Australia Cataloguing-In-Publication data

Martin,Tamara, 1973-

The Fall of Jaz / Tamara Martin

1st ed.

ISBN: 978-0-6483743-5-0 (pbk.)

Edited by Cathleen Ross

Cover Design: Kristyn McQuiggan, Drop Dead Designs

Also by Tamara Martin

Alexandra Deen – A Harrington Family Story
Mrs May's Tea and Toast – A Harrington Family Story
The Rise of Jaz – A Harrington Family Christmas
The Fall of Jaz – A Harrington Family Story

Almost Perfect – A Dystopian Love Story

Running From Me

For my fellow muskateers

Brooke Dell-Sewell
&
Kaye Chaloner

Thank you for taking this incredible journey with me
and
For all the wine, laughs, support and the beautiful
friendship you've brought on the ride xo

Chapter 1

You think you have all the time in the world to do all the things you dream of. Get married, have babies, travel the world. You talk about it over Friday night noodles. We should go to Paris or Munich or South Africa next year, you say as you casually sip your Alicante. You talk dream wedding dresses and reception decor with your girlfriends, share the inspiration pictures you find on Facebook and Insta amid a flurry of approving hearts.

You spy an errant child in a café over brunch and declare: 'When Benny and I have children...' You talk wistfully about the family you'll have together in bed during those dreamy post coital conversations. You imagine the overwater bungalow you'll honeymoon in on a faraway island. You fall asleep imagining the ring he'll buy you and how he'll propose on one knee amid New Year's Eve fireworks or a lavish, romantic picnic at one of your favourite wineries.

But all you really have is now. These very moments before you. Because in the next, in a single blink behind your rose-coloured glasses, your whole world could be gone. Ripped from your trembling hands while you're serving someone their morning cup of French Earl Grey. I know because I had the ground beneath my feet shaken, taken out from under me until there was nothing. I lost it all, all the dreams, the beautiful future and the love of my life.

It's been 3 years since I lost Benny. Well, three years, eleven weeks and six days to be exact. I'd give you the hours too but everyone's already watching me like a hawk, waiting for me to fall apart and crumble in the corner. But I'm not going to fall apart. I'm fine. I'm working. I'm breathing. I'm living. But they, my parents, Ainsley, even Mrs Donovan, had an expectation of my recovery, an imaginary timeline for my grief and I wasn't following their schedule.

I should have finished grieving by now, been moving on to some imagined, predetermined future. You see people on the telly do it all the time. Their loved one's body is barely cold and off they go traipsing back down the aisle. But no one knows their story. No one knows their path or how they got there and it's no one's business. People should just let people walk their path the way their heart dictates and if that means another trip down the aisle before the sun's rounded the earth, then that's their business. Just like me not hopping about the loud, hot, sweaty clubs on the weekend or swiping right on Tinder while watching the Voice on a Tuesday night should be my business.

It's not like I'm in a corner crying into my soup. I'm fine. I'm getting by. Getting up every day. Doing what needs doing, even with a smile but everyone watches me anyway, treads carefully, speaks cautiously like I'm a fragile child.

In the beginning, my parents begged me to come home and get myself together, to think about what I wanted to do next, but I wasn't sure I'd have gotten off the farm a second time. They've almost given up now. All I get is the weekend invitations, just come for a night, the cows are about to calve, you always loved that bit, mum would say. But I didn't love the calving cows. I didn't love any of it. My brother loved the cows. He loved it all. That's why he stayed and I left. They're mostly resigned to their loss of control now, loss of the daughter they once knew and the grandchildren they were expecting. Almost come to terms with this other person that doesn't use the university degree she fought so hard for, who doesn't live in the lovely house with the lovely man she was going to marry.

They don't think I see the defeated look on their faces, the pity, but I do. I'm sad; I'm not stupid. But I don't know what they're worried about. I'm doing what I want to do. There is no next. They don't understand, I'm happy here at Mrs May's, working in the café, it's enough. It's not the life I'd planned. Not the life I would have chosen when I ran from the farm with nothing but an eager wave as I hightailed it onto the city bound bus but it's a good life and I'm fine. Fine enough anyway and that works for me.

Maybe it was this place, Mrs May's? There was something about it. It was in the air and walls. It lived in the café downstairs and the rooms upstairs as though Mrs May herself were still here in the place she'd loved, the place she'd lived with her beloved husband Henry Mayberry, where they'd made their son and had fabulous soirees. Whatever it was, there was a peace here, a knowing that everything would be okay.

And every day there was Ainsley. She was saving me with her light and her goodness. Had been, every day since the day

Benny died. She'd given me a place to stay, to recover, to be me. She let me have the apartment above the café when she moved in with Christian. I couldn't have gone back to the house after Benny died. I never did. Ainsley and Christian went and packed up my things.

I could have had the house if I'd wanted it but I couldn't afford it on my own and I didn't want to be there without Benny. His parents sold it and a nice family lived there now. I drove by sometimes. They'd planted roses and daffodils and the little girl rode her bike up and down the driveway. I'd always thought Benny and I would have children and they'd play hopscotch on the driveway or something, but he'd died so we didn't, and now the things Ainsley and Christian had packed up for me now lived downstairs with what was left of Mrs May's personal effects. The café had been a place of salvation for Ainsley when she'd had nothing. Now it was mine.

Speaking of Ainsley... The back door blew shut as she struggled to get herself inside while calling out a yodelling, 'Hello!'

She waddled through to the main café area, her pregnant stomach arriving before the rest of her. I'd told her to stay home, off her feet but she wouldn't listen. If she wasn't careful, I'd be delivering the blasted child on Mrs May's Persian rugs and I'd never hear the end of it from Christian.

'Does Christian know you're here?' I asked as I poured her a peppermint tea.

She groaned as she accepted it, wishing for the caffeine she'd given up to procreate. 'He's not the boss of me, you know.

He's not God. Geez,' she grumbled, leaning against the counter dramatically.

'You can say that because you can alter his mood with your womanly wiles and adorable offspring. What do I have when he comes in here demanding I make you do things as though I have any control over what you do?'

'My womanly wiles?' she laughed with a snort and a hoot. 'There's not much that's particularly wiley about me right now, I feel like a giant potato.'

'The price you pay for creating humans, for which that man only adores you more,' I told her. 'Speaking of which, where is Henry?'

'Day care, thank goodness,' she told me. 'Having a two-year-old and a child about to fall out of your lady parts is not a good combination.'

I laughed but hoped it wasn't about to happen while I was inadvertently in charge of her safety. Henry had it lucky spending the day at his ultra-ritzy day care centre playing in the sandpit and building Lego hotels. The front door opened, letting in another gust of wind.

'Oh, thank goodness,' I cried at the sight of Mrs Donovan. 'Perhaps you could do something about your obstinate daughter?'

'Ainsley, what are you doing?' Mrs Donovan easily scolded as parents do.

'I'm working, Mum,' Ainsley retorted like a petulant child.

'Not today. Sit,' Mrs Donovan commanded, pointing to a booth already occupied by our resident Russian-in-perpetual-mourning.

Mrs Petrov, our resident Russian-in-perpetual-mourning, well, at least we think that is her name, patted Ainsley's hand as though she understood the frustration of becoming redundant to everything else except your bodily needs. Maybe she did. We didn't know a lot about her other than her husband had died, hence the perpetual mourning clothes she wore while she sat in her booth and remembered another life.

'What will I do with that girl?' Mrs Donovan mumbled, coming around the counter and taking the coffee I offered her with a grateful smile. 'She'll be the death of us both if Christian finds out she's here. She should be home resting.'

'Ain't that the truth?' I agreed as Vivi walked in to make the toasties. Making the café's infamous gourmet toasties was Ainsley's job but she couldn't really do much of anything other than annoy everyone when she was about to pop. Vivi, Ainsley's mother's cousin slash best friend, if you can follow that, was filling in, just as she had when Henry was born and every time Ainsley needed to stay home when Henry was sick. I didn't mind because Vivi was a hoot and always had some adventurous tale to tell because she was always doing something she shouldn't be, according to Mrs Donovan, anyway.

Just as the morning rush began to pour in, I sent Christian a message to come and get his wayward wife before she gave birth on the raspberry velvet cushions. Once she was gone, I relaxed and I lost myself in the hustle and bustle, the chatter and stories as I brewed the coffee and the café hummed in lovely synchronicity around me.

We weren't one of those places without personality. I always had a chat with those in front of me as I brewed their coffee and poured their tea. I'd come to know the regulars, made a point to remember what we'd spoken about before, ask them how things had gone but I looked forward to the stories of new customers too. We'd built a community, a warm, safe place for people to be, to take time out of their crazy days. It's what made us successful but also what had kept me sane. The people of this place had held me together and given me something, purpose and focus, when I'd so desperately needed it. They'd become my family, my connection, the grease in my wheels that kept me going when all I'd wanted to do was curl up into a ball and die. When I'd thought there was nothing left for me without Benny, they were here.

Not an hour after Christian had dragged Ainsley away, Kelsey, one of his accountants arrived to say she was there to replace Mrs Donovan because Ainsley had gone into labour. Like Vivi, Kelsey had pitched in and helped out before when she'd been a junior at Christian's father's company. She'd helped Ainsley when Benny died and I was incoherent in her bed upstairs and Christian had taken Kelsey with him when he'd set up his own company. Kelsey had since moved too far up the corporate ladder to be performing barista duties. She said she loved the opportunity to get out of the office, and I couldn't blame her if that was the truth. But unlike me, she thrived in the confines of an office, the hubbub of water cooler confessions and the predictability and comfort of a nine to five, or in her case, probably more like and eight to six. Really, she was just that loyal to Christian and Ainsley, I think. Either way, we loved having her. She'd been dating Ainsley's brother for the last few years so she was part of the family anyway and, like Vivi, always had a fun adventure to share.

'That was a close call,' laughed Vivi as we watched Mrs Donovan scurry around in a fluster, gathering her things before hopping into the car that had brought Kelsey and going to the hospital, promising to keep us updated.

We settled in to an old, familiar routine and the afternoon went by in its usual flurry of customers. I relinquished the coffee machine to Kelsey until she left in the middle of the afternoon after the final rush of the day, followed by our resident Russian-in-perpetual-mourning. Vivi left soon after, headed for her afternoon bus to go home and get ready for a dinner date and then it was just me.

I had a trickle of customers looking for a late afternoon caffeine hit but otherwise I spent some time in a booth with a piece of Mrs Donovan's leftover carrot cake and the latest thriller I'd picked up from the library.

Mum had taken to lecturing me about my book choices, claiming they were too dark and violent but I just wasn't an Austen kind of girl anymore. There was a lot I didn't love anymore. Don't get me wrong, I was doing fine. Ainsley made sure of it. She'd sent me to see her Dr Bailey when Benny had died and I'd been seeing him on occasion since and he'd been great but things like daydreaming and music and funny romantic books hadn't found a place in my new world. Maybe they would someday but it wasn't now. Dr Bailey never seemed too bothered, always seemed to think it was temporary but it bothered Mum and she frowned over the scattered titles whenever she came for a visit.

I finally shut the doors on the dark blustery evening a little while after Christian sent me a photo of his new daughter. I was still smiling when I shrugged into my coat and headed out into the wind through the back door.

I'd inherited Ainsley's powder blue scooter when she'd moved. Christian wasn't having her ride it while pregnant with Henry and with her new family, it was of no use to her. She drove a fancy SUV now that would no doubt protect them if they drove through a war zone. She was a Harrington, that was their way. Today I left the scooter parked under the back verandah sheltered from the wind and the rain, and walked down the alley to the street and headed over to the hospital on foot. It was a little walk but it was nice to feel the wind and the cool air whipping at my face. It was the first real wintery day of the year after a long hot summer that had mostly kept me bound up inside.

I carried the gift I'd been accumulating in readiness, a bright green giraffe and a collection of the prettiest dresses I'd ever seen. I'd had a collection of boys' clothes too, just in case, because we hadn't known what sex the baby would be but I'd return them to the shop Friday night. Ainsley's daughter probably didn't need my collection of dresses. She would be the best-dressed girl in the country if the Harrington's had anything to do with it but I didn't care. I'd thoroughly enjoyed buying them and I knew Ainsley would love and appreciate them too.

I followed the instructions from the nurse at the desk and stood in the doorway of Ainsley's room for a moment, watching Christian and Ainsley coo over their daughter.

Henry climbed on the bed and looked on in awe. It was a beautiful picture of happiness and serenity. The image of a perfect life.

Ainsley's life had been far from perfect when they'd met, Christian's too, despite his wealth but still... to look at them now, glowing with joy, it was a beautiful, heart wrenching thing to see. A contradiction, I know. But it was what I'd once dreamed of for myself.

I'd eventually heal. Dr Bailey assured me I would but for now I was just happy to get through, keep going. Okay was good enough.

'Aunty Jo,' Henry cried from the bed. 'I have a baby. Come see my baby,' he called, waving me over.

Ainsley and Christian looked up, grinning like fools as I entered and scooped Henry into my arms. 'So show me this baby then,' I told him.

'She's right there,' he told me proudly. 'It's a girl one.'

'A girl one? Well isn't that fantastic?'

He clambered back down onto his mother as I leant in and hugged her before hugging Christian and handing over my gift.

'She's beautiful,' I gushed, all disappointment for my own life falling away as I looked at her perfect, sleeping face. Anything was possible for her. She was brand new, unbroken, the world at her feet. In that one moment, with Henry standing on the bed beside me, his little arms wrapped around me, and his sister sleeping peacefully in front of me, I wondered if there could be any moment more perfect. I glimpsed, for just a second, how happy Ainsley and Christian must be, and I thought my heart might explode.

How could they be full of that much joy without exploding? How did it all fit inside just one person? How could I not want that for myself? But I didn't. I couldn't. I couldn't even think of having this life with anyone but Benny. I wouldn't do that to him. I couldn't have this with someone else while he lay dead in the ground.

It wouldn't be right.

'Do you want a hold?' Christian offered with that stupid grin that wouldn't leave his face.

I nodded. 'What is her name?' I asked as I carefully took her in my arms.

'Anna,' Ainsley told me proudly.

'Henry and Anna,' I smiled.

'If it weren't for them, Christian and I might never have met and these children might not exist,' Ainsley told me wistfully.

'How does your mother feel about that?'

Ainsley chuckled. 'Doing alright, surprisingly.'

Mrs Donovan had never been a fan of Anna's namesake but Ana May had been Ainsley's friend when she'd desperately needed one. When Ana had died unexpectedly, unexpectedly for Ainsley, anyway, she'd left Ainsley the café and it had changed her life.

Long before Ana May had been Ainsley's friend, she'd been Anastasia Mayberry, a high-flying city madam and the wife of notorious thief, Henry Mayberry. He was known as the elusive Bauble Bandit. Henry had eventually been caught by one of his billionaire friends who'd relieved him of his passport and left him in the Joshua Tree forest. The Harrington security team had dug up an old article with a photograph, so we'd gone to find him. We'd found him withering away all alone on the hot streets of Las Vegas hoping one day his Ana would find him.

It'd been an awful sight, the once vivacious, mischievous man, nothing but a bag of bones begging on the street for food money. It'd broken our hearts. He'd died minutes after we'd found him and told him of Ana's death.

I'd known what that heartbreak was like, how pointless it felt to keep going when the person you'd loved was gone. I'd felt like I might die myself when I lost Benny only weeks before. But I didn't. I got to live this seemingly half-life instead. But I had Ainsley and Christian. I had the café, a job I loved more than the high paying, high flying corporate finance job I'd had before. I had Henry, the light of my life, and now his sister Anna who slept contentedly in my arms. I felt my eyes well up and took a deep breath. This had to be enough.

I felt Ainsley and Christian watching me too intently. 'What?' I demanded.

'It suits you,' Christian smiled.

'Hmph,' I grumbled.

'Are you going to like her more than me?' Henry asked innocently.

'What? Why on earth would you think that?'

'Because she's a girl baby and you're a girl lady. You'll do girl things now.'

'Doesn't mean a thing, kiddo. You and me go way back. Nothing's going to change that, okay? Nothing wrong with monster trucks and Lego, you know.'

Little Anna began getting restless so I handed her over to her mother and took Henry to the enclosed playground downstairs to burn off some energy, before leaving the happy family to do their thing. 'Let me know if you need anything. And you, my man,' I said to Henry, 'you let me know when you're coming for a sleepover, okay?'

Henry gave me a big, little person hug that had the tears welling up again and then I was off.

I was glad I'd walked instead of taking the scooter because even though it felt like it had dropped ten degrees outside and the icy wind howled as it slapped at my face, I needed the walk, the headspace, the time to compose myself before I climbed the stairs to my empty apartment above the empty café.

I'd made peace with my reality. This was just my lot in life. I'd been lucky to have Benny. He'd loved me like I was the centre of his world. We'd been so in tune with each other. It'd all been so easy, so beautiful. Not everyone was that lucky. So I'd made peace with it and I was grateful for what I'd had, but seeing the look on Ainsley and Christian's faces, feeling the sweet perfection of that tiny new human sleeping blissfully in my arms, left me feeling empty. Wistful for things I'd never have. I needed the fresh air, the space to get my head straight and then maybe a Netflix marathon to go with the lasagne Mrs Donovan had somehow snuck into my fridge.

Chapter 2

I woke on Saturday with the weekend looming ahead. The café didn't open over the weekend. I'd seriously toyed with doing so many times over the last few years just to fill the hours but neither Ainsley nor Dr Bailey would hear of it.

Dr Bailey had been the psychiatrist in charge of Ainsley's care after she'd decided there was no longer a place in the world for her or a point to keep on going. There were clinical terms for her emotional downfall that led to effective treatment but Dr Bailey had helped Ainsley re-interpret her world that had become so out of focus she could hardly see straight anymore and now he was helping me make sense of my world without Benny.

I trusted Dr Bailey with everything I had and had long ago committed to doing the work and promising not to question it. I mostly stuck to my promise. He was right too, bit by bit, I'd found my way out of the fog. Bit by bit, I'd been able to relinquish the medication he gave me, the sleeping pills, the ones for my sadness. I was on my own two feet now but the road hadn't ended.

We'd replaced the pills with meditation, exercise, a little of this, a little of that. Ainsley had added in essential oils, which she'd discovered thanks to her sister-in-law, Lydia when Henry was being a fussy baby. It meant I often smelt like lavender or mandarins but they helped more than I'd ever admit to Ainsley.

Dr Bailey also insisted on lots of self-care and good food. I really worried about where he'd gotten his degree sometimes, it all sounded very Cosmo inspired. Next he'd be discussing makeup primer and the Kardashians.

I'd only managed to extend my self-care to the occasional bubble bath with the lovely smelling fizzy things from Lush that Ainsley kept buying me and resting when I needed to, which usually involved camping out in front of my television. Whatever worked, was Dr Bailey's theory but I know he analysed me constantly for signs I wasn't okay, that the television time was masking more than a need to rejuvenate. But I always won. Because I was fine, like I kept telling everyone.

The food was a tough one. While comatose in Ainsley's bed in the days and weeks after Benny died, which was now my bed, I'd slept a lot, been unable to eat more than a little soup here and there. I'd lost too many kilos in those days. Mrs Donovan had been making sure I put them back on and then some. I carried more kilos than ever now thanks to the pasta dishes and curries and whatever other one pot meal accompanied by carbs she could think of and snuck in my freezer. Then there was the never-ending supply of cake and muffins. She brought them in under the pretence of providing a service to our customers but extra always found its way upstairs to my benches and it'd have been rude to waste them. That's what I told myself.

Then there were Ainsley's toasties. She served them for breakfast and lunch and they'd become a staple, a major food group for me. She made everything from bacon and egg toasted sandwiches for an on-the-run breakfast with the best gooiest cheese, your regular gourmet ham, cheese and tomato to an apple pie toastie for dessert and every other heavenly combination she could come up with that most people never considered but worked so well. She was the queen when it came to filling two pieces of artisan bread and people loved her for it. I loved her for it. No one had thought it would work, that she could run this place on nothing but fancy toasties but here we were.

Luckily my job kept me busy, behind the coffee machine, toing and froing in the afternoons when I was alone, from upstairs to my apartment to downstairs to the basement. It helped combat the excessive carbs, at least a little.

But on Saturdays there were no toasties, not a lot of toing and froing, so Dr Bailey gave me rules. I'd built a routine based on Dr Bailey's advice and once showered, dressed and caffeinated, I went into Mrs May's living room and searched my phone for a guided meditation from The Meditation Queen. I'd found her on YouTube when I'd first been searching and after having listened to an endless array of annoying breathy women, she'd been a breath of fresh air.

I queued up my favourite centring meditation and just relaxed into the sound of her voice. I often lost what she was saying and forgot to follow where she was leading but I always felt better for it.

I sat for a few minutes when the session finished. Breathing in, filling my lungs and letting the peace work its way through my body. Then I did the next thing on my Saturday list and went for a walk through the mall.

'It doesn't matter where you walk, Jo, you just need to get the blood pumping, burn off some of those unused endorphins, get some fresh air, be out in the world, somewhere,' Dr Bailey told me. So, the where was irrelevant. I'd tried a few different Saturday routes in the beginning, worked my way up to some of the parklands, but none were as enjoyable as a walk through the mall. That had to say a lot for my mental stability, surely, that I preferred the mall with the people than the solitude of another route?

People roamed aimlessly and leisurely, enjoying their day. They drank coffee from paper cups, laughed with their companions, enjoyed the quiet time with themselves as they weaved in and out of shops. It was life going on around me everywhere I looked.

The wind of the last few days had turned to rain during the night and now winter sunshine glowed down on the freshly cleaned pavers of the mall. The mall was a car free zone, so I walked down the centre to avoid ping ponging with the masses on the sides. I had nowhere in particular to go, no shops to pop into. I'd returned the surplus baby boy clothes I'd bought for Ainsley late the night before when it had been quiet so today, I was free to just enjoy the air and the hubbub of activity around me.

At the end of the mall, I waited at the traffic lights, then crossed over Pulteney street with a seeming swarm of people that magically dispersed at the kerb on the other side. I left the safety of the car free zone of the mall and kept walking down Rundle Street, zig zagging between pedestrians. I picked up a double shot latte from the Cibo's takeaway window, then kept going all the way to the end, passing the cafés and restaurants, the high-end boutiques and spas, the uni pubs, the pop-up markets and funky laneways, until I was almost alone at the intersection.

I crossed over East Terrace and went into the parklands, to sit on a bench by the lake. The little café was still open, the row boats still in operation despite the time of year, and a couple of brave romantics were rowing into the middle.

Once a year this space came alive with the Fringe Festival and the V8 car race. I used to drag Benny to the first and he dragged me to the latter. I always enjoyed the frivolity of the festival, the change from the normal, the community of artists that were testing the boundaries. The car race was loud but we always sprung for seating on pit straight, so it made it bearable. I liked watching the mechanics and support crews preparing for the cars to come in, changing their tyres, filling them up with petrol and getting them ready to go back out on the track. We'd eat hotdogs and ice cream and spend the whole day talking about nothing, all the stuff you never usually make a point of talking about. But all those hours sitting still together, you ran out of the important things and I loved it, hearing the nothing of his life and the other people in it. We both worked hard, had friends and hobbies outside of our relationship, so always had something to talk about. He went to the football when he could during winter, the cricket during summer, neither of which interested me much, so he'd go with his mates and I'd go wine tasting in the Barossa or McLaren Vale with my girlfriends, enjoy long lazy days shopping or lunching at the exclusive Q Club. I hadn't been there in so long. Not since I'd left my job.

Q Club was one of those exclusive places with an undisclosed list of criteria you needed to meet before they'd take your money. I no longer met the criteria and no longer renewed my exorbitant membership. There was a mile-long waitlist, so I'd never get back in but that was fine with me. I didn't need the evening cocktails, rooftop parties or the networking anymore, I had Mrs May's.

With my coffee finished, I made my way back the way I'd come. Took the escalator down into Coles for a few essentials, picked up a burrito bowl from the Mexican takeaway in the food court and made my way back home. It was routine, it was nice and it kept Dr Bailey happy.

Once I'd eaten my burrito bowl, curled up on the couch, I spent some time on my journal. With all that had happened with Mrs May and Henry Mayberry, with Benny and Russ, our Vegas guide, Ainsley and Christian's Vegas Wedding and my road to recovery over the last few years, my journal entries sounded more like a fictional novel. Not for the first time, I wondered what a hoot it would be to package it all up and sell it. As what, I wasn't sure, a fictional story, a non-fiction guide, a television show, it could be something if I was brave enough to bare all my innermost secrets.

I smiled to myself at the silly idea, microwaved some popcorn and settled in for an afternoon of Netflix. I'd completed all my required activities assigned by Dr Bailey so the rest of the day was mine and I was going to enjoy it.

My routine was much the same the next day. I'd fallen asleep on the couch and dragged myself to bed in the middle of the night, so I had a kink in my neck that made meditating uncomfortable. But I'd promised Dr Bailey I'd do it, so I did it and then I walked across town to the pretty church in time for a Sunday service.

The Meditation Queen had led me to the universe, which led me to God, which led me here to the prettiest old church on a Sunday morning. I still wasn't sure what my relationship with God was. I was still mad at him for taking Benny, so I was still figuring out how such an entity fit into my world. But somehow, being in the church with all its history, listening, brought me comfort and that was enough. For now. I didn't understand the mechanics of religion, the organisation of it as though if you didn't show up on Sunday there'd be a black mark against your name. I knew it wasn't true. If everything else they said about God was true then he didn't mind where you prayed. Maybe they were all more like me than I realised. Maybe they just liked having somewhere to go on a Sunday morning too, the sense of community, feeling like you belonged to something more than just you, listening to the sermon, feeling inspired, centred. There was a lot I didn't understand though so I tried.

Father John waited, greeting people from the grand archway, wishing them a good morning as they came in, shaking some hands and smiling. He nodded to me as I tried to blend with a family group and enter unseen. Father John often tried to talk me into coming to a later session, joining the community for lunch. I wasn't ready for that, not sure I'd ever be that committed, so I just avoided him as much as I could.

I breathed in the musty smell of the old church as I took my seat in the mahogany pew in the last few rows. I wasn't sure I was even allowed to be there. I wasn't catholic. I wasn't anything. But Father John never asked me to leave and I liked hearing what the priests had to say, considering the thoughts they provoked as I sipped a coffee on the way to Ainsley's afterward. Today was no different.

Father John was my favourite and always left me with something to consider. Today he talked about the importance of acceptance and community, finding people to lean on when times were tough. He said the words with far more flourish than I can recall but they meant the same. I had had a community once, a large one. Colleagues, Benny, friends, other couples we enjoyed spending time with. Now I just had Ainsley.

After Benny had died, I'd been in such a fog I just couldn't return any of the emails or phone calls that came. Then we went to Vegas to find Henry Mayberry where Russ had led us on the most wonderful adventure before leading us astray and when we returned, I just focussed on getting through each day. Not looking too far ahead. Just surviving in this new world, this new life I found myself in and before long, those people stopped calling, they stopped emailing.

It was fine, we didn't have that much in common anymore.

I no longer had the fancy corporate career and most of those friends couldn't imagine being happy as a barista. Why is that? A seemingly simple job, frowned upon by society because it wasn't fancy enough, despite it bringing me joy, despite the importance of it to the people who came in looking for sustenance and that sense of community Father John spoke of.

I never felt like justifying my choice, so I left it at that, just like I did with the friends and couples that I had accumulated with Benny. We'd met when we were nineteen on a pub crawl, a tale of when two students meet over cheap beer. I was head over heels by the time the sun came up. Being so young, we'd grown together, learned together. Over the years, our friends became entwined. Even the ones he had outside of our relationship. I made them nachos and bought their beer and chips for finals season. Without Benny, what role did they have in my life or the couples we dined and vacationed with? There was no fun in being a fifth wheel. It'd have been a constant reminder Benny was gone. That life moved on without him as though he'd never been there at all. But I missed the community, I missed having people. Just a little.

I avoided Father John and Father Michael who stood at the end of the altar as though planning to tag team me on my way out. 'We'll get you, Jo,' they laughed as I scurried past and I couldn't help but smile because they were kind and they wanted so much to welcome me. I knew sometimes my grief was evident in my sitting towards the back of the church and by the way I dipped my head to avoid people as I hurried away like a little mouse. I wasn't ready to open up yet, not to strangers, no matter how kind and welcoming they were.

Ainsley lived on the edge of the city in a lovely home we joked of as a mansion. It wasn't but to two girls who'd grown up in middle class suburbia it was. It was, in fact, a blue stone Victorian manor built in the 1800's and renovated to perfection by Christian and his team. It was always full of love and light and warmth in the winter that came from the multitude of stone fireplaces.

I enjoyed the burn in my thighs as I walked through the parklands sipping my coffee, excited that Ainsley and Anna were now home and resting comfortably and I'd get to see Henry.

The latter was waiting for me on the front step as I turned into their long circular drive. I knew Ainsley or Christian would be watching him from inside and he'd have received instructions in no uncertain terms to not move an inch from that step.

He stood when he saw me, jumping up and down on the spot and waving as though it had been an age since he'd seen me. But not once did he move from the step until I reached him and swept him up into my arms and twirled him around in the lovely morning sunshine, while he giggled and giggled, filling my heart with his goodness.

'I have something for you,' I whispered, conspiratorially.

He gasped as though we didn't play this game every Sunday. 'What did you bring me?' he asked.

I handed over the Freddo Frog I snuck him every Sunday and he squealed with delight as he did every Sunday before, wrapping his arms around me and thanking me as though I'd handed him the whole world on a platter.

We sat on the step for a few minutes while he ate his chocolate and he told me all about his day, about his sister coming home, how his friend, Alistair at day care had peed in the sand pit and they couldn't play in there anymore until there was new sand. When he finished, we went inside.

I found Ainsley all the way in the back of the house where they'd added on a beautiful, light filled living room encased in windows with a vaulted ceiling and a chef's kitchen that would make girls like Ainsley and me cry. In fact, I think she had when Christian had finally unveiled it to her, just as she was about to give birth to Henry.

'Hey you,' she called to me from the white poufy couch that was so soft, it was like air. It also had so much fabric protection on it, there was no way the kids could damage it.

I flopped into the couch.

'Nice walk?' she asked as I cooed over Anna.

'It was, the sun is out and it was lovely.'

'It does look nice. I think Christian's planning to serve brunch under the pergola. You don't mind him cooking, I hope? I'm knackered,' she smiled.

'Of course not. He always does a great job,' I insisted as we took our seats under the pergola, bare of its usual big fat leaves, the chiminea fire giving off all the heat we needed to combat the oncoming winter chill.

'Here you go, ladies,' Christian smiled proudly as he placed plates of waffles, pancakes, bacon, eggs and freshly baked apple cinnamon muffins on the table. 'I can't take all the credit for the muffins. Margot sent me the recipe,' he told us. Margot was his family's housekeeper and even though the Harrington children had all moved out, she still cared for them all as if they were her own.

Christian was proud of his baking efforts as well. Benny had always been like that. Looking for his medal for something I did all the time. Christian was a little different though, more innocent. He'd grown up a Harrington with housekeepers and chefs and someone to tend his every need. He could have food delivered from an elite restaurant with just a call, anything he wanted at any time. That's the luxury of being a Harrington, so it was a proud moment to see him whip up a feast and get so much joy out of it.

'So, how's our little Anna doing?' I asked as I sipped a coffee while Henry sat on my lap sharing another muffin.

'She's gaining weight and doing fine but she needs food ALL the time. She's definitely not as easy as Henry was but she's just beautiful,' she glowed proudly.

'She really is,' I agreed.

'She's all Harrington though,' Ainsley added. 'Christian was showing me pictures his mum sent over of Lydia and Jaz when they were babies and Anna is the spitting image.'

'That's not a bad thing, is it?'

'No, not at all. At least Henry looks like me or more like my brother but he's definitely a Donovan.'

'He has the Harrington charm and tenacity though,' I added.

'Oh, does he what,' she laughed, before telling a story about Henry charming the pants off the staff at day care and getting extra snacks.

We finished the visit on that laugh and a squishy hug with Henry before I made my way back across town. I stopped in at the markets for some fresh salmon and salad greens. I considered some fruit but once you'd had Ainsley's apple pie toasties you couldn't eat plain fruit again.

I climbed the stairs to my apartment above the café suitably worn out from my morning. I felt good for it as I changed back into my comfy pyjamas and eased myself into an afternoon of catch up tv. Working in the café came with early starts, so I missed a lot of evening television and enjoyed spending my Sunday afternoons with fictional friends. The familiarity of the people, the stories were comforting. People were rescued, justice was served, relationships began and ended.

I was a bystander to their lives with a bag of chocolate honeycomb or whatever else I had on hand. Today it was the honeycomb because it had been on sale in Coles. I used to buy it from the outlet store in McLaren Vale when I went wine tasting with the girls. Benny would always chastise me when I came home with it and remind me all week I had to make up for it in the gym. The memory made me smile. But in hindsight, maybe that makes him sound harsh, but he wasn't.

'Do you think, maybe, now that he's gone, you've turned him into a martyr?' Ainsley had asked a while back.

I'd become defensive, saying, 'I had my things too. I wouldn't let him keep his holiday beard because I thought it made him look like a hobo and I didn't want people making the wrong assumptions and judgements about him.'

'That beard looked awful,' Ainsley had laughed. It had, he just wasn't a beard growing kind of guy. 'Do you also remember how you always argued about where to spend family holidays, Christmas, Easter, Mother's Day, until somehow you always decided you'd just have everyone at your place and then you'd end up cooking lunch for twelve people and dinner for eighteen more?'

'Yeah, but then he'd feel bad and send me off to the spa for a massage to alleviate his guilt,' I'd smiled.

It was just one of our things. We were a normal, everyday couple. We had our ways, we knew each other inside out, our triggers, our soft spots, each other's favourite dinner, what counted as comfort food. I hadn't turned him into anything. Love was give and take. Sometimes he was an ass. Sometimes I was. I hadn't forgotten. I missed having someone who cared what I did. But I had no one to mind anymore where I spent holidays or how much chocolate I ate, so I enjoyed every bite and the last of my weekend.

I never minded the weekend ending anymore though. I used to, back in my old corporate life. I'd get a little bitchy on Sunday nights as we'd curl up ready for some reality tv with the promise of my freedom ending in a few hours. I loved my work so much now, I looked forward to it, to the people, to Ainsley and Mrs Donovan and Vivi while we had her and even our resident Russian-in-perpetual-morning.

Chapter 3

M onday came with a flurry of customers desperate for coffee, tea, and bacon and egg toasties to ease them back into the work week after their weekends of freedom. Mrs Donovan bundled in around ten with new pictures and tales of Anna from her morning visit. Vivi swept in soon after like an old Hollywood movie star with her flowing red kimono, matching lips and a dramatic air with tales of her weekend shenanigans that didn't impress Mrs Donovan at all.

'Vivi, you're too old to be behaving like a frisky teenager,' Mrs Donovan scolded.

'Says who?' demanded Vivi indignantly as she sipped her coffee with a smirk.

Mrs Donovan sighed as she always did and turned to serve a customer while Vivi chuckled and finished her tale of Mr Saturday night that turned into Sunday brunch.

We settled into a rhythm, the three of us, and we worked in sync for the few weeks following Anna's birth. Vivi experimented with the toasties here and there with some daily specials, but not enough to bother the customers.

She loved working in the café as much as I did, as much

as Ainsley and Mrs Donovan. We'd all come here from somewhere. Ainsley, like me, had come from a corporate world where she'd supported directors at the top of their game until she fell from grace and no one wanted anything to do with her, not when she started coming to work in her pyjamas, that had been the beginning of her downward spiral and I still kicked myself every day for being too caught up in my own world to have not noticed, for not helping her and giving her a safe place to fall.

Mrs Donovan had been a primary school teacher until the day she came in to investigate this café of Ainsley's. She'd found Ainsley rushed off her feet so she did what any good mother would do and pitched in and loved it so much she never left.

Vivi had been a dance teacher in her day before she'd married and had her daughter. I suspected she and Mrs May would have been friends if it weren't for Mrs May's extracurricular activities and the company she kept. But we were all here together, bringing joy to people, some who loved the high-powered fast track, some you could see were just getting through the day, still figuring out where they fit in the world. It was always an eclectic mix of people and stories and life going on around us and we got to play a part in their days, bring them some light and comfort and we all appreciated how special that was.

Kelsey filled in here and there over those weeks so Mrs Donovan could help Ainsley with Henry and the baby when she needed her. But in just a few weeks, Anna was sleeping better, feeding better and Ainsley was getting back to her usual strength. Christian wouldn't let her return to work. She'd promised him three months but we all knew she wouldn't last that long and she'd be bringing Anna upstairs while she covered the lunch rush before we knew it. But for now, she was enjoying her time off with Anna. It didn't stop her from popping by the café and meddling under the pretence of showing off the baby. We didn't always notice and rarely minded as long as we got a cuddle but now and then we'd see through her little facade.

'So, I was speaking to Jaz the other day when she came by to see the baby,' she said casually, drinking a green tea combination with hazelnuts and cocoa husks, blackberry leaves and chicory root as she leant on the counter. Jaz was Christian's sister, she and her ex bodyguard now husband, Jay, owned a pub down south on the beach where they lived a nice quiet life.

Ainsley had that look in her eye, that air about her that said she was up to mischief so I just nodded and waited for her to go on and for whatever she was planning to all fall into place.

'She said they have a meditation guru of some sort in residence at the pub for the next few weeks and people are loving him. They're turning people away. They've put together this whole retreat thing, she has local craft people coming in so you can try your hand at macramé or painting or Chef will teach you some recipes. It all sounds so lovely and therapeutic,' she told me.

I raised a curious eyebrow. I sensed this was leading somewhere I wasn't going to be happy with.

'Don't get mad,' she added, trying not to grin. 'But while I had Jaz distracted with baby love, I wrangled you a spot into this Bodhi's calendar. Jaz is holding a room for you for this weekend,' she announced.

'What? Don't be ridiculous. Who even is this guy?' I asked. I had delved my way into some of the spiritual, the meditations and the church visits, which Ainsley did not know about, the church that is, she knew about the meditations. It was one of Dr Bailey's go to treatments these days. But these spiritual things were not something you trusted to just anyone, to random strangers passing through regional pubs. It was private and personal. It wasn't a team activity or a spectator sport. Not for me, anyway. It was something personal for me in my living room on a Saturday morning.

'I don't know, some meditation guru. He's supposed to be life changing and Jaz says he does this Reiki treatment, some sort of spiritual healing that takes away all your woes.'

'And you think I need to be relieved of my woes?'

'Don't get me wrong, you're doing great, you've come a long way since Benny died but don't you think you're still holding on a little tightly to the sadness? Don't you think it's time to move on and make a new life?'

'I have a life. One I like.'

'I know you do. But Jo, you need more than this,' she said, looking around the room.

'Why? Who says? Besides, what am I even going to do there? I'm not a macramé kind of girl and I'm not one for lazing around on the beach doing nothing, you know,' I protested.

'Since when? We used to bum around a beach all the time when we were rolling around corporate land with disposable income burning a hole in our pockets. You remember when

Benny and the boys would go to Melbourne for the weekend to watch the footy and we'd fly off to a lovely faraway beach for a couple of days just because we could? We'd drink margaritas and eat too much food and read books all day,' she reminded me wistfully.

I huffed. I remembered the days but now it just sounded like my idea of hell. All that sitting around and being quiet, that was not my idea of fun.

'Come on, what harm can a little hocus pocus and reading by the beach do? Jaz was going on about how he's helped all these people, including her and you know how much crap must be stuck inside Jaz Harrington's head,' she laughed and I couldn't help but smile. Jaz had once been an IT girl, a party girl before she got clean and gave it all up for love. When she reappeared a couple of years ago for her brother Tom's wedding, the media hounded her and sent her back down a dark hole. I could only imagine how much pain still lived inside her but she was the loveliest person and she always managed to make you feel like you were the most important person in the room. 'People are driving up and flying in from all over the place,' Ainsley added.

'Well, like I've told everyone else, I'm fine. I don't need to change my life and I don't need some guru poking about in my head.'

'Jo, you've barely left this café except to follow Dr Bailey's recovery rules and visit me and the kids for almost as long as I can remember, probably since Vegas. You have to do something.'

'You sound like my mother. Where am I not going, that I'm supposed to be going, that has everyone up in arms, anyway?'

'I don't know. You used to love going to Sunday markets and hunting out talented new designers and having dinner on The Parade, a movie, martini's at the bar and late night hot chocolates or even just shopping, going to the beach or going on a hike.'

'I've been shopping,' I defended. The other things, the hiking and the beach and outdoor activities and Saturday nights, I did them with Benny.

'For yourself. For fun, not groceries and gifts for my kids.'

'You don't like the gifts I buy them?'

'You know I do. That's not the point. You don't do anything for fun anymore.'

'What are you talking about? I'm here, this is fun.'

'I'm glad you think so because I do too but you need more than this.'

'Says who?'

'I don't know. You just do,' she insisted.

'You're making this stuff up, aren't you?' I smiled.

'I bet Dr Bailey agrees with me,' she said with a victorious smirk.

'Of course, he does. You're like his star patient. He'd agree with anything you said.'

She laughed. 'I don't know about that. I put in the work. I try. I didn't always but once I met Christian and I fell pregnant with Henry, I had so much to lose, so I worked my butt off to be better. Depression never goes away. I still have bad days. It's something you live with for the rest of your life. But I do what Dr Bailey says, and I try, for Christian, for my kids, for myself.

You need something worth trying for and I really think this could be the start, a chance for you to reset and move forward.'

'What if I don't want to move forward? What if I'm happy with my life as it is?' I asked, always surprised at how easy people thought it was for me to just let go of Benny, of our life together, all the plans we'd made. How do you just move on? How do you leave all that behind?

'I've seen you with my kids, Jo, I know you want more than this. I see it in your heart.'

'Well, it's not going to happen, is it? Benny's gone and that's that.'

'Nothing is ever as simple as that.'

I shrugged. 'For me it is.'

Our resident Russian-in-perpetual-mourning tugged on my arm as she was prone to do when she had something to add. 'Go, rest, get better, it be good for you,' she insisted, with her strong accent and broken English.

Our resident Russian-in-perpetual-mourning was hard to argue with because the one thing I'd learnt over the last few years of working at the café and seeing her every day was that if she had something to say, which wasn't very often, she was usually right. Also, I knew she wouldn't stop tugging on my arm until I agreed with her.

'Fine, fine,' I conceded before escaping back behind the coffee machine and leaving them standing there in their smug victory. There may have also been a part of me that didn't want to be in my golden years, lost in nothing but long-gone memories. Every day our resident Russian-in-perpetual-mourning sat in her booth remembering, as though that one pocket of time she'd spent attending Anastasia Mayberry's fancy soirees and hobnobbing with the underworld elite was all she had left to cling to.

Anastasia Mayberry had abandoned the café in the late seventies when her husband had gone missing. She'd changed her name and disappeared into the suburbs to raise their son, never to return. Had our resident Russian's life halted then too? We knew she'd married, that was the point of the funeral clothes she wore every day in memory of her dead husband. But had she not done anything else in that time worth remembering? Travelled? Built a family? She wasn't one for chatting and sharing though, not even with Vivi who was the queen of sucking out your inner most secrets. So our resident Russian's life remained a mystery outside of the few snippets she'd shared about the café's history. I'd never pitied her. I'd learnt not to, you could never fully know a person's story.

She'd been kind to me after Benny, like a kindred spirit, the only person who seemed to understand the aching cavern of loss inside of me. My pain had taught me not to judge another person's grief, so I would not pity her now. But something stirred inside of me that made me want more in my golden years, to remember a fuller life, more than just a few wonderful years with a beautiful man who'd loved and adored me. It was more than a lot of people got and I felt guilty for thinking I could have more. But because of it, I let them have their victory and agreed to go to the pub and see this guru, but I refused to partake in macramé.

'Good. I've sorted it all out with Jaz. It's not going to cost you anything so if it doesn't work, you'll just have a rest at my expense and maybe some killer cocktails. I'll have a car come for you Saturday morning at eight and we'll see you in a week,' she smirked.

'A week? I don't have time to be away for a week. Not with you off with the baby.'

'Hogwash,' she said, waving me off. 'Mum's back on deck and Christian's sending Kelsey. What else is there? You can watch Grey's Anatomy on catch up tv when you get back,' she added smugly as though she knew exactly how I spent every moment of my life. The fact that she was right was completely beside the point.

'Bloody hell, you're a nightmare now you're a Harrington, you know. All the power's gone to your head,' I scoffed as I turned on the coffee machine to drown out her gloating.

Chapter 4

A car collected me from in front of the café Saturday morning as promised. The sun was barely up as I waited in the crisp morning air. It really wasn't R&R at the beach kind of weather but there'd been no reasoning with Ainsley and here I was at the crack of dawn too tired to argue.

Jaz and Jay's pub, The Old Colonel, was nestled on the edge of the ocean. It had been a broken-down old place when they'd bought it, now it was a highlight of the peninsula.

It was built of sandstone and tiered like a wedding cake. The pub was on the ground floor. There was a floor above it that served as cheap, serviceable accommodation when needed. One row of rooms had a balcony overlooking the ocean. The other side overlooked the carpark, the bluff and national park beyond. They'd renovated the top floor into a lush apartment which is where Jaz and Jay lived their quiet, unHarrington life.

The clouds parted and some winter sun forced itself through as we pulled into the carpark. The sun was all for show though, and the cool air nipped at my arms as the Harrington driver placed my bags on the ground beside me and I wished for the coat I'd packed in my suitcase.

As the car drove away, I sighed, exasperated that I had to force myself to partake in some guru's life changing shenanigans, most of which I could do myself at home. For me, meditation wasn't a group activity, I'd read the combined energy did magical things but I didn't want other people's energy murking up mine. Besides, Saturdays were for curling up on the couch with Netflix. But then I looked up and Jaz Harrington stood in the doorway between two enormous potted peace plants. Her smile was full of sunshine, her hair a crazy mass of black curls reminding me I'd chopped off my lovely long hair in an act of defiance and control one Saturday night as though if I could control this one thing, I might have some say in everything else.

Ainsley had lost it when she'd come in on Monday. She'd called Vivi who promptly dragged me down the mall to get it tidied up. We'd never spoken of it again and I started going to St Francis' on Sundays, not long after that.

As Jaz stepped forward, I put on my happy face and implored my grown-up manners. It wasn't Jaz's fault I was here. She'd graciously gone to a lot of effort to make space for me so when she leant in for a hug, I gratefully accepted the goodness she offered. She was that sort of person, full of light and it infected everyone.

'I'm so glad you're here. Come, come,' she insisted as though I were one of her oldest friends. In fact, we'd only met a handful of times and always through Ainsley. Either Jaz came into the café for a catch up, or I caught her at Ainsley's for brunch or there was that one time Ainsley had dragged me out to the pub with her little family for the weekend where I'd curled up on the balcony and barely moved for 48 hours. But Jaz was good, kind people and not bothered by semantics. Ainsley considered me a part of her family. Which meant, to the Harringtons, that I was a part of theirs.

Jaz led me inside and down a long hallway painted in the lightest freshest aqua. This wasn't one of those pubs with dark, woodsy bars full of old men. This was a pub in which Jaz Harrington had infused all her light and talent. It didn't mean she'd eliminated all the cosy corners, they were still there but they weren't dingy and they somehow managed to keep that old beer smell out of the building.

I'd forgotten how good it felt to be here, forgotten the energy that seeped from its walls, from its people. Light attracted light and the people that came here, all had one thing in common: they loved life. Halfway down the hallway, we turned and went up the stairs that led to the first floor and beyond.

'Thanks so much for making space for me,' I said, as we climbed the timber stairs, sanded and lacquered to their original perfection.

She waved my thanks off as though it were no big deal. 'I'm so glad to have you here. We're fully booked right now so it'll be nice to have a familiar face around,' she insisted as she opened the door to my room. 'Shhhh... don't tell anyone, but you've got the family suite.' she said conspiratorially. 'This is the one I had done up for when the family visit. As you might remember, the others are nice too, they're serviceable and have nice linen and a comfy mattress and we've put ensuites in all the rooms so you don't have to share but we wanted something nice and homey for the fam and seeing as we're fully booked and I'm not expecting any family visits, this is all yours.'

'It's lovely, thank you,' I told her, having trouble imagining any space Jaz couldn't make into something special. She worked as a designer for Christian these days, had found she had quite the knack for creating beautiful spaces and this one was no different. It was the first in a long row of rooms and seemed to take up the space of two regular rooms. There was a queen size brass bed in the middle that looked nothing short of lush with pink and grey linens and two equally plush lavender sofas by the window that looked like they folded out into beds. In the corner was what looked like a lovingly restored antique cabinet with a small television on top.

'We're serving breakfast down in the T-bar and dinner in the dining room for guests, both are included in the accommodation package but you can get lunch in the dining room as well if you don't feel like walking to somewhere else. There's tea in the T-Bar overlooking the ocean all day and we'll switch them to Martinis at sunset. This is your charge card, just hand it to the server or bartender whenever you order something and everything will be taken care of.'

'Really, you don't have to do that, I can pay for things.'

'I know,' she smiled. 'But Ainsley insisted, and I tell you, she's gotten quite forceful since she became a mumma. When she gets fixated on something, there's no stopping her.'

I laughed. 'Don't I know it.'

'Well, you get settled in and when you're ready, I'm downstairs doing some work in T-Bar so come join me for a cuppa. The fire's lit so it's all nice and toasty,' she said with a proud grin.

I promised I would and then she was gone and it was just me and the quiet. I took a deep breath and unpacked my toiletries, leaving everything else in my bag, mostly tracksuit pants and leggings, some big sloppy knit jumpers. I wasn't planning on doing much or going far. Ainsley could force me out of my home but she couldn't force me out of my comfort clothes. I put my toiletries in the small but beautifully appointed ensuite with lovely shiny taps and rich blue towels and then there was nothing to do. I sat on the welcoming brass bed loaded with lovely pillows and Jaz was right, it had a really nice mattress that felt like a cloud. It was the Harrington touch. Christian had it too. When I'd stayed at his old penthouse, the entire place had been a hodge podge of sloppy design bought off the internet, but the mattresses, the small creature comforts, they'd been all Harrington and nothing short of top notch. It'd been a little slice of heaven. The Harringtons didn't know any other way. It was in their DNA. Now the rest of the world benefited from their fine sense of style and comfort.

As much as I'd have liked to curl up in the cloud mattress, I'd promised Jaz I'd have tea with her. That's what I told myself as I collected my things and hustled out of the quiet room anyway. But there was no Internet attached to the television in the room which meant all that was on was morning talk shows. I needed more noise, more action and I only had one bar on my phone, not enough to stream anything without driving myself nuts with buffering. With no television to drown out the noise in my head, my brain would start up. It was like an old lawn mower, it'd rev and rev and then finally catch and once that happened, there was no stopping it and it would be a frightening downward spiral from there so I grabbed my things and the charge card Jaz had given me and took the stairs nice and quick to try and burn it all out of my system.

Turning right at the hallway we'd come in on, led me into a wonderfully light filled room full of windows that overlooked nothing but ocean. The serenity of it almost shocked me. The walls were the same soft aqua that was throughout the rest of the building. The upholstery almost turquoise like the ocean, mixed with the orange of the sunset. I noticed Jaz had taken some notes from Mrs May's since I was last here and had installed big circular booths and bank seating along the wall in the same lovely upholstery as the rest of the room.

I found Jaz over by the windows. She looked up and a grin lit her face when she saw me.

'Sit, sit,' she insisted.

'Are you sure I'm not interrupting your work?' I asked.

'No, of course not. I'm glad for the break. It's not urgent anyway,' she assured me.

'What are you working on?' I asked as I sat. Unlike the lovely velvet seating at the café, these were poufy, with deep seats you could curl up on, tuck your feet up onto and spend the afternoon. The fire was on the other side of the room in a big stone fireplace and the room smelled glorious and was warm and toasty. I didn't feel like I was in a pub at all, it felt like someone's lovely home. That's why Christian had hired Jaz to decorate all his hotels. She created the same feel in them and people knew that whenever they went to a CH hotel, they were going to feel at home, be cared for and have every need taken care of before they even realised they needed it.

'Just some design work for one of Christian's new projects. It's not due for a while but I love doing it. He's given me free reign on this project. Want to see?' she asked with a glint of conspiracy in her eye that told me it was one of Christian's top-secret projects, so of course I nodded with a grin.

She pointed out some of the rooms, 'It's in the desert, he loves building things out there,' she smiled. 'I'm going to do lots of soft colours, take the edge off the overstimulation of the desert, let the outside be the star and the inside a soft place to rest at the end of the day. It's hopefully going to be a beautiful haven,' she said as she led me through the design.

'Here you go,' interrupted a waitress delivering two pots of tea we hadn't ordered.

'Jade is the one you like, yeah?' she asked, remembering what I'd had last time she'd had tea with Ainsley and me at Mrs May's.

It's amazing how something so simple as remembering your choice of tea can have such a profound effect on you but it did. It filled me with something I couldn't quite name, made me feel seen and to feel seen by someone like Jaz Harrington, added a special bit of something. I remembered seeing her on the cover of gossip magazines when I was a teenager, she was always in the who's wearing what spreads, wearing the most amazing clothes, going to the hottest places with the who's who even though we were almost the same age. She'd lived the most glamorous life, jetting off to amazing places and attending important functions and she was now remembering my favourite tea.

She was a long way from the girl she'd been. I understood how much a person could change after hitting bottom. Our bottoms were different, hers was one of addiction and mine was one of grief but she'd made her way out. She'd decided a new path, who she wanted to be, the way she wanted to live and she'd done it all without the backing of the Harringtons, just her own tenacity to be more than she'd been, and Jay.

'Yes, thank you,' I smiled and waited for her to continue with her tour of Christian's new desert hotel.

When she finished, her face was alive with excitement. She loved what she did, and she spoke of Christian like he was some kind of messiah. She clearly adored him as much as his offspring. Her happiness was infectious, and I couldn't help but feel better for it.

'Now,' she said, changing direction. 'You're not here for a sneaky peak at my brother's new hotel, you're here for Bodhi.'

'Apparently,' I said. The enthusiasm I'd had for Jaz's project disappeared as I remembered the forced participation in some stranger's hocus pocus.

Jaz giggled. 'I know, I know, some of it sounds way out there. But my sister's friend, Bex, met him while travelling and raved about him and then suckered everyone she knew in to hosting him for a couple of months at a time while he travelled around Australia as though he's the bloody Dalai Lama. Anyway, I let him do his thing on me when he arrived just to test it out before I told the world he was here. I tell you, Jo, it was like nothing else I've ever experienced. It was like years of crap was just gone from my body. I was almost weightless and slightly euphoric for a few days. It was extraordinary.'

'So you spread the word?'

'I didn't have to do much. He has this whole following on Facebook. He just asked if I could manage the bookings for him as he wasn't so good at keeping track of things and next thing I know, we've got people coming from all over the place and the pub's booked out for a month, as is the caravan park and half the bnb's. We always keep a room spare though in case friends or family come to visit. Okay, in case Christian's bringing the kids,' she grinned.

She took a breath, a sip of tea. I followed suit.

'So, anyway,' she said, pulling out a diary. 'I know, a diary is a bit old school but we don't have a system to manage bookings for someone like Bodhi. Like me, you've been through some stuff, how are you doing by the way?' she asked, even though I hadn't been through nearly as much stuff as she had. But that wouldn't have mattered to her.

'I'm doing okay. Not well enough according to Ainsley,' I laughed. 'But I'm doing okay. I feel good.'

'She thinks you should move on?'

'I don't know, something like that, I guess.'

'I don't blame you for not. I don't know what I'd do without Jay, he's my rock,' she said, reaching for my hand.

I nodded.

'But we do what we can with what we have, right? People were on at me for years to behave, to get clean. My family did everything they could but I had to want it. I had to do it when it was right for me and I did. It took having to choose something

I loved more than booze to put a cracker up my behind, but that was my time. You move on when it feels right, not because it's on a schedule. You have to let your heart heal, and maybe Bodhi can help with that. And then you have to find out who you are as this new, unexpectedly single person, and it sounds like you've been doing good with that. So you just let whatever happens happen when it's time.'

'Thanks,' I smiled, squeezing her hand. It was nice to have someone who understood that getting your shit together wasn't always as easy as just doing it.

'So anyway, you're here for the meditations. Bodhi will gather everyone up when it's time and you might find random people appear and sit in as well, that's just his way, go with it. Then, I'm guessing,' she continued. 'Like me you'll need a few of his lovely healing sessions. Bodhi says the first will get rid of a lot of the surface emotion and drama and blockages but then after a few days or so you'll have some older stuff pop up. It'd probably be good for you to stay for a few weeks but I get it, you have a life to get back to, so we'll just have to try and get you sorted in a few sessions. So I've booked you in for one this afternoon and then another on Wednesday and then one next Saturday before you leave,' she said as she confirmed things in her book while I just nodded. 'Then in between, I have some local artist friends coming by each day so you can try their trades. You missed macramé, that was yesterday, but we have a lovely lady who knits coming by tomorrow and I've booked a jewellery maker and a painter for during the week, so if there's something you fancy, we'll probably set them up on the patio if the weather plays nice, just come on by. Oh, and there's board games in the bar if ever you feel like passing the time.'

'Thanks,' I smiled, impressed with the level of detail. She could have just invited the guru and left it at that. People still would have come and they'd have been happy but bare essentials wasn't Jaz's way. 'So how do these healing sessions actually work?' I asked.

'You don't have to do anything. You just lie there. It's bizarre, I promise, it makes no sense. He'll just wave his arms over you, push and prod here and there, I don't even know and then voila, done.'

'So I just lie there.'

'Yep, nap if you feel like it, there are no rules. He'll let you know when he's done.'

'He's not some creep who's going to cop a feel while I'm asleep, is he?'

She laughed. 'You've been watching too much crime tv,' she said, waggling her finger at me. 'No, he's just a sweet guy. I'm not actually even sure how he identifies to be honest.'

I nodded. 'Well then I guess I can do that. I don't have much to lose, do I?' I said. 'Not sure about group meditation though,' I added, trying not to let my face show how uncomfortable the idea made me. I liked The Meditation Queen. I'd put my headphones in and it was just her and me, so it felt like an intimate moment with myself. I didn't like the idea of doing that as a group thing.

'I know, I wasn't sure about all that quiet. I'm not good at being still, I like to be busy but it's really helped with my energy and focus. You won't even notice anyone else is there. Once the session starts, they'll all fade away. I think you'll like it. It helps keep your mind still for a bit,' she assured me.

'He doesn't do all that coaching you to a better life business as well does he, cos I'm definitely not up for that?' I added. The Meditation Queen ran some popular programs through her website but there was a lot of talk about opening your heart to love and letting go of the past. If I was going to entrust anyone to that journey it would be her but I wasn't up for any of that.

'Nope, that's it, not unless you ask anyway. He seems to be very good at steering people in the right direction. But unless you ask, it's just the healings and meditation and those tend to focus on your chakras and centring your energy and bringing in the light.'

I nodded. Well maybe there'll be something worthwhile in the experience after all, I thought as Jay came up to the table. He was an imposing man if you didn't know him. He'd served with Jaz and Christian's brother Tom, before he became Jaz's bodyguard, when she was an out of control teen. He could make people wither and cry with just a look but these days he was all smiles and when he let one of those loose on you, it was nothing but charm.

'Hi Jo, how you doing?' he asked.

'I'm good, Jay, you?'

'Excellent,' he replied. 'I'm going to need to steal my wife for a while though, do you mind?' he asked.

'Of course not, go, do your thing. I'm going to curl up on this bench and enjoy the rest of this pot of tea and that gorgeous view,' I said, indicating the ocean.

'It's nice, isn't it,' Jaz agreed. 'I'll get some cake sent over. I think we have lemon today, that okay?'

'Perfect.'

'We'll see you for dinner?' she asked. 'We've got some space in the dining room sectioned off for our guests at the moment, to add to that whole community feel. Bodhi thought it would be good for everyone who's taking the journey together to have a place to eat together. So just come in whenever you're ready. We'll be there and someone will come and find you for your appointment with Bodhi this afternoon at three.'

'Thanks. I'll see you at dinner,' I agreed and then they were gone.

Chapter 5

I tucked my feet under me and held the warm teacup in my hands, breathing in the comforting smell of the open fire and let the peace of the view flow into me. Beyond the glass folding doors was a grassed area that sometimes had a market on Sundays, then there was the golden sand and beautiful blue ocean as far as the eye could see. *How did anyone get any work done?* I wondered, captivated by the view as I sipped my tea.

There were a few guests in the room. Waitresses were bringing pots of tea and slices of cake. There was a soft, gentle hum of chatter. Just enough to break the quiet. Just enough to keep my brain distracted.

As I sat enjoying the life going on around me, a girl who looked more apparition than human with long, dark hair curtained around her face scurried through the room from the patio doors and towards the hallway carrying a bakery style paper bag. She didn't look up, she didn't smile, she just scurried and was gone.

The fire crackled across the room. A couple came in from one of the downstairs rooms, the lady in a flowy blue dress, a big hat and sunglasses, the man beside her was beige; sandy blonde hair, beige polo shirt, beige slacks. They shared hushed but heated words as they settled into a small table on the other side of the room.

I wondered if they were all fellow guests here to see Bodhi or just regular tourists passing through, enjoying the view. They certainly didn't look like Jaz and Jay's locals. I took in the people in the room, the older lady reading a newspaper as she sipped her tea, the businessman with slicked back hair who looked ready to head into the office, not the beach for a meditation session. Jaz and Jay tended to attract an eclectic group of surfers, artisans and generally chilled people. Could you even tell the sort who'd seek out a meditation retreat or a healer? I'd assumed they'd all be hippies like Lydia's friend Bex. But perhaps hippy types had already transcended and no longer needed someone like Bodhi?

I mentally shook my head free, I spent too much time in the café trying to figure people out, what they needed, if they needed a shoulder or a laugh, some of Mrs Donovan's motherly wisdom or just a quiet corner to reset for a minute. This was the time to let my brain rest.

'Thank you,' I smiled to the waitress as she cleared away my tea things. Like a lot of Jaz and Jay's staff, she was young and had that permanently suntanned, joyful air about her. It was common among the surfing crowd they attracted. People who lived their bliss and regularly overdosed on vitamin D. Ainsley had often joked that if the waves were good, you'd have to serve your own tea because the staff were prone to disappear. I guess I was lucky there were no waves. But those were their people. They didn't take life too seriously. They waited tables so they could surf or create or whatever else filled their souls. They had no interest in the corporate jungle or being chained to a desk and confined to a nine to five. I understood. I'd spent years chained to a desk and I'd been miserable. I wasn't sure if making coffee counted as creating but Ainsley and I, Mrs Donovan and Vivi, we'd created something special at Mrs Mays, just like Jaz and Jay had created something special here, so I decided it counted.

The soft waves of the ocean outside came and went as if beckoning me to come and play, and as the hubbub of activity increased in the room with people coming in for lunch, I could resist its call no longer, so I wrapped my coat around me and headed outside.

The air was cool and salty. It had that fresh, new feel of infinite possibilities. It was an ocean thing I'd found. It always renewed me. Perhaps it was because I was a Pisces, a water sign. I'd never given it much thought. But I didn't go to the beach anymore. Benny and I had spent many hours at many beaches, lunching, walking, eating ice-cream, swimming to cool off from the hot summer sun. His family had a holiday home up north and we'd spent hours just sitting on the balcony overlooking the water, reading, renewing. He'd BBQ in the evenings and we'd drink wine as the sun set, and go for a walk after dinner or hike the nearby national park on long lazy Sunday afternoons.

As I breathed in that familiar air, tasted the salt on my lips, I almost felt him walking beside me. Almost heard him laugh as a friendly dog ran up for a scratch. But it didn't make me sad like I thought it would. My heart remained intact and the tears remained at bay. It was nice to remember. It gave me strength.

It was too cold to take off my shoes and walk through the water's edge, so I stuck to the sand and just walked and walked. I didn't even mind the quiet, I just enjoyed the sound of the ocean and the gulls playing in the sky above. I didn't mind seeing the families from nearby holiday homes playing frisbee and beach cricket or building sandcastles.

I rounded a bend and came into a secluded bay with just a fish and chip shop and a grassed picnic area. On the other side of the grass was a playground already full of children, their sounds of play and laughter carrying on the breeze. There was a caravan park up on the hill with a spectacular view of the ocean but nothing else you could see, it was a little hidden paradise.

After buying some lunch, I avoided the families and found a nice, quiet piece of grass for myself overlooking the water. There'd been enough sun to dry the morning dew from the grass, and there was still enough sun to make the water sparkle like diamonds. I hadn't seen much beauty in a while, always in too much of a hurry to hustle back to my cave to look up, look around and appreciate what I saw. But I took a moment and as the steam wafted out from the chips in the paper bag, I even smiled.

The fish and chips were old school, wrapped in paper, straight out of the fryer, they were nice and greasy and heavy on the salt, the fish coated in thick crunchy batter. It reminded me of those long lazy summers I'd spent with Benny.

I couldn't remember the last time the memories of Benny hadn't engulfed me with pain. I avoided thinking of him, drowned the memories out with noise, music, the television. I kept busy and kept them at bay. But there was nothing to distract me here and I felt him more than I'd felt him in a long time. It made me feel safe and happy and hopeful.

When I'd finished eating, I bought an ice cream despite the winter chill and began making my way back down the beach. I passed the lady I'd seen in the T-Bar with the big hat, still bickering with her companion. I smiled at them but they didn't smile back. They didn't know who I was, I reminded myself. They'd been bickering and too focussed on each other to have seen me. I'd been busy hiding in the corner of the booth enjoying the fire and my tea. I did a lot of hiding. A lot of shrinking into the shadows. I was safe in my bubble. My sad, lonely bubble. But the bubble was where Benny still lived. Even if it was only in my pain, in my grief. I felt him, or at least I felt the loss of him. Was that the same? I wondered as I sat on a secluded bench overlooking the water.

It wasn't, I knew it wasn't. I felt the best of him today, in the memories, the good, happy ones. As I watched the waves build and flow and crash and recede and begin all over again, I realised it was time to let go of the pain. Time to release the grief. It didn't keep him closer, it just turned him into something else and I was missing the good memories, all the wonderful things we'd done together to build our life, that made him who he was. I was forgetting them. I was forgetting his smile and the sound of his voice and the silly things he'd say just to make me laugh.

I'd been gripping onto the pain so tightly for so long, afraid to see anything else. I began letting it go on an exhale as the ocean receded. Breathed in deep as a fresh wave built. Exhaled as that one crashed onto the sand. My whole body seemed to sigh with the exhale, my muscles let go as though I'd been gripping the edge of a bridge above a canyon.

I barely felt the tears fall down my cheeks but the ocean blurred so I knew they were there, that there were more to come. I looked around but I was alone. No one knew me here. My sunglasses were on and there was nothing but the ocean and the gulls, so I let them fall until there were none left. There was no howling or hysterics, just a quiet, knowing release. A quiet sense of relief. And just a little pinprick of light shining in through the dark.

I felt better, lighter by the time I returned to my room at the pub. I washed my face and was putting away my coat and thinking about what library books I'd brought with me when there was a knock on the door.

'Hi, Jo?' asked the person on the other side. 'I'm Bodhi,' he introduced.

Bodhi was about the same height as me, perhaps a smidge taller. He had a beautiful serenity about him, it almost glowed from his soft, smooth skin. He was a strange blend between masculine and feminine, the timbre of his voice was even stuck somewhere in between and with an accent that was not quite distinguishable. He had dirty blonde hair he'd pulled back into a man bun. Benny would have called it hippy hair but this person was beyond hippy, he was the embodiment of light.

'Hi,' I replied, suddenly feeling self-conscious about all the shaken-up emotions inside my body and what must still be an awfully blotchy face and red eyes from my crying jag on the beach.

'Are you ready?' he asked, seemingly not noticing any of the chaos whirling inside of me.

'Sure,' I shrugged. I had nothing to lose. Jaz had made it sound so easy and if it didn't work then who could argue with a nap in the middle of the afternoon?

Bodhi led me down the hallway and around the bend to one of the rooms that overlooked the carpark and national park beyond that he was using as his treatment room.

The overhead lights were off. Just a salt lamp in two corners giving a soft light. The faint smell of sage hung in the air. I recognised it from the essential oils Ainsley had come to love. I breathed it in, appreciating the familiarity of the smell and the comfort that eased through my body.

In the middle of the room was a massage bed laid with the usual towels for comfort and warmth. I sat on the edge of the bed and awaited further instruction.

Bodhi sat on a rolling stool, scooted up next to me and I got a fresh waft of that sage as though he'd bathed in it and it had clung to his skin. 'So, what brings you here?'

I took a deep breath. This was part of the letting go, I told myself, letting people in and finding peace. I'd already begun the process on the beach, it was time to truly set it all free and trust in whatever this process was so I had a chance of moving forward.

Bodhi had the loveliest kind air about him and as I hovered over what to say, I remembered the girl with the bakery bag. I didn't want to become a ghost woman scurrying around in the shadows. It was time to share the pain and see what he could do with it all. I had to try. It would all still be there whether

I held onto it with a death grip or not, my story, my loss, my broken heart. It wouldn't hurt, it wouldn't change anything if I let go just a little, so, I politely and unemotionally told Bodhi, my story.

'Three years ago, I quit my corporate, soul sucking job, even though it paid well, went to work as a barista in my friend's café after she tried to commit suicide. She'd inherited the café from a madam she'd befriended near her parent's home. Then my boyfriend died. I gave up my home, moved into my friend's apartment above the café and she moved in with her billionaire boyfriend. She married him while we were in Vegas hunting down the dead Madam's long-lost husband, a notorious thief known as the Bauble Bandit who went missing in the seventies. My dear friend Ainsley, the café owner, went on to have some babies with the billionaire and still lives in their swanky home and I still live upstairs from the café and do more of the running of it now she has a couple of little ones.'

'Wow, that must have been a tough year for you.'

'Year?' I chuckled. 'No, that was just a few months. It all happened a little fast, I know and it took some time for my head to catch up and the legalities to fall into place, but it was a lot for a short period of time. Ainsley's babies took longer, obviously, but the rest, not so much.'

He raised his eyebrows in surprise but clearly had no words. 'And so how have you ended up here?'

'Ainsley made me come. She booked it, worked it all out with Jaz and shipped me off like prized cattle and here I am.'

'Why did she make you come?'

'She thinks I don't get out enough and that I'm not living my life to the fullest. She thinks since Benny died, I've cut myself off and she read somewhere it's not healthy to be a hermit.'

'Have you? Cut yourself off? Become a hermit?'

I shrugged. 'Maybe. Not intentionally. I'm happy enough. I feel fine enough. It's not like I sit up in my apartment wallowing.'

'But?'

'How did you know there's a but?'

He smiled.

'I don't like the quiet. I get anxious in the quiet. But I just walked on the beach in the quiet and it was nice. I remembered Benny for the first time in a long time and that was nice too. I'm already doing better for being here but God, don't tell Ainsley,' I laughed.

He nodded, trying not to smile.

'She doesn't know about the anxiety though,' I added defensively. 'I've not told anyone but my shrink that. She just thinks I need to get out more and that by not getting out, it's a sign I'm sad or something. She really needs to re-evaluate where she gets her information. I'm not. Sad that is. Well, I am but not unnaturally so. It'd be abnormal for me to not still be sad about Benny, right? It was sudden. He was the love of my life.'

'You think there's only one love for everyone?'

I shrugged. 'I haven't thought about it. I can't imagine replacing him though.'

'You think loving again, feeling good, moving on with your life, is disrespecting him?'

I shrugged. Dr Bailey and I had had this conversation and it always ended the same, with me shrugging and him agreeing to discuss it again in a few months.

'You think he wouldn't want you to move on and be happy?'

'Why does everyone say that? I'm not sure I'd like him to be moving on lickety split as though I'd meant nothing.'

'Three years isn't exactly lickety split.'

'Three years isn't very long either.'

'How long would be long enough?'

I shrugged. 'It is what it is and I'm fine with it.'

'Are you?'

I shrugged. 'I can't imagine having a family or living life or being in a relationship with anyone else. We had been together for a long time. We had our way. How could I have that with someone else? It's not really fair to him, is it? And what if I don't like it with someone else?'

'What if it's great? What if it's better?'

I scoffed. I couldn't do that to Benny. How would he feel if I was having a jolly old romp without him and showering some man with praise because he did things differently, did things better, how would that make Benny feel? 'Anyway,' I said, changing the subject. 'This is Ainsley's sister-in-law's place. Ainsley sorted it out and here we are.'

'Ah, she's a Harrington then?'

'By marriage, yeah, and a right pain in my arse with it,' I smiled. 'I'm kidding. I love her to bits. She's the best friend a girl could have and I'm bloody lucky to have her,' I told him.

He smiled. 'It sounds like you are indeed. Alright then, shall we start? Why don't you lie on the bed and just relax? All I ask is that you promise to surrender to the healings and the meditations while you're here. Don't think too much about it or have too many expectations, just surrender and see what happens. Do you think you can do that?'

'I guess so. Sounds easy enough.'

'Excellent,' he smiled and I swear sunshine burst from his pores. What must he see when he looks at me, I wondered? Then I wondered why I was wondering and I chastised myself before giving up and doing as he'd asked, surrendering to the process, lying down and readying myself for a little nap.

Bodhi started by pressing his thumbs into the soft area around my collarbone and my breath caught in my chest, it was hard to breathe.

'It's okay, it happens. Just breathe as best you can,' he told me and he kept doing what he was doing for a while longer and slowly, my breathing eased.

As he moved on, I sucked in a lungful of air and felt better for it. I felt him as he moved around my body, felt his hands hovering just above my arms and my stomach and my feet. He poked at my arms here and there and spent more time hovering over my stomach. I wasn't sure if I was so aware of him because of all the crime tv I watched and subsequent paranoia of knowing how awful humans could be, if it was the difficulty breathing in certain places or the heat coming from his hands. It was like a fire burned from him through my clothes and onto my skin but not in an unpleasant way, it was comforting. He seemed to move methodically. As though following a pattern. I was aware of each movement for a while but then lost myself to his rhythm.

I was just starting to drift off when he spoke. 'There you are, all done. How do you feel?' he asked.

'I'm not sure,' I told him as I sat up. 'That was strangely intense. And I couldn't breathe.'

'I know, I felt that, my own breath caught as well. I almost stopped but you really needed me to keep going.'

'Is that supposed to happen?'

'It's where you've been holding onto a lot of stuck energy, here in your solar plexus,' he explained as he touched my stomach, his hand still warm.

'How are your hands so warm?'

'It's the energy. It's how I do what I do. I can tap into it, turn it on and off when I need to, to some degree but it's always there, just a part of me, I guess. But I wasn't alone in this process.'

'What? Who else was here?' I asked looking around.

He smiled that beatific smile of his. 'Spirits, Jo. I connect with the spirits. I could see the other dimension, I saw them moving around you. You had a man sitting at your feet smiling at you, helping me to take away your pain and fill you with new energy. I suspect from the look on his face, he may have been your Benny. He held his hands together in gratitude when we were finishing. He wants you to move on, Jo. He's grateful you're here.'

'What?' I asked, my eyes welling. 'Benny was here?'

'Sweet girl, he is always with you in spirit.'

'See, that's what I mean. How can I move on if he's here watching? That's not fair to him,' I said, as a tear fell down my cheek.

Bodhi held my hands in his. 'He is not here to stop you from moving forward. He is here to help you move forward.'

'And if I do, will that mean he will be gone for good?'

'When you don't need him anymore, he will move on. He will do other work. This life that we live is not all there is, Jo. But he will stay until he's sure you're okay.'

'What other work would he do?'

'Help other people through their pain, maybe. I'm not really sure, none of us can be, not entirely, until we're there, but he will always come to you if you need him.'

'But until then I'm stopping him from doing good work?'

'I don't think that's how it works,' he smiled kindly.

'But I am, in some way,' I said, almost to myself, deciding I was being selfish by holding onto him. 'I have to let him go, don't I?'

'When you're ready,' Bodhi insisted. 'We have a week. Don't rush it. See how you feel after our final session. In the meantime, I think you need to get all that fresh, clean energy flowing through you. I'm going to go down to the beach to do some yoga before evening meditation. Would you like to join me?'

I looked at him with what I suspected was that same scrunched up face I gave Jaz earlier.

'It will be painless, I promise,' he insisted. 'I'll go slow but I think it will be good for you.'

I nodded. Tentatively, apprehensively. He smiled that smile in return that made me think everything would be okay.

Chapter 6

I followed Bodhi down to the grassy bank by the sand, the same grassy bank surrounded by big gum trees on which Jaz had married Jay. It was a lovely spot overlooking the ocean. Ainsley had brought back pictures of the wedding. Jaz had filled it with tiny twinkling lights and just enough people to keep it intimate but still a beautiful celebration. It still felt like all that love was in the air, all that hope and joy.

I was just in my tracksuit pants and sloppy knit but Bodhi waved off all my concerns. 'It's not a fashion show, Jo, you can do yoga and meditation in anything, a ballgown if you fancy,' he smiled.

I guess we didn't really need to dress for everything. I blame all the advertising, societal expectations to play a part, look a part, to fit in.

'Why don't you grab a mat?' Bodhi suggested, indicating a pile rolled up against a nearby tree.

I did and brought it back to where he stood. 'Are you not using one?' I asked.

'I like to feel the energy of the earth beneath my feet. But it's coming in cold and the dew might make the grass slippery, I don't want you to fall,' he said.

I took off my shoes and he was right. The sun was sinking towards the ocean and the grass was already icy on my bare feet and I could feel the dampness rising from the earth. It had a magical feel to it but I think that might have just been where I was, the view, Bodhi.

I wasn't accustomed to yoga. To things like balancing on one foot. I was smart. I was efficient. I wasn't particularly coordinated. So I appreciated his insight and stepped onto the mat.

In my corporate life, many colleagues had popped across the street in their lunch breaks for a quick yoga session, a class at the gym but I had always been busy running errands, so I didn't have to do them after work or I'd spend the hour enjoying some fresh air in the park with a book. The whole exercising in the middle of the work day felt like too much hassle. Changing into your workout gear, changing back into your work clothes, having to redo your hair and makeup. It was too much.

Back then, I kept fit by getting off the bus a stop early, going to the gym when I remembered or Benny dragged me along on a Saturday morning. I did okay with a decent metabolism. And since I'd joined Ainsley at the café, I'd been too busy hustling here and there, down to the basement and up to my apartment to be worrying about things like yoga and workouts. I woke energised, I went to bed exhausted and satisfied and it worked fine.

We started the yoga session with our legs crossed, focussing on our breathing. Listening to Bodhi's voice, following his direction helped keep the noise in my mind at bay.

When Bodhi was satisfied, we rolled on our backs stretching and easing muscles and then stretching out our hips. He walked me through pose after pose. Helping here and there. Aligning my body. Keeping me safe. It was nice. The stretching. The flow of energy. Being taken care of. The touch of another human.

I struggled with balance but he was patient and as the sun began to sink into the ocean, we sat back onto our haunches and stretched forward and it was a lovely end. We sat back up with our legs crossed and finished with some meditation. It wasn't too different to something The Meditation Queen would lead me through, drawing energy from the centre of the earth, letting in light.

'You look peaceful,' Bodhi commented when we finished.

'I feel peaceful,' I smiled. Looking around, I realised other people had joined us during the meditation. Suddenly I didn't mind. Jaz was right, I hadn't noticed them at all. 'I feel more peaceful than I have in a while,' I admitted. 'Thank you for helping me.'

'Of course. I hope you might join me for meditation in the morning. We start at six.'

'In the morning? On a Sunday?' I asked.

He smiled that smile but said nothing.

'Sure,' I sighed but not sure I really meant it. 'I'll do my best. But right now, I feel so relaxed I might never get out of bed,' I admitted, thinking about how beautiful that cloud bed had felt.

'Well, you have a little while before you can sleep. Come on, you'll want to freshen up, dinner is in half an hour.'

The last of the daylight had gone by the time we reached the stairs to the first floor. He left me at my door and continued on. As I let myself into my room, I felt relaxed and calm and for the first time in a long time, my brain was quiet, not racing, not erratic, not sad, just quiet, so that was something.

I dressed in my only pair of jeans and my nice jumper. Ainsley had been right when she said I didn't shop for myself anymore. Not beyond the necessities anyway. If my jeans had a hole in them, I bought new jeans. Serviceable, practical shopping, that's what I did, but for fun, for fashion, to feel pretty, not since Vegas.

Even in Vegas, it had felt very out of body. Benny had not long died. I'd only just managed to get out of bed and back to work and in a blink we were in Vegas looking for Henry Mayberry and it was like for that week I was someone else, someone with a different life, someone whose boyfriend hadn't just died on his way to work one morning. It was that other person who'd shopped for Ainsley's wedding dress, my bridesmaid dress, sunhats for by the pool and pulled Harrington style strings to get an improvised, impromptu number from the Thunder from Down Under while we had a mani pedi. But I'd come home and that was that. No more shopping. No more frivolity or drinking or dancing. I was fine. I was happy, enough. I didn't need all those fancy things anymore.

Something changes to your priorities after losing someone that should have lived another sixty years. I still had all my fancy clothes from my other life. The suits and work dresses, the pretty frocks and fancy jeans. All the boxes from that life were in the basement. Piled amongst the remnants of Mrs May's life. I couldn't bear to look. I'd taken a jumper once and ended up a blubbering mess. Everything still smelled of our home, of us, of Benny. I'd popped down the mall to Target for the essentials and I replaced them when they broke and that was that. So I wore my comfortable, serviceable jeans and soft, functional jumper downstairs to dinner. The Old Colonel wasn't the sort of pub you had to dress nicely for, anyway. People didn't walk around like bums but it was a casual, no judgement kind of place. No one would have judged me if I'd gone to dinner in my fleece pants. But for the first time in a while, I felt the need to do better.

Jaz and Jay were busy over by the bar, so I waved and looked for a seat. I couldn't see Bodhi, the only other familiar face. There were some small tables already occupied. There were a few people filling up a long communal table. I wasn't sure yet if I was ready for the company of strangers so I sat at an empty table. I was a bit out of practice at making friends. I met a lot of people at the café, I chatted a lot but it was inane stuff and mostly, they talked, I listened. I didn't actively make friends, sometimes in part because I'd learned the first question people asked when given the opportunity was 'Are you married?'

My marital status or more so, the story behind it was not something I wanted to be discussing with strangers, or with anyone at all. I hadn't even mentioned it in so long before I'd sat with Bodhi because everyone I spent time with knew everything there was to know, so there was nothing to discuss.

Ainsley was right, I had been cutting myself off, avoiding people and life, to avoid having to talk about Benny, about my new life, my new reality. Now I realized how I lived, how I'd been protecting myself, I saw how unhealthy it must have looked to Ainsley. No wonder she'd been so worried about me.

To me, it was just comfortable and easy but I saw how she might worry. Was she right to? Should I be doing more, making new friends, getting out more? Meeting another man? What would life even be like with someone else? Learning new coffee routines, hobbies, tv preferences, even going to the movies would be a whole new experience.

Benny knew where I liked to sit, that I liked to be there in time for the ads and the previews, that I didn't eat the sugary snacks because I was a popcorn girl but I'd have to explain it all to someone new, learn someone else's rules for life, go through the whole polite faze before we got down to the real business of the truth and that I didn't like to share my popcorn. And what about sex? What would that be like with someone else? What would it feel like if they touched me where he'd touched me? And what if I didn't do things right?

Benny and I had been together so long, I could barely remember anyone before him. What if Benny had forgiven my lack of experience because the rest of our life was so good? Or what if Benny and I had gelled so perfectly because we were two halves made for each other and with everyone else, it would just be disappointing? I didn't want to spend my life going from one disappointment to another. Always looking for something that measured up but never finding it because I'd already had what I was searching for.

What if with someone else, it was just awkward and awful and I couldn't look at him in the morning and it ruined everything else we had started and I'd just have to start all over again with someone else? I'd never given any of the practicalities any thought before now. I'd resigned myself to being done with all those things. Without Benny to do them with, there didn't seem to be any point. Even Dr Bailey hadn't managed to get into my head and make me see any of it. What had Bodhi actually done with his hocus pocus? He'd opened something up in my head, cleared a way for new thoughts. I had no idea how, but he had.

'Hello,' an older lady I'd seen in the tearoom earlier said, interrupting my internal monologue as she pulled out a chair and sat down on the other side of the table.

'Hi,' I replied, although it may have sounded like a question.

'You don't mind me sitting here, do you?' she asked as an afterthought.

I shrugged because I no longer minded the company it seemed. Or maybe it was just the lovely energy she seemed to bring with her.

'Margaret Packersham,' she introduced as though it were all one word.

'Jo,' I said as the waitress offered me a glass of wine. I nodded and she poured.

She offered the bottle to Margaret Packersham and Margaret hesitated as she considered.

'Go on, you're on holiday, right?' I said, full of peer nudgery.

She giggled as though we were old friends and we egged each other into mischief all the time, then nodded at the waitress.

The waitress poured and moved on to the next table where the ghost girl sat alone with her head down. She shook her head at the offer of wine without even looking up and the waitress moved on.

'Why is she all alone?' I asked, almost absently and not really expecting an answer.

'She's been like that since she got here a few days ago. I've tried talking to her but I don't get much more than a single word response,' Margaret Packersham explained.

'She looks sad,' I added.

'Yes. Doesn't she.'

I watched the Ghost Girl for a moment. She looked in pain, more than pain, perhaps something else, as though she was hiding behind the shadow she created for herself with her hair. She hung her face and wore clothes so baggy they could have been for a bear of a man and she was just a waif of a girl. I couldn't sit there and leave her in a room full of people all alone and in pain. What kind of person would that make me? What kind of person did that make everyone else in the room?

I walked over to her table. 'Hello,' I said.

She looked up, surprised but she didn't say anything.

'Would you like to come and sit with us?' I asked, indicating the table where Margaret Packersham sat.

She seemed to consider the offer for a moment but then shook her head. 'No,' she mumbled. 'But thank you,' she added, before hanging her head and returning her attention to the game of Candy Crush she was playing on her phone.

At least I'd gotten more than a one-word answer, I guess.

That sounded like an improvement to the response Margaret had received, albeit only a little.

I returned to my seat as the lady that had been bickering with her companion in the tearoom earlier sat down at a table in our sectioned off area with her companion, which meant both her and ghost girl were also guests here to seek Bodhi's healing powers.

'What do you think is wrong with her?' I asked, referring to the bickering lady. Other than the bickering, she looked put together and in control.

'That's Karen. She's some famous author, so one of the girls was telling me, and he's her publicity manager, apparently, but I'd say he's something more. They share a room and what kind of manager holidays with an author?' Margaret Packersham offered without me asking.

'Famous, huh? You know what for?'

She shook her head. 'The girl I was talking to didn't know. Said Karen had been really cagey and not very chatty. I think she writes sexy books though. Don't you think she looks the sort?'

I hadn't realised there was a sort.

'I bet she wrote something like that shady book that everyone devoured but were too embarrassed to admit to reading.'

I smiled because I liked this Margaret Packersham even though I didn't agree with a word of what she said. I'd seen the woman who wrote the book she was talking about and she just looked like an ordinary lady, but I had hidden my copy from Benny, she'd been right about that. I'd had to read it and see what all the fuss was over and had fallen in love with the fun banter of the characters. I'd thought it was supposed to be about the hanky panky bedroom shenanigans but I'd liked their banter. It did made me question what my own neighbours did in their homes because she looked like all of them. *Who else had such an interesting imagination*, I'd think when I put out the bins on a Sunday night and would catch one in a friendly wave? So, I just smiled at Margaret Packersham's amusing assessment.

'So, how are you finding things?' Margaret Packersham asked as she sipped her wine.

'I'm not sure yet,' I admitted, 'I'm feeling rather unlike myself, to be honest,' I told her

'Ah yes, well, that's Bodhi for you,' she said.

'You sound like you know him?'

'What? Oh no, no dear, I've been here for a week already, that's all,' she said. 'He's very good at what he does.'

'So, Margaret Packersham, how's this place treating you?'

'Oh, lovely, dear. I lost my husband a while back. Bodhi has been helping me along, helping with the pain of it. It takes some getting used to. Being without someone after so long. You never think you're going to be the one who's left behind,' she commented thoughtfully.

I nodded, because I understood her loss. At least some of it.

'How long were you together?' I asked.

'Forty-two wonderful years,' she smiled.

'Children?'

'A daughter, who lives in London now. She comes home with her son when she can but she's busy, he has school and soccer and things. We do a lot of that face timing.'

'It's nice that you have her.'

'And who do you have?'

'What do you mean?'

'You feel the pain too, I can see it in your eyes.'

I smiled. 'I lost my boyfriend three years ago. We weren't together as long as you and your husband, but it hurt. It still hurts. But I have people. My friend Ainsley organised all this for me, organised for someone to cover my shifts at the café where we work even though she has a newborn and a toddler.'

'That sounds like good people.'

'She's the best.'

Just as I was about to go on about Ainsley, Bodhi walked in with another man. Tall, tanned, his hair too long, his beard the same. He looked up and our eyes locked and the biggest grin broke out on his bearded face. Russ.

I felt my whole body sigh at the sight of him. He cut Bodhi off from whatever he was saying and weaved his way through to where I sat with Margaret Packersham. I stood to meet him and he instantly wrapped his arms around me in a bear hug, stopping just short of twirling me around like a prize he'd just won.

He let go, keeping his hands on my arms as though afraid I'd disappear if he let go. 'Jo?' he asked as though he almost couldn't believe it was me.

'Russ... what are you doing here?' I asked unable to resist hugging him one more time to be sure it was really him, that he was really there. My whole body sagged into him with a sigh as his arms wrapped around me, as the warm, spicy honey smell of him filled my senses. My body sighed as though something inside of me was recognising a familiar place that had felt like home for a little while.

I stood back to look at him, hardly comprehending he was standing in front of me after all this time. I'd last seen him when we'd danced our way down the Las Vegas strip after a night at the Excalibur. It'd been a month after I'd lost Benny and Ainsley and I had gone looking for Henry Mayberry and Russ had been our guide. Then Ainsley and Christian got married and while they were celebrating, Russ had kept me company. He'd farewelled me that night at the door to my hotel with a flourish reminiscent of a knight and then he was gone, and I hadn't seen or heard from him since. Not a phone call or email or a single peep to know he was even alive.

'My mother brought me here if you can believe it,' he said.

'Your mother, why? Wait what are you even doing in the country?'

'Long story. One that ends with my mother being so desperately worried she brought me here to see Bodhi,' he laughed.

'I suppose that story would also explain why you look like you've been living in the mountains eating bear?'

He laughed, a big, loud laugh that lit up his face and made his dark blue eyes sparkle. 'I look that bad, huh? I guess I've been a bit... distracted,' he added thoughtfully.

Bodhi called to him as the first of the meals came out of the kitchen.

'Well,' he glanced at the small table I was sharing with Margaret Packersham, then said, 'I'll leave you to eat your dinner. I promise I'll tell you all about eating bear later,' he smiled. He pulled me in for another tight hug. 'It's really good to see your face, Jo Jo,' he whispered into my ear before walking away, leaving my whole body buzzing with happiness.

Chapter 7

'Well, isn't he a dish?' Margaret Packersham said, as I watched Russ walk away. Whatever had happened to turn him into a mountain man, he still cut a nice figure from behind I noticed before chastising myself for noticing.

I waved Margaret Packersham off. 'He's just Russ,' I told her, putting the way his body moved out of my mind.

'The way he was looking at you, love, I don't think you're just Jo to him.'

'What? Don't be ridiculous,' I said as a waitress put my schnitzel parmigiana with chips in front of me.

'Ahuh,' Margaret said with her eyebrows raised before thanking the waitress for her dinner.

'What's that supposed to mean?'

'Nothing. It's just I saw the way your face lit up when you saw him. It was like finally you'd been let out into the sun after being locked away for the winter.'

'Pah,' I grumbled. 'We're just old friends. He was good to me when I needed a friend,' I told her.

Thankfully there wasn't much conversation after that as we began devouring our schnitzels, so it was easy enough to change the conversation to benign subjects. She talked about the small town she was from where she'd built a good life amongst the community and I tried not to glance over at Russ.

'It's hard though when you lose someone,' she said. 'You just don't always fit without them and that's how I felt. Going to barbeques with friends didn't feel right without him anymore. I was always just a little bit lost on my own and I felt lonelier than when I was at home on my own. I miss going to dinner together though and having someone to talk with about what's on the telly or what's growing in the garden. It's the little things I miss the most. But I'm feeling better after Bodhi's treatments. I have a few more to go but I'm already feeling better,' she said.

'I'm glad. And I understand,' I said, reaching for her hand as her eyes welled. 'Nothing is the same when they're gone.' I told her about not being able to even clear my things out of our house and she sympathised as only someone who'd been through that kind of heartache could.

Margaret Packersham made for lovely company. We'd shared our pain and we'd giggled our way through dinner like old friends. Although that could have been the wine. Bodhi's treatment left me feeling like I'd detoxed and the wine went straight to my head. But in that lovely way that made you feel light and happy.

I looked around the room at our companions as everyone was finishing their dinner. I made a pact with myself to sit with Ghost Girl the next chance I got. I'd force myself on her because sometimes we needed it. That's what Margaret Packersham had done when she'd sat down at my table for dinner and now I had a lovely new friend. I wasn't sure what pain Ghost Girl felt or if it was the same pain as me but I could see she was hurting and she looked like she needed a friend and I knew what that was like.

Karen, the famous author, and her manager slash lover, got up and left as soon as they placed their cutlery on their plates. Karen the famous author's manager, slash lover, gave a quick thanks to Jay as they passed then he hurried after Karen before she got away.

There was big group at the communal table that appeared to be making the polite conversation of strangers happy to make friends they'd probably add to Facebook but never actually see again.

Two women sat across the room, a bottle of wine upturned in a bucket as they giggled. They looked like they'd stepped out of a Lorna Jane catalogue with their soccer mum-esque active wear outfits. They had dark rings under their eyes and that exasperated look of mother's too used to running after little people.

Then there was Bodhi and Russ eating with Jaz and Jay. I hadn't realised Jaz and Jay would stay in here to eat or I'd have sat with Jaz. I felt bad for a moment for not having been more gracious, she'd gone out of her way to make space for me. But I was glad to have met Margaret Packersham and I knew Jaz wouldn't have minded, she wasn't that kind of person.

As the room emptied out and Margaret Packersham thanked me for a delightful evening before leaving, I went over to thank Jaz and to see Russ.

'You're not going up yet, are you?' Jaz asked when she saw me.

'I hadn't really thought about it, why?'

'We're going to go into T-Bar for cocktails, or mocktails for me. Come, spend some time with us,' she asked. 'Oh, have you met Russ?' she asked, clearly not having seen our display earlier.

'Indeed, I have,' I smiled. 'Russ and I met in Vegas when Ainsley and I went looking for Henry Mayberry,' I told her.

'You're that Russ?' Jaz asked, snapping her head around to look at him as though not quite believing it.

'What Russ is that?' he asked. 'How do you know about that?' Jay asked.

'You know Jaz is Christian's sister, right?' I asked Russ.

'What? Are you kidding? You're that Jaz?' Russ said.

She laughed.

I shook my head.

'Come on, I think we need those drinks,' declared Jay.

Bodhi, Jaz, Jay, Russ and I moved into the T-Bar. Jay organised drinks for us, drinks that seemingly appeared as though his staff were reading his mind. We squished into one of the big semicircular booths designed for large groups and I had a view of the ocean outside the window glistening under the moon. It was a beautiful place to be.

'So, I have to know more about how you and Russ met,' Jaz insisted.

'Christian set it up, for Russ to help find Henry Mayberry. Christian was supposed to go with Ainsley but your dad did his thing and made up some crisis, although I think it was his heart, so not entirely made up. But anyway, he was just trying to keep them apart, so Christian went up north to help out your dad and I went to Vegs with Ainsley instead. My boyfriend had just died so I needed a break from everything I knew and then waiting at the other end was Russ. So, we spent a week traipsing up and down the strip together looking for Henry, who bloody well died right after we found him. Then Christian came, and he and Ainsley got married. Russ and I went to the Excalibur show so I wouldn't be sitting around all by myself while they did their marital things, and that was that. It was nice to have a have a friend, to be silly and drunk and to laugh with a mate over mindless things.'

'Well now, wasn't that chivalrous of you?' Jaz smirked.

He shrugged as though it was no big deal.

'He's a chivalrous kind of guy,' I told her. 'He's very good at catching damsels.'

'I think you're the only damsel I've caught with any kind of chivalry, Jo,' he said, leaning in closer to me with a naughty smile on his face. 'I'd like to say I'm renown for it,' he told the table, 'but I'd be lying. Jo's good people though. We have history. And Ainsley would have sliced my balls off if I'd taken advantage.'

'That's the only reason you didn't take advantage of my misery?' I asked curiously.

'No. If I'm taking advantage Jo, I want you to be seeing my face while I'm doing it,' he declared.

Jaz and Jay raised their eyebrows. Bodhi stirred his cocktail intently.

My heart beat a little faster and my breath caught in my throat. 'Russ...'

'What? I have a pulse, Jo. I have eyes.'

'Right?' I said with an understanding smile but somewhere inside I caught a glimpse of my heart sagging in disappointment, that to him, I had just been another pretty face in a city full of pretty faces.

What was that? I wondered. This is Russ. We ate turkey legs like animals together. We drank beer from tankards and yahooed like yobbos and sang Australian pub songs walking down the Vegas strip. He hadn't so much as tried to kiss me. Not then. Not on the vodka fuelled night when Henry Mayberry had died. We'd drunk so much that night we could barely stand. We were just lucky Christian Harrington owned the hotel or they'd have thrown us out. Yet still, with all that vodka flowing through his veins, Russ had been the perfect gentleman. We were mates. He'd come through for me. He'd heard stories. I'd cried on his shoulder. We shared things. Personal things. He'd seen me at my worst.

Why would I think he'd fancy me after that? Of course he hadn't looked at me beyond seeing a pretty face. A pretty face like all the pretty faces he'd slept with. He wasn't the kind of guy that even saw much else. It was who he was. I knew this about him. I knew he liked to play the field, keep things free and easy. It's why he avoided bedding the locals, kept to the tourists passing through town. Less complications, an unspoken understanding but he was my mate and we'd laughed about it. So why was I suddenly so disappointed that he hadn't seen me as anything more?

'Jo Jo... that came out wrong,' he begged, his voice panicked.

'Don't be silly. It's cool Russ. Another time, another place, I might have gone there too, fling away and all that.'

He looked around at our companions who were intently watching our exchange. 'We will talk about this later,' he said, with that serious look of his you never expected when you saw the rumpled shirt and the three-day growth he usually sported as though it were a uniform. But that was Russ for you, a contradiction.

Jaz did what a good Harrington does and redirected the conversation but it didn't last long. A couple of laughs later and everyone called it a night. Bodhi seemed to hover as though he had something to say but eventually Jaz delicately led him away amid a conversation on spiritual awakenings.

'Will you walk with me?' Russ asked. 'Please?'

'Sure,' I agreed, unable to stay cross at him. What was I even cross about? I couldn't be mad at Russ for being who he was.

As Russ led me outside and across the grassed area to the sand with his hand on the small of my back, I wondered if he'd been that tall in Vegas. Had he had that same, self-assured air about him then? It was almost arrogant. But amused at the same time. By himself. By what people saw. I don't know. It was like I was seeing him for the first time despite him being so familiar. The feeling of his touch though was just as I remembered. He had a way of making you feel safe and seen with the smallest of gestures. He moved his hand from my back to my elbow to lead me onto the sand. A cold chill swept across where his hand had been and raced over my skin sending a shiver through my body.

I took a breath. Let it go. 'It's been a long time,' I told him.

He nodded, looking at me from the corner of his eye with a smile as though he too couldn't believe he was seeing me.

'Not a single email,' I added.

'Ah you didn't need me popping into your inbox with all you were going through,' he told me, draping his arm across my shoulders as we walked along the quiet beach with just the hush of the ocean. He'd done it before, the familiarly draped arm. Many times. He'd done the same with Ainsley. It didn't mean anything. He was just that kind of guy. But this time, unlike the other times, I wanted to lay my head on his shoulder and sink into his warmth.

The night air had a bite to it and it nipped at my nose and my ears. But the need to sink into him came from somewhere else. I didn't want to know where. I didn't want to think about that. What I'd said to Bodhi before our session was true. I couldn't imagine sinking into the warmth of anyone but Benny. But something had happened to me on the beach earlier and then something else I couldn't define happened in that session with Bodhi, in the meditation before dinner, and my pain didn't sit so heavily inside me anymore. It had been there for so long, a weight buried deep inside my stomach, the loss, the missing Benny, the sadness over our lost future, our lost dreams but now it was like Bodhi had taken the weight of it away and left in its place something that felt like hope. And as Russ pulled me closer and kissed the top of my head, I didn't seem to mind the idea of it even though it was just a Russ kind of thing to do.

'I really am sorry, you know,' he said into the quiet.

'For what? Being you? Don't be ridiculous.'

'You think that's who I am?'

I shrugged.

'Okay, maybe sometimes. Maybe a lot,' he chuckled. 'But it's not all I am and it's not how I see you.'

'Why would you see me any differently to any other woman?' I asked curiously.

'Because you're Jo Jo,' he said as though it were an explanation.

'What does that mean?'

'It means you mean more to me than just a pretty face. You're my Jo Jo.'

'Thank you,' I said, not entirely sure what I was thanking him for, but grateful for some kind of validation that I was more than just a pretty face, more than whatever it was he saw when he took his women to bed. Not that that was what I wanted from him. Was it? Oh shit. No, of course not. That would be crazy. I justified my wayward thoughts as a waking libido smelling the hope Bodhi had left behind with his hocus pocus. It didn't mean I fancied Russ. It didn't mean I was ready to jump his or anyone else's bones. It just meant a weight was gone. I had to get used to the new feeling. I was misconstruing simple bodily feelings, the smell of a man and the comfort of his arm holding me close because I hadn't felt them in so long.

'You alright?' he asked.

'I should be asking you that,' I said, looking up at him. 'What's with the mountain man look?'

He pulled me close as he looked out to the ocean before answering. 'Now that's a Vegas story that probably won't impress you and it's too nice a night to be seeing disappointment in your eyes when I finally get to see you for the first time in three years.'

'Can you at least tell me why you're here, at this place, in the country without so much as a phone call?'

He smiled down at me and it lit up his whole face. 'Are you cross I didn't call?'

I shrugged but couldn't help smiling.

'I like that you're cross about that, I think,' he said, considering it for a moment and then nodding. 'My mother heard about Bodhi through her friends at the golf club, thought it would be good for me and dumped me here like an errant teenager.'

'Right. So that somehow links in with the Vegas story?'

He nodded. 'And why I didn't call you. Or Christian for that matter.'

'Are you in hiding?' I joked.

'Not from the mob or anything,' he laughed. 'But yeah, kind of, I guess. From life. From everything.'

'What on earth would Russell Whittington III have to hide from?'

He smiled.

'Right,' I said, thinking it must be one heck of a story.

'I'm glad you're here though,' he said. 'I didn't realise how much I needed a friend until I saw your face.'

I wrapped my arms around him in a hug.

'Now, why don't you tell me why you're here?' he asked with a smirk.

I smiled. 'Ainsley made me. You know, Harrington BFF, Harrington hosting the guru, the two of them put their meddling heads together and here we are. You know Ainsley has two babies now?' I said, changing the subject.

'What? That's incredible. I'm not sure I can imagine Christian as a dad.'

'You really didn't know?'

He shook his head.

'So you've not kept in touch with Christian, either?'

'Is that your polite way of telling me off?'

I shrugged. 'Maybe.'

'I haven't kept in touch with anyone. I've kind of been swirling around in my own bubble.'

'I suppose that's part of this mysterious story?'

'Not so much mysterious as miserable. You've avoided my question, you know,' he said, tilting my chin up with his finger so I had to look in his eyes. 'Are you okay, Jo?'

'What? Of course,' I insisted. 'It's just Ainsley thought I was too sad and this guru guy was going to take it all away.'

'Are you? Too sad?' he asked, his eyes on mine, melting something inside me, something I'd been holding on to without even realising. My breath caught for a second and sweat pooled in my armpits. It was as though his eyes could see into my deepest darkest corners and I didn't know what to make of what was happening to my body.

'Honestly, I'm feeling better than I have in a really long time,' I assured him, ignoring my current inner turmoil.

He watched me with those eyes, his face moved just a fraction closer and I thought this is it, time to decide what side of the fence you're on with this moving forward business. But, just as I thought he was going to kiss me, he tapped my nose, kissed my forehead and said, 'I'm glad. Come on, let's head back, it's getting a bit cool out here.'

My whole body deflated on a sigh and I wasn't sure if it was from relief or disappointment. He draped his arm across my shoulders and we walked back down the beach and I nursed a little something in the pit of my stomach. I was disappointed. Disappointed he hadn't kissed me. Disappointed he'd tapped my nose and kissed my forehead with the love and kindness of a brother. What the hell was happening to me? What had Bodhi done in that session? I'd been different ever since. Now I was disappointed my old friend Russ hadn't kissed me. I was losing my bloody mind.

Chapter 8

As morning neared, I lay staring at the ceiling as I had for most of the night. I'd lost track of the time. It was still dark outside the window but it felt like it should be morning.

I'd been going around and around all night thinking about Russ and my reaction to him. I'd come here certain in who I was and what the rest of my life looked like. I had made peace with things like love and a family. I'd had more with Benny than many people ever got and I was fine with that, grateful.

Now there was Russ and I'd stood on the beach looking into his eyes like a lovesick teenager wishing for him to kiss me. How had everything changed so drastically and so quickly? I wondered as someone knocked on my door.

Throwing on a hoodie to brace myself against the cold, I opened the door to Bodhi standing on the other side with a sleepy looking Ghost Girl beside him, a way too perky Margaret Packersham and a trail of other faces obscured by the dark.

'Are you coming to meditation?' he asked.

I looked down at my pyjamas.

'As you are is fine,' he assured me with a smile.

'I'm in my pyjamas,' I said, in case he hadn't noticed.

He waved me off as though it were no big deal. Ghost Girl's outfit consisted of striped flannelette pyjamas. She uncomfortably crossed her arms across her chest. Poor kid. She deserved to have someone in her corner so I shrugged and stepped out.

'He got you too?' I asked her, ignoring her reluctance to make eye contact as we followed Bodhi down the stairs.

'Yeah, you'd think I'd be ready for him by now,' she mumbled.

'You and Russ sort everything out?' Bodhi asked before I could engage Ghost Girl any further.

'Sure, nothing to sort out.'

'You look a lot lighter today. That Russ? Something happen?' Bodhi asked.

'What? No. I suspect it was whatever you did in our session yesterday. But it was nice to see him. I haven't in a long time.'

He nodded but I couldn't quite read his face. He was clearly considering my comments, but there was nothing to consider, the whole thing was very benign. The version I gave him anyway. Before he could voice his thoughts on the subject, Jaz caught up to us and hugged me. 'You and Russ good?' she asked.

'Yep, all good,' I assured her.

'What were the odds of you two running into each other?' she asked.

'He says he hasn't kept in contact with anyone but this has Ainsley written all over it,' I told her.

'That a bad thing?' she asked with that same look Ainsley got when she was up to mischief.

'It's good to see him,' I told her, refusing to divulge anything else, especially not while Bodhi was giving me a weird side eye look. Jaz noticed it too and looked at me with raised eyebrows.

I shrugged, I didn't know what it meant or why he was interested in any of the goings on in my life. We reached the grassed area already set up for our session so I put Bodhi's weird look aside and stood on the mat next to Jaz.

A few other guests had already gathered. The Lorna Jane mums were perfectly kitted out for the occasion but then I suspected they lived in readiness with their active wear but otherwise everyone appeared to be in an array of whatever they rolled out of bed in or what had been on the floor next to them. But there was no Russ.

It wasn't the same as the evening before when Bodhi and I had meditated together or at least had begun together. It didn't feel as intimate but it was nice just the same. Focussed. Calm.

'He's pretty bossy for a guru, isn't he?' I asked Ghost Girl to make conversation as we walked back up the grass towards the patio that led to the T-Bar.

She shrugged. 'I've never met a guru so I wouldn't know,' she mumbled.

Fair enough, I thought as we all headed into the T-Barfor breakfast. She was going to take more work than I thought, but I could do that.

I really should have changed out of my pyjamas but no one else bothered and we seemed to move as one through the T-

Bar, like a pack of wildebeest on migration to the beautifully laid out buffet.

I'd been at the pub for breakfast before, dragged along that one time on a family weekend with Ainsley, Christian and Henry, so I knew that breakfast here was usually a la carte. It was a popular place to eat on the weekends with the local surfers and with a good enough reputation to attract the tourists passing through. With so many people in residence though, it seemed they'd gone for a buffet set up instead. It worked fine for me and I filled a plate with eggs, bacon and mushrooms before going to sit at a table with Ghost Girl. Margaret Packersham joined us a moment later.

Ghost Girl stared down into her sad bowl of fruit. She seemed uncomfortable to have company but I was on a mission and she clearly needed a friend.

'We haven't officially met,' I said, interrupting the quiet. 'I'm Jo and this is Margaret Packersham,' I said.

'Natalie,' she replied quietly.

'So what brings you here?' I asked.

'My parents dumped me here hoping for a miracle,' she grumbled. 'You?'

'My best friend did much of the same. I called her a busy body.'

'Who? My sister-in-law a busy body?' laughed Jaz as she passed cups coffee to each of us.

'With the best intentions full of love, of course,' I added, even though I knew I didn't need to with Jaz.

'Of course. Although when you're on the receiving end you

just want to shove her good intentions in a less than sunny place,' she smiled sweetly.

'Well, seeing as I'm eating breakfast in public in my pyjamas at the crack of dawn, right now those are my sentiments exactly.'

'I should have warned you, Bodhi can be demanding,' she said smiling as though she wasn't the least bit sorry. 'I see Russ managed to avoid the meditation round up,' she said as we all turned to watch Russ walk in with Jay, both wearing boardshorts and hoodies, shoeless, their hair wet from surfing, looking far better than anyone had the right to this early in the morning.

Or limp in, I realised watching Russ. If you didn't know him, you'd barely have given it a thought. But I knew him. We'd walked up and down the Las Vegas strip for two days looking for Henry Mayberry. We'd walked down it drunk as skunks barely able to stand. But not once did he limp. I wondered what had happened to Russell Whittington in the last three years? What had brought him home? Why did he look like a mountain man? He'd always had a casually dishevelled look about him. The usual three-day growth on his face, his rumpled shirts and shaggy haircuts, worked in his favour. But he never looked out of control. Not up close. Not once you knew him. He was cool, calm, and as switched on as anyone. This version of my casually dishevelled friend had nothing casual about him.

'What happened to you two last night, anyway?' Jaz asked.

I shrugged. 'Nothing, just went for a walk, caught up on old times,' I told her as Russ caught sight of me and a big stupid grin crossed his face.

'Sure,' laughed Jaz as she moved on to another table to distribute coffee.

Margaret Packersham looked like she was about to say something about the nothing that happened the night before between Russ and me, when the man himself approached and sat next to her. Suddenly Margaret Packersham had nothing to say. She kept trying to find the words but just looked like a guppy, gave up and focussed on her food. I looked over to Natalie and for the first time saw the hint of a smile on her face.

'How did you get out of morning meditation?' I asked him, keeping my eyes on his face to avoid thinking about how he'd just been shirtless, wet and covered in neoprene.

'Easy, I ignored the knock,' he replied matter-of-factly.

'Just like that?'

'Just like that.'

'Do you not care for your recovery?' I asked.

'Surfing is just as good as meditation, trust me, and this wasn't my idea, it was my mother's. But if I'd known you were going to show up in your jammies...' he grinned, giving said pyjamas a once over.

'Shut up,' I said, suddenly feeling self-conscious about my pyjamas, my morningness and wishing I'd gone upstairs for a shower, after all.

I hadn't considered ignoring Bodhi when he came knocking. I'd answered instinctively and then once the door was open there was no escape. I knew better for tomorrow. Although I didn't mind the meditation. I felt strangely peaceful for it, even still, but I minded the crack of dawn wake up call.

After we'd all finished eating, everyone went their separate ways to shower and get on with their day. I lost Russ to a group of surf lovers as I headed upstairs. I was glad for it because I needed some thinking space.

It seemed it wasn't so much that I didn't want to do all those things I'd done with Benny with anyone else. It seemed I didn't want to do them with just anyone. Turned out I might want to do them with Russ. Not exactly the same things but I wanted something from Russ I hadn't thought about wanting in a really long time. Things that hadn't so much as crossed my mind in a passing thought and now filled my head whenever I saw him.

He made my skin buzz with excitement, my heart beat faster and I just wanted to curl up on a couch somewhere and snuggle and talk and while away hours with him. I wanted to know his story, where he'd been, what had happened, why he was here? I wanted to know what his skin felt like under that hoodie, what his bare thighs would feel like when I touched them, how they'd contract from pleasure, from anticipation.

I'd had all these things swirling around in my head while I'd eaten my breakfast. While the four of us had talked of inane things. While Natalie slowly and tentatively opened up a little, contributing to the inane, I wondered what Russ had looked like tucked up in his bed, eyes still heavy with sleep as Bodhi knocked.

Whether I could actually go through with any of the thoughts in my mind, the snuggling, the touching, the sharing, was another story. But the thoughts were there. They were more than passing and feelings were waking inside my body that I'd thought were gone for good. I'd resigned myself to it, content with it, accepted being alone for the rest of my life. But now as I thought of him touching me, my breath caught and my dormant sex drive woke up to say hello.

Dressed and ready for whatever the day had in store, I lay on my bed staring at the library book I was trying to read but suddenly it was too angsty, too violent. When had I stopped liking them? Thrillers and mysteries had become my go to's over the last few years. Anything too happy, too fluffy, too funny, just didn't sit right anymore. But now even these didn't feel good. What was I left with? Where did I go from here?

A knock on the door interrupted my thinking. On the other side stood a freshly shaven Russ in fresh boardshorts and another hoodie.

He walked in and collapsed on my bed as though he did it all the time. 'Why is this room nicer than mine?' he asked looking around at all the nice furnishings while I stood by the door like a silly teenager.

'It's a Harrington family guest room,' I told him finding my words.

'Ah,' he said understanding. 'What's wrong?'

'Nothing. Why?'

'Why are you standing by the door?'

I shrugged.

'Jo? What's going on?' he smiled, as though he knew exactly what was going on, his arms behind his head pulling the hoodie up to show his bare stomach.

'Nothing. I have to go,' I mumbled, running from the room and leaving him lying on my bed.

I'd lost my mind. All I'd wanted to do was climb on the bed beside Russ and wrap my arms around him and sink into the warmth of him, to feel his heartbeat and his breath on my skin. It had been such an intense, visceral need, I'd vibrated with it and it terrified me. So like any maladjusted woman, I ran. No bag, no shoes, no coat.

The sky was a perfect blue but even the sun couldn't take the chill off the ocean or the fear from my insides. A month ago, it would have been too hot to walk barefoot on the sand, now the sand felt like ice. We lived in a land of dramatic contrasts. My brain seemed to have taken on those same contrasting affects.

A month ago, I knew exactly who I was and where I was at, what my life would be and I was okay with all of it. My life was good. It was full enough. I found joy in the small things like sleepovers with Henry and sun-filled walks through the mall picking up a treat for Henry or something the coming baby or enjoying a piece of cake Mrs Donovan snuck into my kitchen upstairs with a quiet cup of coffee and catch up tv.

There were so many things in my life that were joyful and beautiful and I was happy. Happy enough. My life wasn't full of parties and nights out and whatever else it was Ainsley thought I was missing out on, but it was a good life, a nice life. My life.

But suddenly I didn't know which way was up, like the earth was turning too fast. I couldn't catch my breath, my head felt like it was spinning out of control and my heart was doing this thing that I couldn't remember it ever doing and I didn't know how to make it stop.

It wasn't just about how beautiful Russ looked freshly shaven and leisurely lying on my bed, his arms behind his head, his hoodie rising up, just a little, revealing his bare skin underneath with that smart-arsed smile on his face, and trust me, it was a sight indeed.

The second I'd seen him walk into the dining room the night before, I'd felt the most beautiful sense of relief. It wasn't just for the sight of a familiar face, for seeing a friend, someone I cared about. But something else. Something else, I couldn't quite put words to.

We'd been friends. We'd been through things, shared things, stories, monumental things. I'd been trying to tell myself, it was just the relief of seeing a friend. Maybe in those first moments, I could have lied to myself and said that that was the case. But then we'd walked and I'd wanted him to kiss me and since, something else had been building and building like a pot getting ready to boil and seeing him lie on my bed, I realised I was somewhere I had never planned to be again.

I'd found myself somewhere so unexpected and strange and I didn't know what to do, about the feelings, about Russ, about that thing that was screaming inside my gut, that feeling of wanting to throw my body against his and taste his mouth on mine and get lost in all of it, in him. It terrified me so much, it had driven me out here onto the damp sand in the morning chill.

Leaving my shoes behind wasn't enough to send me back in there. I didn't care that my feet hurt from cold. I ignored the pain and walked on, let the icy water wash over my feet. I needed to feel something other than lust for my friend.

I kicked at a wave as it crashed over my bare feet. How had I gotten here? Just a week ago, just a few days ago, everything was fine, my life was fine. But suddenly fine wasn't enough. I wanted what Ainsley and Christian had, the way they looked at each other like the rest of the world faded away in those moments. The way they'd looked as they'd held their family, their newborn daughter and it terrified me. How could I even want any of it without Benny? What kind of person did that make me?

I walked back up the sand. The cold powdery sand caking to my numb, wet feet. Natalie was lying in the sand, her arms and legs out wide, baking in the sun like a starfish in her oversized black jeans, her black jumper, boots and coat. She'd closed her eyes to the sun, which made her look mythically golden.

I was going to walk past, I didn't want to disturb her peace with my chaos but she broke the silence. 'Hey,' she said, without seeming to open her eyes.

'Hey,' I said, collapsing down onto the sand next to her.

We didn't speak, we both just lay there staring up at the sky. It was nice. The space. The quiet. For a moment my brain stopped swirling.

'Aren't you cold?' she asked.

'Maybe,' I admitted.

'You running from that guy?'

'Maybe,' I smiled.

'Don't blame you. They're all more trouble than they're worth.'

'I don't know about that. It's complicated.'

'Not if you're both consenting.'

'I don't know if he is.'

'Oh, trust me, if you're offering, that man is consenting. I saw the way he looked at you at breakfast. He's more than consenting.'

It was the most words she'd said in a row, and an opinion, observation thrown in. It made me smile. There was a person inside that body after all. A funny, clever person.

'Jo,' I heard Russ call from up on the grass before we could continue.

'Told you,' Natalie smiled.

I huffed as Russ called my name again. He was closer this time, so I got up from the damp sand to avoid having the conversation we were going to have in front of Natalie.

I met Russ halfway down the beach after having watched him limp towards me. 'You okay?' he asked.

'I should be asking you that,' I suggested, nodding to his leg and purposely avoiding his question.

He huffed. 'I'm fine. Why did you run out? You're barely bloody dressed and didn't even put on shoes. Jo, it's freezing down here.'

I shrugged. 'I can't feel it now.'

'That's because you probably have frostbite.'

'Geez, it's not that cold. Drama queen. You surfed in it this morning,' I chastised with a small smile as I started walking back towards the pub.

'I wore a wetsuit. You didn't answer me,' he said, catching up to me.

'I'm fine.'

'You said that already. Why did you run out of the room?'

I stopped walking. Looked at him as grey clouds swept across the lovely blue sky over head, smothering Natalie's sun and turning the waves from something relaxing and therapeutic into a something else, something sinister that kind of matched my stormy mood.

I watched him for a minute, deciding how much I was going to say. I decided I wasn't ready to come clean with my lustful feelings. 'No reason. Just needed a walk.'

'Don't bullshit me, Jo.'

'It doesn't even matter, Russ. It is what it is and I am who I am.'

'What is what and I know who you are.'

'Do you?'

'Jo, I would never want you to do anything you didn't want to. That you weren't ready for. I get it, you loved Benny and you don't want to go there with me. How could you, you barely even know me? I barely even know me anymore. But I like you. Every time you look at me, it's like being sucker punched. I lose my breath somewhere in my throat. It's like my heart cries out for you, to be near you and my heart has never had an opinion before. But I know you don't feel the same. It's okay. I'm a big boy. I can deal with it. It's not why I came to your room just now either. It doesn't change the fact we're mates.'

'That's just it, Russ,' I confessed. 'I think I feel that too,' I whispered, tears pushing at my eyes.

'Then what's the problem?' he begged, leaning his forehead against mine.

'Because you're also right. I loved Benny.'

'Come on, let's go inside and talk about it.'

'What's there to talk about? I just don't think I can do that to him.'

'But you want to?'

'I don't know anymore.'

'Come on, you're freezing,' he insisted, draping an arm around me and pulling me into his warmth and leading me back to my room.

I went into the bathroom and took off my damp clothes and put on my fleece pants and a hoodie. I found him lying on my bed when I came out and realised he'd put on pants to come and find me.

'Jo, would you sit down?' Russ asked.

It's just Russ, I reminded myself and sat on the bed.

Suddenly it seemed neither of us had anything to say. 'So, do I get to hear the story now? Are you going to tell me what you're doing in the country?' I asked.

'I'm allowed to come home,' he answered defensively.

'To hide out at your parent's?'

'Who said I was hiding out?'

'Russ you looked like you'd been living in the mountains, you had a full beard, your hair's long past cool, casual, floppy and you have dark rings under your eyes. You don't look like yourself at all.'

'Did you become an investigator since I last saw you?'

'Don't be smart. I'm a barista. I see people. I know people. I know you. You're not yourself.'

He shrugged.

'Russ, what happened?'

He shrugged again, stared at the ceiling. After a moment,

he took a deep breath and spoke softly. 'Things got a bit out of control. The drinking. The partying. D and I got into some trouble,' he said, referring to his mate who worked in security at one of the big hotels. He took a moment to gather himself, gather his thoughts, took another deep breath. 'We were yahooing. D got hurt. We both did, I guess. I don't even really know how. We can't really remember. I don't even remember how long it had been since I'd been sober. But there were girls. A fight we think, well, the cameras showed the fight, with men, not the girls but they were there. Then D and I were in hospital. He had a broken arm and a fractured cheekbone. I had a broken leg, broken ribs and a fractured hand.'

'Jesus, Russ, how did you get there? To that point? I know you liked a drink but you're a happy drunk. You don't go around picking fights. That's not who you are. Not to mention, you have a bloody awesome constitution.'

He smiled. 'It was a thing of beauty, right?'

'What happened?'

'I don't know really. After you and Ainsley left, it was just a slow downward spiral.'

'Russ, that was three years ago. You've been spiralling for three years?'

He shrugged.

'Because of Henry?' I asked. I wouldn't blame him. When Henry found out his beloved wife, Ana, had died, he died moments later. The police interrogated us for half the night. Then we'd gone to Christian's fancy hotel to wash the cop shop cooties out of our system with premium vodka until we couldn't stand up.

'No. Not Henry, Jo.'
'Then what?'
'You.'

Chapter 9

'Me? What about me?' I asked, my breath catching in my throat.

'When you left, I don't know, I just felt lost. I guess I kept trying to get that back. Us. What we had. Whatever that was. I wasn't even sure what it was. We were mates. We had a blast. It's not even like we were sleeping together or had *fallen in love*, but I just couldn't seem to find my feet again. I was off kilter. But I tried. I really did but it seemed the more I tried, the more and more out of control I became and I took D down with me and then after that night, a couple of important people had a conversation with me and suggested it might be best if I go home.

'That's how far I'd spiralled. They were asking me to leave Sin City,' he laughed. 'So, I came home and my parents shipped me off to their weekender. They send me shrinks and physiotherapists and everything I need. Groceries show up at my door and to be honest, I don't think I left the house in three months. Mum heard about Bodhi and did what mother's from her world do, harassed someone, probably poor Jaz, to get me a spot in the schedule and drove me here herself.'

'Three months?'

He shrugged.

'And you haven't spoken to Christian?'

He shook his head. 'I've not spoken to anyone but my therapists and the delivery guy from Coles.'

He looked so sad, so broken, so alone. My heart ached for him and I pulled him to me instinctively, wrapping my arms around him and holding him tight. I knew what it was like to feel like you'd fallen apart, and I knew what it felt like to have a friend holding you together. That's what Ainsley had done for me. She'd held me together when Benny had died. She'd lain on the bed and just held me to stop all the pieces of me crumbling and it had worked.

After a few moments, Russ pulled away, tapping my nose. 'See, this, us, you're just you, Jo Jo. No wonder there was a giant hole when you left.'

I looked up into his eyes and that was it, I was gone. I stretched up until my mouth met his and he needed no further invitation to take over.

He was gentle and soft, his hand holding my face as though afraid I might disappear. It was a few deliciously agonising moments before his tongue came to find mine and I sighed into the kiss. He kept his hands still, the one on my face, the other on the small of my back but they didn't wander, his body didn't move, not even when I was practically climbing him, the need to be closer, to pull him closer, consuming me.

My instincts had taken over, my desire controlling my brain and my body. My hand crept up under his hoodie to find bare skin. I pulled him closer, may have groaned and then his hand stopped mine.

'What?' I asked breathlessly.

He smiled at me. Kissed me chastely and rolled away onto his back and stared at the ceiling.

'What's wrong?' I asked, my heart sinking to my toes. Had I done it wrong? I wasn't even sure what I'd done. I'd just let everything else take over.

'Hey, don't look like that,' he begged, pulling me down so I snuggled into him. 'I don't want you to do anything you're not comfortable with.'

'Did I look uncomfortable?' I asked, afraid to look into his eyes.

'Oh, no, you seemed very comfortable,' he said and I could hear the smile in his voice. 'But an hour ago you ran from the room because you were afraid to be alone with me.'

'I wasn't afraid to be alone with you, I was afraid of what I was feeling and what that meant.'

'Semantics. You were afraid.'

'And now I'm not.'

He kissed the top of my head, held me tight against him. 'I just want you to be sure. Take a minute and gather your thoughts. There's no hurry.'

I stretched up, held his face in my hands. Felt the smoothness where he'd shaved. Ran my thumb over his mouth, the same mouth that had just ignited something in me that I couldn't ignore. I wanted him. Just him. My heart and libido had been waiting for him.

I didn't know if I was in my right mind. I didn't know

whether it had anything to do with Bodhi's healing treatment, whether he was pulling my leg when he said Benny was there helping me to let go and move on. I didn't care anymore. It all made sense with Russ, lying with him, with his arms wrapped around me, felt right. I held his face still. He watched me, unsure, uncertain, as I lowered my mouth to his.

Sure he wasn't going to pull away, I let one hand find its way down to the band of his fleece pants. I pushed it inside his pants. He'd forgone underwear and my hand easily instinctually wrapped around him.

Russ' mouth pulled away, breathlessly. 'Jo...'

'Russ, I want this. I want you,' I told him.

'Are you sure?' he begged, his eyes afraid.

My thumb found his mouth again. I ran it across his bottom lip before kissing it. 'I am so sure, Russ. Seems my heart was just waiting for you.'

He smiled, rolled me onto my back, his mouth claiming mine, his hands roaming. His mouth soon followed his hands and my head fell back on a sigh. I'd missed this. This feeling of desire, of being devoured and needed. His mouth claimed my body, did magical things until I could barely take another moment.

'Fuck, Jo Jo,' he said, his lust-filled eyes boring into mine as he panted with the same need that controlled my body. 'Are you sure?'

I nodded, pulling him to me so he knew I meant it. 'Yes. No doubts. I want you, Russ.' I didn't know the entirety of what I meant, and I don't think it mattered. I wanted him, right now and I hadn't wanted anyone since Benny.

He didn't need any more convincing, searched the floor for his wallet and the condom inside it. With that taken care of he paused, giving me another chance to change my mind. I nodded and he slid into me. I closed my eyes, sighing from the beauty of it.

'Look at me,' he begged.

I did as instructed. Losing myself in those infinite dark blue eyes.

'I need to know you see me,' he whispered, his hand holding my face to his.

'I see you, Russ. I see only you,' I confirmed as I pulled his mouth to mine.

He did magical things with his hips, he ground in and out and the exquisite pleasure of it made my eyes roll back. His mouth did beautiful things too, we were losing ourselves in each other, in the heat and the desire.

'God,' he exclaimed his voice husky and desperate.

My whole body was alive, electrified from his touch. But I knew an orgasm wasn't on the cards, the build came and it went without the in between. It's not something that happened for me. There were other ways, that's how it had always worked with Benny.

'It's okay, you go ahead, I don't think it's going to happen for me,' I whispered.

He stopped dead still suddenly losing all his momentum. 'What?' he asked.

'No, no,' I said. 'You go ahead, don't feel bad, sometimes it happens.'

'What do you mean sometimes? How many times?'

'A lot really but it's fine. I am having a nice time and all.'

'A nice time? Are you fucking kidding me?' he asked.

Suddenly I felt bad. I'd put my foot in it. Benny had always been fine enough about it, he'd sort me out other ways, owe me, that kind of thing.

Doing this with other people hadn't crossed my mind as inappropriate. Steeling myself, I waited for Russ to kick me out of the bed.

'No, no,' he said shaking his head. 'That won't do at all. You know that's not how it's meant to be, right?'

'I read that for some women it's just the way it is,' I told him.

'Well whoever wrote that crap was justifying the fact they'd never had a proper orgasm in their whole life. You however, will have multiple before the night is done,' he told me matter-of-factly. A shiver raced up my spine.

'Let me just clean up a minute and we'll start fresh, yeah?' he said, with far too much enthusiasm.

'I really think you're making way too much out of this,' I told his beautiful retreating body.

He switched on the bathroom light but didn't close the door. Was this part of his game? I didn't care. I couldn't take my eyes of him. He was a little rounder in the middle than when he'd spent the night on the couch in our Vegas suite but he still looked alright, better than I remembered from my grief-stricken state at the time. His back and shoulders were broad and strong, his butt divine.

He returned, took a long swig from the water bottle on the bedside cupboard, then passed it to me, leaning down, whispering in my ear, 'You might need the hydration for what I have in mind.'

I nearly spluttered the water out my nose. Benny and I had had perfectly nice, perfectly satisfying sex, perfectly enjoyable shenanigans to make up for any missed orgasms on my part, but never did I require hydration. I was suddenly terrified and drank half the bottle in one go.

He laughed warmly, taking the bottle out of my hands, his whole face lighting like a kid at Christmas.

He looked at me and smiled with a naughty glint in his eye. Where had my friend gone? He'd been replaced with this man. This beautiful, lust filled man. Fire burned behind his eyes, in that wicked smile.

I wondered what he saw when he looked at me. A broken twenty something. Broken well before I should have been. I'd chopped off my once lovely long chocolate curls that Benny had loved so much. It had grown back some but I still kept it shorter, it felt better that way. But I'd lost that little bit of wild, like Samson losing his power when Delilah cut off his hair. But I hadn't needed the wild, what would I have done with it over the last few years, anyway? But I felt more whole with Russ than I had in a long time. More alive, more everything.

I sat on the bed and waited for what was next with my arms wrapped around my knees to stop my hands from shaking. I was nervous, afraid, excited. I was afraid my faux pas had ruined everything but his eyes locked with mine as he put a fresh condom on the bedside and ambled smoothly to the bed, kneeling in front of me.

My fear didn't put him off at all, he just smiled and leant in, 'Just relax and let it all go,' he whispered.

'I'm sorry,' I told him. 'You're just the first since Benny. I just don't know how any of it's meant to work with someone else.'

'There aren't any rules, Jo. You just need to lie back and relax and let me do what I can until you beg for mercy,' he smiled. 'See, nothing hard about that, right?'

'It seems a little one sided.'

He smiled as his mouth went to mine, drawing the first groan. 'Actually, there is one rule,' he said.

'What?' I eventually stumbled as he grinned.

'No faking.'

'What?'

'No faking. I need the truth. Promise me?' he begged, that hint of fragility sweeping across his face.

'Fine. No faking,' I promised breathlessly.

He kindly took my hands from my knees, kissing each of my palms in turn as he did.

'Fuck, Jo Jo,' he said, his lust-filled eyes boring into mine as I lay open and vulnerable in front of him.

I'd never been entirely comfortable with being nude and on display but the way he looked at me, the unbridled desire in his eyes, left my skin flushed with desire.

He smiled, that arrogant, lusty grin that sent tingles throughout my body. Then that mouth was on my body, on my most private parts, it was everywhere doing magical things. His touch left goosebumps and made me groan like an animal. Finally, my eyes glazed over. He chuckled against my skin and kept going. Filling my body with so much desire I thought it'd explode. My skin burned and my insides begged for him, needed him.

By the time he sheathed himself, my need for release was almost unbearable and then he slid into me. This time wasn't like the last. Everything inside me was so alive, electrified. I threw my head back, crying out.

'That's my girl,' he gloated. I didn't care, he could gloat all he liked as long as he didn't stop. I was lost, gone, somewhere else.

I couldn't see straight. I could hardly breathe or think or grasp anything he was doing and before I could comprehend anything more, my entire body rocketed with pleasure. It seared and it throbbed and he covered my mouth with his as I cried out and let go of everything I'd been holding on to, all the things that had been holding me back. I had no control over it, over any of it, it just exploded through me with a force so powerful I could barely breathe. I barely felt his breathing increase or heard his groans as he found his own release, too lost in the electrical current running through my body.

I lay panting as my head slowly stopped spinning, as my breathing found its right place, as my heart returned to my chest. I was completely immobile. Completely and ridiculously elated. Unable to move a single muscle in my body. His fingers trailed up and down my arm and my leg, leaving heavenly delicate goose pimples in their wake but still, I couldn't move, I could barely breathe.

His breath was warm on my neck as he whispered, 'You okay?'

I nodded. Or at least I think I nodded.

'Take a minute to catch your breath,' he whispered. 'I'm not done with you yet,' he smiled before going to clean up.

I could feel the smile in his voice. He was having fun. I briefly wondered if he did this with all his women, but was in such a state of euphoria, and so alive with anticipation, I didn't care, not a bit.

I didn't know what this was other than what it was in this moment. We were mates. That's all I knew. That's all that mattered as I pulled the sheet over me and waited for him to return, waited for what came next.

He climbed back into bed and pulled me to him on a sigh. Russ had woken something in me. Woken me up to something new and I was more than happy to see what else he could do.

Chapter 10

I woke as the sun was sinking outside my window to a knock at the door.

'Ignore it,' Russ mumbled beside me, tucking me in closer to him.

I assumed it was Bodhi coming for evening meditation so I did as Russ asked and ignored it. The knocking went away and I lay there staring at the ceiling, a growing ache in the pit of my stomach, a desperate, black, clawing ache as what I'd done sunk in. Sadness, regret, betrayal. I felt it all filling me, eating me from the inside out as tears pricked at the backs of my eyes.

I pulled the sheets up to my chin but there was nowhere to hide, nowhere to go.

'What's the matter?' Russ asked, his voice still heavy with sleep.

I shook my head, unable to speak for the fear of falling tears.

'Jo,' he asked concerned, raising himself up to his elbow. 'What's wrong?'

I shook my head again.

'You regret it all, don't you?' he asked, and I heard the devastation in his voice.

I shook my head again. 'It was perfect. All of it. Every second. You were perfect.'

'So, what's the matter?'

I turned to him as the first tear fell. 'Benny. What did I just do to him?'

'Jo,' Russ commanded, his finger under my chin, gently forcing me to face him. 'You did nothing to Benny. He wouldn't have wanted you to be celibate and alone for the rest of your life.'

'Of course you say that. Everyone says that. But who knows? I'd never have wanted him to move on. I know, it makes me a selfish cow but I don't know if I'd have been that generous if I'd died.'

He smiled. 'Right at this moment I know how you feel.'

'Don't,' I smiled. 'That just makes it worse.'

'What worse? You're going to have to tell me everything that's going on in that pretty head of yours,' he said kindly.

'He was never able to do to me what you did. I never did to him what I did to you. Well not quite like that and I never liked it quite so much.'

Russ just raised an eyebrow with a hint of a satisfied smirk.

'Stop it. What if he's up there watching? You know how they say our loved ones are always with us? What if he saw that? What if he hates me for it?'

'Hates you for what exactly?'

'For liking it better,' I admitted quietly as the avalanche of tears took over.

'Hey, come on,' he said pulling me to him.

'No,' I said, pulling away. 'I don't know if I can do this to him.

It feels disrespectful somehow. Like I didn't love him enough and I did, Russ. I really did. But it was different. And I don't know what that means.'

'That's all it means, Jo. It was just different.'

'But what if he thinks I didn't fancy him enough and that's why he couldn't do what you did? What if I robbed him of a life with someone he could have had that with so easily? You made it so easy.'

'I've had a lot of practice, remember?' he smirked, trying to lighten the mood.

'Well that's true,' I agreed with a smile.

'Jo, it's just sex. Good, incredible, mind-blowing sex. Probably the best I've ever had. But it was just sex.'

'The best. You? With all you've had?'

He smirked, pleased with himself.

'It wasn't just sex though, Russ, was it?' I asked, my heart near breaking at the thought that what we'd experienced together wasn't as special to him as it was to me. It had meant something to me. Changed all the cells in my body. Repaired my broken heart and filled it with a glorious bright light.

'I don't know, Jo. I know sex. I know good sex. Anything else, your guess is as good as mine but no. That was not garden-variety sex, I know that much. There was something extra going on in that but my head is still spinning and I'm not sure I can put words to it.'

'Maybe it was just because I was three years out of the game. You've been out for what three months, that's equal to me in your world, right?'

He laughed. 'Maybe. I guess. Where are you going with this?'

'Maybe we were both just so darned hard up?'

'If that's what's going to make you feel better, then sure, that's why.'

'You don't believe it though, do you?'

'I'll believe whatever you want me to believe today.'

He got it. He understood how hard this was for me and he wasn't frightened or threatened by it. And my traitorous heart fluttered.

'I don't know what to do, Russ.'

'You live your life, Jo. That's all you can do. You had a great life with Benny. You had something special with him you'll never have with anyone else. You did things, had your ways. There are jokes you shared that no one else will ever get and memories that will always belong to only you and him. But that doesn't mean you can't have special again.'

'But...' I interrupted, sitting up with the sheet wrapped around me, ready to protest.

'But nothing, Jo. He's not here. He's gone but you're still here and hopefully you will have a really long life to live, you have to live it. You can't exist as a husk of a person in the shadows of what might have been. You can't hide from life. Having great sex with me, laughing with me, creating memories with me, if that's what we do, it's not disrespectful to Benny. It's not better or worse, it's just different.'

'Do you believe in soul mates?'

'I don't know, maybe, I guess, why?'

'What if Benny wasn't my soulmate and I robbed him of knowing his?'

'If there's such a thing as soulmates then that indicates

there's such a thing as a higher power, God, the universe, fate, whatever, and if that's the case, don't you think they would have intervened and sent Benny to whoever he was truly meant to be with if it wasn't you?'

'I don't know.'

'Do you believe in soulmates?' he asked, watching me with that cautious look in his eye.

'I thought I did. I thought it was Benny. But now, now I feel bad he didn't get to feel what I feel right now. It's like something inside clicked into place and my heart, I'm not even sure I have the words for all the feelings right now.'

'How do you know he didn't feel all those things?'

'Because he never looked at me the way you're looking at me right now and I never felt what's happening to my insides when I was with him and it's tearing me up inside.'

'Oh, baby,' he scooped me to him and held me together. 'I know enough that if there is such a thing as soulmates, that there are all different types. All different types of soul connections. Every one of them has a purpose and a reason and none invalidates the other. And if you ask me, you're the bloody luckiest person on earth to have had three of them.'

'Three?'

'Benny, Ainsley and me. I don't know what our connection is or its purpose or what happens now, but I believe if there's such a thing as soulmates and destiny then we are somehow destined.'

'Destined, huh?'

'It's definitely something, Jo.'

I snuggled into him. He was right. There were so many

different soul connections and like my connection with Ainsley didn't invalidate my connection with Benny, neither did my connection with Russ invalidate either of the others. And maybe if Benny had had as much practice in bed as Russ, he'd have had more moves too, I thought with a smile. But I liked that Benny and I had learnt so many things together, had so many firsts together, found our way together. Maybe Benny wouldn't be so mad after all.

'So, you feel this too? It's not just me finally getting laid and letting my imagination run away with all the increased oxytocin?' I asked quietly.

He laughed. 'No, baby, this is definitely something and I promise, I don't know what it is or where it's going but bloody hell, I'm holding on tight.'

'Is it ridiculous? A bad sign that after one go in the hay, we're all oooh, soulmate connection?'

'Jo, I have felt like this about you for three freaking years. I bottomed out because of how I feel about you. I didn't know what to do with all the feels, and now, multiply it by a hundred. You can thrash about as much as you like, I'll call in your Dr Bailey so you can work through your survivor's guilt if you need to. I can be a patient man but this is not just one go in the hay. If you hadn't been so blinded by grief when we first met, we may have started this then. I like that we had that time though, that we were friends, that we could be drunk and stupid and have fun together with no sex on the table.'

'You really never thought of throwing caution to the wind? Even when we were stumbling down the strip, you weren't tempted to let your libido take over?'

'It crossed my mind for a millisecond. I'd had a week long hard-on, but like I said, not so eloquently in the bar, no. I wanted you to look at me and see me when I kissed you, when I made love to you. I've never cared that much before, never even thought about what they thought or who they saw. I couldn't care if they'd been seeing Chris Hemsworth when they looked at me but you, I cared who you saw and I didn't want you seeing him. Benny, not a Hemsworth, just to be clear, although I'd rather you not see one of them either,' he smiled. 'So, the thought may have been fleeting but even as inebriated as we were, no, I had no intention of crossing that line. Not knowing who you'd seen would have crushed me more than you leaving.'

I snuggled in a little closer, held on a little tighter.

'What happens now?'

'Now, we have to get healed by that guru so we can get out of here,' he declared.

'What happens when we do?'

'When we do what?'

'Get ourselves healed and get out of here? Will you go back?' I asked, suddenly terrified he would go back to Vegas if he could.

He held my face gently between his hands, forced me to look at him. 'No,' he said emphatically. 'While we have this thing, I will never go where you can't follow. I'm seeing this through.'

'You say that like it has an inevitable end.'

'I'll no doubt fuck up whatever this is because I don't know how to do anything else other than what I was doing. But that's not me and you. Me and you, we're something else. All I know is I like waking up with you beside me. So I hope that no matter how many times I fuck it up, I keep waking up to you.'

'You think this is something more than right now?'

'I think this is anything we want it to be. But it feels like it could be. The only way to know for sure though is to get the hell out of here and see, but until then, I'm going to make the most of having you in such close proximity,' he grinned with a naughty glint in his eye.

I kissed him then, because how could I not? And I sank into the most beautiful, loving, toe-curling kiss of my life.

When he'd taken his fill, his voice heady with lust, he said, 'Come on, we better go down for dinner before Jaz sends a search party for you.'

'Mmm,' I groaned, knowing full well how a Harrington operates but not wanting to leave the warmth of the bed. But after another languid kiss, I left him there to shower.

How had I even gotten here? I wondered with a smile as the hot water beat down on me. Letting go of the guilt wasn't as easy as he'd made it sound but I'd found a place for it. It had eased. Because he was right, I had a long life to live, hopefully. I could live another seventy or eighty years. I didn't want to do that alone in Mrs May's ghost filled apartment. I loved it there. I loved working at the café. But for the next seventy years? There'd come a point when I needed more.

I wanted more of what Russ had shown me. I wanted some of what Ainsley and Christian had found. A family. A life. Something worth waking up for beyond a job that brought me joy. I couldn't be sure what this thing with Russ was, it was too early to tell but I wanted to see it through. I needed to try.

It felt good to have the water beating down. Good to take a moment to think. My whole body buzzed with a new energy, with excitement, hope, something. Feelings I'd forgotten. This was good. Yes, I was okay.

I wrapped the towel around me and stepped into the bedroom. Russ was gone. The bed made. A note on my pillow.

'Gone for shower and clean clothes, see you downstairs. Save me a seat xR.'

xR. I smiled like a stupid teenager. I didn't care. I was going to enjoy it. I knew how short life could be. I knew what it was like to lose someone in a second. I was going to enjoy this. Every minute was a gift. I was going to make the most of every one of them.

Chapter 11

'Well don't you look all shiny and new,' smirked Jaz as she threw her arm across my shoulder. I'd barely stepped off the internal stairs and hadn't even seen her coming.

'I don't know what you're talking about?' I told her.

'Ahuh. And I guess that bloke sitting in the dining room looking like the cat that got the cream doesn't know what I'm talking about either?' she asked.

'Still don't know what you're talking about,' I said, trying not to smile.

'Well, I'm guessing Ainsley is going to feel pretty pleased with herself regardless,' she giggled.

I groaned because I knew exactly the reaction I was going to get from Ainsley. 'Well, let's not go and tell Ainsley about theoretical events until there's something worth telling, or she'll just get her knickers in a twist over nothing. How are you so perceptive anyway?'

'It's a superpower. And you were the only two people who were missing from afternoon cocktails and no one could find you for the evening medi. Oh, and you both have that stupid look on your face,' she grinned as we walked into the dining room.

I tried schooling that stupid look as I found Russ sitting at a table with Margaret Packersham and Natalie. 'See you at after dinner drinks?' Jaz asked, before she headed off to play hostess.

'Sure thing,' I agreed.

'Hey,' grinned Russ moving along the bench seat so I could sit next to him. Margaret Packersham and Natalie shared the bench on the other side.

'You alright?' he whispered to me as his hand found my knee under the table.

I couldn't resist looking up to smile at him. I was more than alright, I thought.

'And how are you both? How was evening meditation?' I asked Natalie and Margaret Packersham.

Natalie shrugged watching us with a smirk. Margaret Packersham talked about the lovely light as the sun had set over the ocean.

Jay came up behind us, leaning on the back of Russ' chair talking about surfing conditions.

'He scrubs up alright,' Margaret Packersham joked, leaning in to whisper.

I did nothing but grin because she was right, after a shave, he did indeed scrub up alright. You could now see his handsome face. He didn't have the harsh strong lines of Jay, he was softer, more classically handsome. More boy next door, than disarming. Until he turned on the charm. Although I was feeling utterly disarmed regardless. Or perhaps that was from the memory of what he had done with that mouth.

'Drinks?' interrupted the waitress. 'It's a Barossa Valley blend,' she told us.

'Please,' I said as she poured.

Margaret Packersham also nodded, seems I'd started something there, but both Russ and Natalie asked for soft drink.

Not that it bothered me that someone wouldn't be drinking but I guess in a culture so accustomed to it, I was surprised and looked at them both with an inquiring look.

'Nothing good ever comes from me drinking,' said Natalie, her voice soft and shamed, making my heart sad for her. But she didn't expand and I didn't ask. We'd just met and we were at a table full of people she didn't know, so I would wait until a suitable private moment, to make sure she was okay.

'Recovering from a downward spiral,' Russ added as the waitress brought him his Coke.

'But you were drinking last night?' I asked, confused. He'd drunk the same coloured cocktails as I did.

'Jaz and I had mocktails. The beauty of a cocktail bar run by a recovering alcoholic, everyone is catered for with no judgement,' he smiled.

Now he mentioned it, Jaz had also had the same coloured cocktails but I'd already known hers would be non-alcoholic, I just hadn't thought about it. I looked at my red wine then, wondering if I should drink it or if I should be more supportive.

'Drink it,' smiled Russ. 'It won't bother me, I promise.'

I smiled back but was sure it would be my last of the night.

Finding she had a comrade in the aversion of alcohol seemed to be all Natalie needed to warm up to Russ. She was intrigued by his life in Las Vegas and listened intently as he told stories of debauchery and excess from a city where anything goes.

'I don't know how you survived all that,' she said.

He waved her off. 'The magic wears off the locals soon enough,' he assured her, leaving out the parts about his downward spiral.

We were halfway through our lasagne when Jaz came over, her usually sunny face serious and cloudy. 'Excuse me, Russ,' she said, interrupting Margaret Packersham's tale of a childhood beach holiday gone wrong. 'Sorry to interrupt, but someone just delivered something for you to the front bar.'

'Really? Who would be delivering me something? No one even knows I'm in the country,' he told her.

'Not sure. You might want to come check it out,' she added.

'You can't just bring it in here?' he asked confused.

Jaz looked at me then back to Russ. 'I think it's best you come and have a look,' she said.

I let Russ out of the booth then watched them walk away to where Jay was waiting for them in the doorway as though guarding the entrance to the front bar.

'Well that's strange,' remarked Margaret Packersham before finishing her story.

Ten minutes later, Russ still hadn't returned so I politely excused myself and went to search for him.

Jaz met me near the doorway Jay had previously guarded. 'You might not want to go in there, maybe just wait in here or the cocktail bar for Russ?' she suggested.

'Why? What's going on?' I asked.

Then I saw him holding a baby, deep in conversation with

a woman in a boho maxi, and long wavy blonde hair. They looked more intimate than I was comfortable with. As though sensing me, he looked up and our eyes locked.

'Jo...' he called trying to get up without dropping the baby he was holding tightly to his chest.

I tried backing away but backed into Jaz whose arms wrapped around me. 'Nothing is ever as it seems,' she whispered in my ear.

What it seemed was Russ had another woman, a family and everything we'd shared that afternoon was a great big fat lie.

'Let him explain,' begged Jaz.

'Jo, it's not what it looks like,' Russ begged standing in front of me.

'It looks like you have a family, Russ.'

He looked down at the baby in his arms as though it were a foreign object. 'I didn't know,' he insisted, his voice cracking.

'And now that you do?' I asked, not even stopping to wonder how a person doesn't know they have a family.

Before he could answer, the blonde came over and linked her arm through Russ'. 'I'm going to go,' she said in a soft American accent, stretching up to kiss his cheek.

'What? Lana, wait, you can't just leave me with the baby.'

'His name is Nico,' she said, walking away.

'Jo, I'm sorry,' he said, turning to run after the woman and leaving me standing alone in the doorway between rooms, as though a doorway between worlds, between realities. On one side, I'd found a path forward. Found a man who might love me when I thought I'd never be loved, could even love again. A love that promised hope and dreams and all the things I'd thought

I'd lost. The other side was emptiness. Again. Loneliness, nothing but loss.

I turned and tried smiling at Jaz in thanks for her comfort. 'I'm just going to go upstairs, I think,' I told her.

She nodded. There was nothing else to say. What could anyone say in such a situation?

I lay on my bed shell shocked, hardly able to comprehend what had just happened. What did he even mean he didn't know? He didn't know he had a family? He didn't know they were coming to surprise him? What exactly didn't he know? He didn't know he still loved her? Did he love her? It didn't even matter. I wasn't going to be the one who came between a family.

As I was trying to decide what to feel, what I felt, was I angry? Heartbroken? Disappointed? All of the above? I wasn't sure of anything. It hadn't sunk in yet. There was a knock at the door. I ignored it. I didn't want to see him, that much I knew. I wasn't sure I wanted to see anyone.

The door opened anyway and Natalie came in with two tubs of ice cream with spoons sticking out.

'Jaz sent me,' she said. 'Margaret's downstairs keeping an eye on things. I think she's ready to rip his man bits from his body,' she added with a slight smile.

I couldn't help smiling in return. It was nice to have people who had my back, especially when my usual people were far away.

Natalie joined me on the bed. 'Chocolate Chip or Boysenberry Ripple?' she asked.

'Boysenberry please,' I said, accepting the tub of ice cream.

We didn't speak for a while. We lay there eating, looking at the window opposite but Natalie's company was comforting. I'd been tempted to call Ainsley to come and get me. She'd have wanted to know why. She'd have asked for all the details. I didn't have the words. I couldn't say them out loud. Not yet. So I appreciated Natalie filling the void.

'Are you okay?' she eventually asked.

'I don't know yet.'

'Do you know any of the story?'

'What's to know. A woman showed up. It was clearly his kid. Did he know, didn't he know? I'm not even sure it matters. He has a family. I think all I feel is stupid.'

'For believing in him?'

'Not even that. For believing that maybe I could have it all, what other people have. But now I think I was right all along. I had my chance at all that and then he died. Maybe you really don't get do overs.'

'I was kind of rooting for you. Hoping you did get to have do overs. I could have really used one.'

'Natalie, are you okay?'

She shrugged.

'Does it have anything to do with what you said earlier. About bad things happening when you drink?'

'Everything bad that's ever happened to me has happened when I've been drinking.'

'What is it exactly you do when you drink?'

'It's not what I do. It's what other people do.'

I reached out and held her hand because I suspected nothing good could come from that comment.

'The first time I was at a party, one minute everything was

fine. I'd had just a couple of drinks, then next thing I was waking up in a strange bed with no underwear. The guy laughed. Said I'd been begging him for it. That he had video evidence to prove it so I didn't say anything to anyone. I was mortified. So ashamed. After that I stopped drinking. Stopped wearing pretty dresses that might give people the wrong idea. My parents were worried, didn't like the change so as soon as I finished school, I moved out, got a job in a call centre.

'Then one Saturday night, my housemate had a few friends over. I tried just minding my own business, sat on a chair in the corner, just to be polite and avoid looking like a freak. Or more of a freak, they just couldn't understand a person who didn't drink. It's our culture, you know. It's ingrained in us that you must or you're a party pooper or something. Anyway, my housemate's boyfriend thought it would be a hoot to spike my drink. I don't know what he used. The last thing I remembered was him carrying me to my bed with my roommate gushing about how kind he was. I couldn't move, my body was so heavy and my head spun so I couldn't see properly. The next thing I know, I'm waking up to him having sex with me.

'I reported it. Lost my best friend and roommate. I had to move back in with my parents. Some people thought because of the way I dressed I was the kind of person who did drugs, that would have been up for anything. I couldn't win either way. The others called me a liar. It was his word against mine and my roommate was saying there was no way in hell he'd have touched me and that he wasn't even in my room long enough. My lawyer said it would be hard to prove I hadn't willingly taken the drugs in my system. They were standard party drugs. To the outside world, with the black baggy clothes I wore, I looked like a druggy. So people told me. The guy used a condom so he hadn't left any semen. I'd been too out of it to struggle so there was no bruising. It would be hard to prove it hadn't been consensual if I could prove it happened at all, so I dropped it. I didn't want to be called a liar in a court full of people.

'After that, I stopped leaving the house. I didn't really have anywhere to go anyway. I lost my friends, my job. I couldn't look anyone in the eye. I barely trusted my own parents. Refused to let them pour me a drink and I saw the look on their faces, the shame, the embarrassment at what I'd become. Then my parents heard Bodhi was coming to town. Thought he could fix me. I thought maybe he could take away the pain. The shame. Make me better again. And here we are.'

I squeezed her hand. 'People suck.'

'Yep.'

'You deserve better.'

'Thank you. I haven't heard that in a while.'

'I could help you ruin him, if you want? Jaz knows people.'

She smiled. 'Thanks. But I just want to move on with my life now.'

'Well, I have a guy who can help with that. My shrink is kind of a genius.'

'Yeah? I could use a genius.'

There was a knock at the door. 'It's me,' called Margaret Packersham.

Natalie got up to let her in and then came back to resume her place beside me and Margaret Packersham dragged over one of the nicely upholstered chairs.

'What's going on down there?' Natalie asked her. I was too afraid to ask anything, too afraid of the answers.

'He barely knows the girl apparently. Didn't know she was even pregnant. She went looking for him once she'd had the baby but he'd left the country. She spent the last three months trying to track him down and here we are, probably spotted his credit card transaction when he checked in if she had people looking,' Margaret said.

'Right,' I said, trying to take in the new information.

'She's gone though, just walked out and left him with the baby.'

'She left her baby? What kind of woman does that?' asked Natalie horrified.

'I don't know, he's just a tiny little thing and she handed him over and walked away. But Jaz and Jay are doing a ring around trying to find her,' Margaret added.

'Are you okay?' Natalie asked me.

'Just a little shell-shocked. He won't let her go. He's not that kind of guy. I know he seems it sometimes, he has that carefree, devil may care look about him. And he certainly shagged his way through Vegas like Hugh bloody Hefner but he's not that guy. If she has his kid, he'll try and do the honourable thing.'

'But I could see the way he feels about you, this won't change that,' Margaret insisted.

'How he feels or felt about me won't matter. He's too good a guy,' I said as I scooped up some more ice cream.

'Then maybe you're better off having it all done with now,'

she said, patting my leg kindly. 'He'll be coming with a lot of baggage now and with all that you've been through, dear, it's probably for the best. You go and get an extra session with Bodhi tomorrow, he'll take care of you,' she added.

I nodded. Not at all sure what was for the best anymore. 'It's late, you two should probably go and get some sleep,' I suggested.

Neither spoke for a minute.

'I will go see if I can be useful somewhere,' Margaret eventually suggested.

'I'll stay here, you could use a friend,' Natalie insisted. But after the story she told me, I should have been the one being her friend. I guess if she stayed, it could be win win, so I didn't argue.

Natalie put the remnants of our ice cream in the freezer of the little mini fridge and when she returned, I pulled the blanket up over us. I didn't want to be under the covers where I'd still be able to smell him, to feel him. I wasn't ready to face that yet, to face the loss of more dreams.

I'd really thought for just a minute, that I could have that life, that perhaps I'd have something meaningful to wake up to over the next seventy or eighty years. I still had all those other things that I'd had before. I had Henry and Anna, and Ainsley but they were fragments of someone else's life. Borrowed moments that weren't really my own. I didn't think I'd wanted it all without Benny. But with Russ, everything seemed possible, marriage, children. With Russ, life seemed possible. For just a moment, I'd believed the life of Jo wasn't over yet. That there really was more to come. I felt stupid for having believed it could be mine. For buying into everything Ainsley and Bodhi and Dr Bailey had said. For believing in destiny and fate. Russ was someone else's destiny.

Chapter 12

'No. She doesn't want to see you.'

The sound of voices woke me. It was the middle of the night, far too early for Bodhi, the sky was too dark.

'Please, I need to see her. I just need to explain,' he begged.

'No, you're not waking her. It took her forever to get to sleep. I don't think she can deal with more right now, she needs to rest.'

'She needs to know the truth. I would never hurt her.'

'Not intentionally. She knows that. But she knows you're a good guy. You have a family Russ.'

'It's not a family if I don't know the bloody woman. I don't even know if this is really my kid.'

'And until you know, you'll do the right thing?' she asked.

He didn't answer and I imagined him shrugging his yes.

He begged and argued with Natalie a little longer before giving up and calling out my name.

I didn't move. I couldn't look at him and have him tell me to my face he was sorry, that we were over, that he had to try everything we'd imagined with someone else because it was the right thing to do. His apologies wouldn't change what was.

They wouldn't stop my heart from breaking. Tears rolled down my face, choked my voice so I couldn't even speak but I didn't move. He eventually gave up and left.

Natalie came back to the bed. 'Are you okay?'

I shook my head.

'Do you want me to call your friend?'

I almost said yes. But I knew Ainsley would come without a second thought. If I called, she'd be here by the time the sun rose. But she had a newborn and she had Henry and the café, so I said, 'No,' and closed my eyes. I didn't sleep though. I lay there, my mind a fog until Bodhi came for us.

'No, not today,' I told him.

'You need to,' he insisted.

I shook my head, desperately holding back the tears.

I could barely lift my arms, my eyes were raw and my heart too heavy. Bodhi came into my room, his voice soft as it was always soft and knowing and wise. He squatted beside my bed and looked into my eyes.

'Jo, you need this. You need to connect with you, with your own heart. Your life, Jo's life, does not depend on someone else. Does not depend on a man. It depends on your heart. The life of Jo is built from in here,' he said, pressing on my solar plexus. 'This is where you find, Jo.'

I nodded. With tears filling my eyes, I got up and followed Bodhi and Natalie out onto the balcony where Margaret Packersham and the Lorna Jane mum's waited with Karen, the famous author, and her manager slash lover, and followed them down the stairs and to the grassed area overlooking the ocean where some of the other guests waited.

As the sun came up, bright and strong, the gentle swish of the ocean in the background, Bodhi led us through a meditation that opened our solar plexus, expanded our hearts and activated our throat chakras as though he had created the entire session just for me.

'Deep breath in, hold it, one, two, and release. And so it is. Namaste,' Bodhi said, ending the session.

I opened my eyes to the morning light. Sat for a moment breathing in the fresh morning air, listening to a bird in a nearby tree. I felt tranquil and peaceful, as peaceful as I imagined I could. I breathed in again and on the exhale, as though my body had a mind of its own, I glanced up to the second-floor balcony. There was no one there. I watched his door like a stalker, wondering what he was doing inside.

Had he tracked her down? Was he with her now? And then, as though attuned to my thoughts, she walked out in an oversized t-shirt drinking a cup of coffee. One of his t-shirts, I guessed by the size of it and I thought I might be sick. She'd spent the night. In his little one bed room in his shirt. Russ followed her out, spoke closely to her as though cajoling her. Inside? Back to bed? Then I heard the wail of the baby and they both disappeared inside.

'You coming?' asked Natalie. Margaret Packersham stood beside her watching me with concern. They both followed my eye line to the now empty balcony. I felt stupid. It was just one day we'd had and I'd gone and lost myself. But still... I couldn't sit on the grass staring into space like a crazy person, so I followed Natalie and Margaret Packersham into the breakfast room.

I threw an egg and a piece of bacon between two slices of bread and headed out the front door. I was halfway across the car park when I felt him before I heard him. 'Jo, wait, please,' he pleaded. 'Where are you going? We need to talk.'

'Nope,' I said as the wail of a baby came from inside the doorway. I couldn't see it, but I could hear it, a constant reminder Russ belonged to someone else.

Natalie came out, pushing past Russ who stood between the planters of peace lilies. She linked her arm through mine and led me away.

'Jo, come on. I didn't know,' begged Russ from behind us.

'I just can't watch it,' I told Natalie. 'I need some space to do what Bodhi said, to focus on me without seeing him and her and the baby and all the dreams evaporating like smoke.'

'I know,' she said, leaning her head on my shoulder. 'Where are we going anyway?' she asked.

'I have no bloody idea,' I laughed.

We just kept walking. On and on until we reached the local town.

'You want to stop, have coffee?'

'Are you okay to keep walking?' I asked. My brain was too busy trying to make sense of everything that was happening. I needed open space and quiet and movement.

We walked up and around the bluff, feeling the burn in our thighs. We stopped to inspect the wild life, to rest against a tree and appreciate the display from mother nature. We came back the same way. Stopped at a takeaway shop and headed to a picnic table in the park to eat.

'So tell me, what does the life of Jo look like? Without him, without any man. If you could be anyone, have anything, what would it be, how would your life look?' Natalie asked as she picked through her bag of chips for the small, crunchy ones.

'You've been spending too much time with Bodhi,' I told her, pulling apart my piece of roast chicken.

She smiled. 'He has been good for me. So have you.'

It made me happy, all the words coming out of her mouth, the small smile lighting her face that had been so clouded when I'd met her.

'Well I'm glad. The life of Jo, hey?' I said, dipping a chip in sauce as the seagulls surrounded us, watching us, waiting for food. 'It's been so long since I've thought about what I wanted my life to look like. Hey, isn't that Margaret?' I asked, interrupting myself.

'Where?' When I pointed toward the café on the other side of the park, she saw her. 'Oh yeah, and is that Bodhi?' she asked as she began waving to them. They seemed intent on their conversation though, huddled together. I guess even someone like Margaret had private things to say that she mightn't want anyone to overhear. I got it, you didn't want everyone knowing some of the things you spoke to Bodhi about. He was a lot like Dr Bailey that way, he got you to open up easily.

'I guess they don't see us,' she said. 'Well go on, the life of Jo,' she encouraged.

I smiled. 'Well, when Benny was alive, we travelled; we had a long list of places we wanted to see. We were planning to have a family someday. In the future. But since, I haven't thought about it. But my best friend just had a baby. It's her second. And I watched her and her little family and they looked so happy. It had been the first time in so long, I missed the hope of it and I thought with Russ, maybe... So I guess that's a sign there right. I really do want a family. Even if it's not with Russ and even if it's not tomorrow, but someday with someone who makes me as happy as Christian makes Ainsley and Jay makes Jaz. I don't know what else. I like my job. I probably can't be a barista living in an apartment above the cafe forever but for now it makes me happy. I don't even know what I want to do beyond the cafe. How about you, what's the life of Natalie look like?'

'I'm not so sure. Before I came here, I had no idea at all. I just wanted to get through the day. That was my only plan when I woke up. *Don't die today.* But now, I like the impact Bodhi has through the healing and the meditation. I really like the meditation. So maybe I'll look at that when I'm better. Do more of that. Some sort of natural therapy maybe. Some sort of coaching maybe. I'm not sure anyone would want me to coach them but I like the idea of it.'

'I think you'd make an excellent coach,' I told her.

'Really?' she beamed.

'Really.'

'Maybe after a few more days of meditation and another healing session you might be able to see clearer too,' she suggested.

'I already do, so I can only imagine what a few more days will bring.'

'What did you want to be when you were a kid? Sometimes that helps. I wanted to be a teacher but then stuff happened and here we are, so I guess coaching isn't too far from that.'

'I used to like to write. I used to study all the tv shows and movies and break them down and then write my own episodes all the time, some original stuff but I stopped when I hit year twelve. I just got too busy focussing on a career in finance. I was an investment advisor,' I told her as though it mattered. 'Anyway, then I went to uni and life took over, parties, boys, all that. I met Benny in my second year at uni and then I got a job and just focussed on working my way up, until my chauvinistic boss told me I was as far as I could go. I hated the work anyway so I quit and that's when I went to work for Ainsley and I just love being in the cafe.'

'Well maybe you take everything you learn there and that's where you start. Or maybe you use all that down time up in the apartment writing something and just seeing what happens?'

'I don't even know if I can do it anymore. I write in my journal, Dr Bailey makes me, and sometimes that sounds like a crazy tv show but I don't know. Maybe.'

'Well you start and you let the universe send you the rest. Meditate on it and ask for the answers and see where it leads you?'

I nodded. Letting the idea sink in. I'd never used meditation like that. I knew you could but I hadn't needed guidance or answers before. I'd just needed peace. 'I like that. See, you're an amazing coach,' I told her.

'Thanks,' she smiled. 'It's getting late, we should probably start heading back or it's going to get dark,' she said, with the slightest shake in her voice. She was doing better but she still had some way to go if she didn't like being too far from home when it was dark.

We walked back to the pub along the beach as the day was ending. We went around the back of the pub, headed for the outside stairs. I felt better for the air, for the walking, for the company. I felt better for having made a friend, having someone in my corner to bring me ice cream and just go for a walk with me when everything was too much. It had been a long time since there had been anyone but Ainsley.

We arrived back to find evening meditation already finished and Jaz setting up benches around a campfire.

'Hey, there you both are,' she said, upon seeing us. 'We're having a night under the stars. Chef's doing a barbeque, we have marshmallows and music and martinis, it's going to be great.'

'Thanks, it does sound great, but I think I'm just going to head up,' I told her, not in the mood for all that chatter and frivolity.

'Nooo... you can't. It'll be good for you. He probably won't even be here,' she pleaded.

'I'm sorry Jaz, I'm just not in the mood,' I told her.

'Please stay...' Natalie begged. 'Just for a little bit, please.'

Natalie gripped my arm begging. She was finally coming out of her shell. She'd been good to me, a good friend and she needed a friend too, so I agreed. I could do this for her after all she'd done for me.

'Fine, let me have a shower and I'll be back down in a little bit.'

Chapter 13

I came back down the stairs to a sea of people sipping martini's as the sun gave up the last of its light in a beautiful array of colour. The smell of the fire filled the air. That's where most people were, so that's where I headed. The fire pit Jaz had set up on the grass was blazing and sending off a lovely warmth to combat the cold night. Benches circled the fire with blankets laid on each of the seats. The benches were already filling with people with blankets on their knees and cocktails in hand.

The pub's head chef had set up a barbeque and serving station closer to the building and I could smell onions frying. Someone played a guitar on a stool by a tree, lost in his own musical world. I found Margaret Packersham and Natalie rugged up on a bench and joined them.

'Hey,' Natalie greeted. 'I was starting to think you weren't coming,' she said, clearly pleased I had. It made me glad I'd forced myself to dress and come down the stairs despite every fibre of my body begging to go to bed and wallow.

'How are you doing?' Margaret Packersham asked kindly.

'I'm okay,' I said, looking around the circle of people.

'He's not here,' she added. 'And he better bloody well stay away,' she said in my defence.

I smiled, squeezed her hand in thanks as Jaz brought me an espresso martini. Natalie was drinking a hot chocolate, I noticed.

'Mine's an Irish coffee,' Margaret Packersham told me with a smile and I suspected she'd gotten a head start on me.

The Lorna Jane mums sat on the bench next to me with their espresso martini's also, already chatty and happy.

'You ladies are in the spirit early,' I commented to make conversation.

'You bet. No kids wanting anything, it's heaven and we're making the most of it.'

'Or husbands,' commented the other. 'They want more than the bloody kids sometimes.'

'Ain't that right,' the other replied before they downed half of their martini's in one go before sighing with relief.

'How many kids do you have?' I asked, forcing myself to make conversation and drag myself out of my misery funk.

'Seven between us, the first answered.'

'Seven too bloody many,' the other replied with a laugh. 'I'm kidding, I promise. They're great but bloody hell, all we ever do now is talk about brain food and milestones and live according to someone else's calendar. It's exhausting,' she said.

'Is that why you're here? For a rest?'

'You bet. It's not easy to get approved time out with my girl, she said, laying her head on her friend's shoulder. 'Anything that rings of self-development though is a sure-fire winner with the mother-in-law who has to help with the kid wrangling while I'm away, because god forbid the hubby do it all by himself,' she said, with dramatic hand movements and a laugh.

It was nice getting to know some people, hearing their stories, getting out of my own head for a while. I mingled a little around the serving table with a middle-aged couple who were empty nesters between business investments, a slick businessman who looked very out of place in a guru-esque retreat who told me about his corporate burnout. I sympathised with him for a while and we both went our separate ways with a smile, it was always nice to find someone who understood the ugly side of the corporate world.

There were plenty of add-ons too, I noticed, people who'd come to see Bodhi just for the day and stayed on for dinner, some locals who stayed after their surf to hang out with Jay. I was feeling quite relaxed, feeling into me, seeing life again, feeling as though the old me, or at least a version of, was still resurfacing and it felt good.

It was turning out to be a lovely evening until I was sitting on my bench seat about to take a big bite out of my sausage in bread loaded with sauce and onions, and Russ walked up with the mother of his child. Russ' lady friend had the baby strapped to her in some convoluted concoction, her long blonde wavy hair hung free and looked like she'd spent the whole day frolicking in the ocean like a mermaid. She wore a loose but lovely maxi dress with one of Russ' jumpers as though she'd come not knowing it was winter, and she stood there grinning, eager to find a spot to sit and take part in the festivities.

Jaz, ever the graceful host, found them a spot, squished an

extra bench in opposite me. Russ looked up, regret clouding his eyes. '*I'm sorry*,' he mouthed.

Too late now, I thought, turning away.

Bodhi was sitting on the bench beside him. He caught my eye. He mouthed, *you okay?* I shrugged. Margaret Packersham patted my arm, giving Russ' lady friend some serious daggers, but Russ' lady friend seemed completely oblivious as she made conversation with the surfer next to her.

'I think I'm going to head up and let you young folk enjoy the night,' Margaret said. 'Will you be okay, dear?'

'Of course. Sleep well,' I told her.

Russ watched me from across the fire, I could feel him, sense him but I refused to look at him. I couldn't. I thought my poor, fragile heart might break.

I soon lost track of Russ and his lady friend when I got speaking to Mr Slick who took the place of the Lorna Jane mums when they went to mingle. He looked out of place as usual with his slicked back hair and his buttoned up shirt, the top few buttons undone to give the appearance of casual. I had a laugh with Natalie as we roasted marshmallows and then stretching my legs, I found myself standing next to Karen, the famous author, and her manager slash lover, while we waited for a fresh batch of martinis to come out from the bar.

I asked her about her work and spent the next few minutes enraptured with her stories, how she weaved the worlds she wrote and built her characters and how much effort she put in to the raunchy scenes because she knew her readers loved them. I turned as the waitress brought me my drink and turned back to Karen, the famous author, just as her manager slash lover was storming off in a huff.

'Is everything okay?' I asked

She looked up, surprised that someone had noticed. Then she looked around realising she had no buffer without him and then shot me a wonderful megawatt smile. 'Just fine, thanks for asking,' she insisted, taking a martini from the waitress.

Karen took a long sip of her drink, closed her eyes and sighed as though the drink were medicinal and just what she'd needed. 'He's a sweet guy, really,' she insisted.

'He seemed so, yes,' I agreed.

'But he bloody fusses like an old lady. It's not sexy, it's not endearing, it's just annoying. When he works, he's a powerhouse, he always gets what he wants, but when it comes to me, he's a sap. Now look at your hunk of spunk, he knows how to do sexy, but I bet he still knows how to have your back without fussing like an old lady.'

I smiled. 'I don't think he's exactly my hunk of spunk anymore but yes, I suppose he can manage that.'

'What happened?' she asked and then as she remembered added, 'Oh shit, sorry. You mean the baby Mumma?'

I nodded.

'Bugger, I was hoping he could give Robert some lessons?'

'Well, I don't know if it's something that can be taught.'

'Oh, I know, you're right,' she agreed, waving the idea off. 'I write about these sexy, manly characters, you'd think he'd at least get the hint about what I find sexy.'

'One thing I've learnt from that great hunk of spunk,' I smiled, even though my stomach sank with just the mention of Russ, 'is that every person and every relationship is different and sometimes you just have to be very clear about what's what before you all disintegrate. Robert seems to be a very sweet man and he thinks the world of you, hence the fussing, I'm sure. But perhaps you just need to have a direct conversation about what is sexy.'

'Oh, well, wouldn't that be offensive?' she asked.

'Isn't it more offensive to constantly fight with or eventually break up with a man who clearly adores you because you didn't have the conversation?'

She sighed, a deep, heavy, weighted sigh. 'You're right. Here, do you mind?' she asked, handing me her empty glass and hurrying after her manager slash lover.

She left me thinking about Russ then and I looked for him, instinctively, something other than consciously, but he'd vanished. His lady friend was still there, in an intensely animated conversation with Bodhi, seemingly unaware of what she'd done, the upset she'd caused my life. But why would she even care? She had every right to come and find Russ. She had his child. Her child deserved to know his dad. I was the one intruding, threatening their happy family.

I went to get a chocolate martini before all that espresso had me awake for a week, I didn't need insomnia on top of my misery. I got talking to Jaz about the latest project she was working on with Christian. Time passed as though it didn't exist. Jaz was like that. Easy to talk to. Natalie came by to say she was heading up. I saw the mums head off while Jaz was showing me a photo of her brother, Tom's unborn baby, gushing over the 3D picture and the fact she was to be an aunt again. I noticed most other people had gone too.

'Can I help you clean up?' I offered.

'Oh goodness, no, you're a guest. Besides, I have people, they need to earn their keep,' she smiled.

My chocolate martini was still almost full. I considered just taking it up to my room to finish off but it was so nice out. Despite the cold, the sky was clear and full of stars the moon big and bright. I was enjoying the peace. Needed the air. I went back to the abandoned fire and sat on a bench, staring into the flickering flames. Some locals laughed nearby. But otherwise, it was just me. It was nice. Quiet. A good opportunity to reflect on the day, on things, on me, the life of Jo. A life that was coming together. With or without Russ. I had Natalie and Margaret Packersham. My sense of self was returning. I'd come to appreciate the calming effects of meditation more than before and Natalie had sparked an old love I'd had for creating entertainment.

'How are you, Jo?' asked Bodhi coming to sit beside me.

'I'm okay. I think. Yes, I think I'm going to be okay.'

'A shock this business with Russ?' he asked. 'What do you know about his friend?'

I nodded, agreeing it was indeed a shock. 'I don't know anything about her,' I told him. 'She just showed up. You were talking to her, you'd know more than me,' I told him.

'She didn't say much,' he said evasively and I concluded it must have been one of those conversations practitioners didn't like to share because she'd certainly looked like she was saying a lot. 'Are you sad?' he asked.

'Very. It had looked promising. But you were right, I have to focus on here,' I said, indicating my solar plexus. 'Then I can focus on other things.'

He smiled. 'Good. You know there are other treatments you can try too. Have you ever experienced reflexology?' Bodhi asked softly.

'What is that?'

'When the pressure points in your feet are released.'

'Oh, I think I've heard of it but no, can't say I have tried it.'

'It can change the makeup of your whole body if done right. Heal a headache, ease muscle strain, even heal a broken heart, whatever you need.'

'Is that so?'

'Depending on the practitioner of course. If you have an expert, that's when it will change your life,' he smiled.

'Right.'

'Would you like a demonstration?'

'Which sort exactly would you be?' I asked suspiciously but I was curious too. Everything he'd done so far had made a huge difference, opened my mind to alternative treatment possibilities and I wondered what this new one he was suggesting might bring.

He smiled a little crookedly and it made me wonder what exactly he was suggesting? He had a wicked glint in his eye. Like Jaz, I hadn't yet decided on which side of the fence he sat. He looked neither feminine nor masculine. His accent and tone were almost unidentifiable. Was he Australian? American? British? Something else? I couldn't quite tell. It was a guru thing, I suspected. He'd transcended the ordinary. He lived in a more awakened place. But it meant I couldn't quite tell if he was hitting on me. I wasn't exactly sure where I sat if he was. I was still sad about Russ. Mad even. He had a family now, I had to move on. I wasn't sure if I wanted to, wasn't sure if I could. It had been for Russ everything had awakened, so something new wasn't on my radar.

But that glint in Bodhi's eye intrigued me. Too many martinis had disrupted my rational thinking. I felt reckless and impulsive. I was a grown ass woman, I reminded myself. I could be anything I wanted.

'The expert sort,' he grinned a little mischievously.

'Are you some weirdo foot fetish guy?'

He laughed. 'No,' he said, so emphatically that it did a little something deep inside my tummy, and I was more curious than ever. 'May I?' he asked, indicating my foot that I'd tucked onto the bench under me.

I'd had more than a few martinis. They'd kicked into my freshly zenned body. I was emotionally drained and I'd had that healing work or whatever it was, and I was feeling flippant and free and quite unlike myself and in need of feeling something other than pitifully sad.

'Go on, then,' I agreed boldly as though I were someone else, as though my act of defiance was a fuck you to Russ and I tentatively uncurled my feet. Bodhi had insisted I surrender to the process while I was here, after all so I surrendered.

He took my left foot in his hand, gently smoothing his hand over the top and bottom as though he really was a creepy foot fetish guy but then he started in on the pressure points. He started at the front, working the balls of my foot, moving to the arch and slowly, bit by bit, working his way towards the back.

I sighed from the exquisite pleasure of it, the buzz that ran through my intoxicated veins and then he hit a new pressure point at the back of my heel and my head fell back as I let out a groan. I had no idea if we were alone and I didn't care. Whatever he was doing went straight to my hoohaa. I felt him watching me as he worked the points, as he worked others and came back to the magic one, but I didn't seem to care.

'What is this?' I asked, my voice breathless to my own ears.

'Shhh...' he smirked, pulling my foot against him, his thigh, I hoped it was his thight, before his fingers robbed me of any decorum left.

My heart pounded and my breath caught in my chest, came in fast short spurts. Surely, I wasn't about to... oh god.

'Oh shit!' I ripped my foot free of his grip.

'What?' he asked, surprised.

'What was that? I didn't ask for that,' I stumbled, my voice shaking.

'Jo, I'm sorry, I got carried away,' pleaded Bodhi but I saw his pants tenting and suddenly felt dirty and all sorts of wrong.

I didn't know what to say and bolted from the bench with a mumbled, 'It's fine.'

I drank the rest of my martini as though it could wash him away and then walked until I couldn't see the fire or hear the last of the revellers chatting, until it was quiet and I was alone. I stopped then, breathed deep, let out a long sigh.

'I fucked it all up, didn't I?' Russ said softly in the dark shadows. He was sitting alone on a weathered bench drinking a beer while the moon lit his handsome, troubled face. 'I told you I would. Somehow. You know I didn't even remember her name,' he said, taking a long drink from the beer bottle he held.

'Does it even matter now?' I asked, defeated.

'It matters to me. You matter to me.'

'You have a family, Russ,' I reminded him as I sat next to him on the bench.

'No, I have a child with a woman who until yesterday, I'd forgotten existed. That's not a family. If the kid's mine, I'll do right by it. But that's it. You're what matters to me, Jo. For the first time in three years I thought I'd finally found solid ground. I could see where I was going. I was excited by the future. I don't think I have one without you.'

'I saw her this morning. Coming out of your room in your t-shirt. You followed and whispered to her.'

'The pub is full. There was nowhere for her to sleep. She didn't bring anything to sleep in and I came out to ask her to take care of her fucking kid who wouldn't stop crying. Sorry, it's not the kid's fault but he's always crying. And all I can think of is you and how hurt you must be and how much I need to talk to you about it,' he said sadly.

My heart broke at the tone of his voice, the cracking in the words as he spoke. I knew what it was like to lose hope, to have a future you were excited about ripped away from you. 'How do I, we, even fit in your new world?'

'We, you and me, don't change. I'll make it work anyway you want.'

'You can't promise me that. There's a child involved. He needs his dad.'

'If it's even mine. Jay's tapping into some Harrington resources to expedite a paternity test.'

'Chances are it is though. If she's come all this way to find you.'

'I know. And she'll leave as soon as she gets what she wants, I'm sure.'

'What does she want?'

'I don't know yet.'

'Maybe that's because she wants you?'

He shrugged. 'She can't have me. There is no scenario in which she gets that.'

'And what about when she goes back to wherever she came from? You need to be wherever your son is.'

'I told you, I'll never go where you can't follow. I'll figure something out. Christian's sending me a lawyer as soon as the paternity test results are in.'

'You've been busy.'

'I need to sort it out before you disappear on me again. Jo, I can't lose you,' he begged, his eyes glistening in the moonlight.

My heart broke for him. We wanted the same thing. It wasn't fair that we had to lose that. I leaned forward, put my hand on his shirt and he pulled me to him, enveloping me in an all-consuming hug so great I couldn't tell where one of us ended and the other began.

'Please stay. Please... don't go, nothing makes any sense without you. There's no point, no purpose. I need you. I want you,' he pleaded.

'Are you sure you're not just afraid?'

'Hell, yes, I'm afraid. I'm afraid of being a dad. Of what Lana wants. Of what comes next. Of losing you. But that's not why. Everything made sense when we were together. In the grand scheme of things, it was just a minute. A fleeting flash of a minute. But it was the truest time I know. I was me. One hundred percent me and I liked who I saw for the first time in a long time and it felt right. You felt right. Everything that had been floating and higgledy finally found its place and I smiled. I bloody smiled. It's stupid that something so simple could be so important but it is. That's all you. I want to know what it's like to wake up with you every day and plan a life with you, Jo. With you, no one else.'

I reached my mouth up to his because I didn't want to plan a life with anyone else either.

I still had the blanket from the fire wrapped around my shoulders. Russ laid it on the sand and in the glow of the moonlight, as though we were in a romance novel, he made love to me in the sweetest most beautiful way.

Then, because I also wanted to know what it was like to wake up with him in the morning, I took him back to my room.

Chapter 14

'Russ, you in there?' Jay called, knocking on my door before dawn had even cracked.

I rolled into the warmth of Russ. He'd been right, waking up together was pretty perfect. His arms tightened around me as he slowly registered the call of Jay.

'Russ? Jo?' called Jay again.

Russ got up, put on pants and went to open the door.

'What's up, man?' he asked.

'You have to do something about the baby. It's been crying for an hour.'

'What? Where's Lana?' he asked, not really expecting an answer. 'I'll be back,' he called to me with a regretful look on his face that I'm sure I mirrored.

Checking the time on my phone, I saw it was almost five so I showered and threw on my leggings and a long sleeve tee and favourite oversized hoodie ready for some morning meditation. I wasn't sure I was ready to see Bodhi again after what he'd done. But the meditation was too important. I wasn't going to let his one stupid, misguided decision ruin that for me. Besides, I'd be with a group of people. It should be easy enough to keep my distance from him and I'd figure out how to deal with my next healing session later. Bodhi and co knocked on my door just as I finished brushing my teeth.

'Well don't you look cheery,' smirked Margaret Packersham with far too much cheer for that time of morning.

I shrugged. Not sure how much I wanted to divulge among a group of near strangers. Especially with Bodhi watching on with that curious look on his face. I just felt creepy about everything that had happened. I gave him a look I hoped said go away and he mouthed another apology. I nodded then blended into the safety of my friends.

'We'll talk at breakfast,' Margaret Packersham said as we all followed Bodhi down the stairs like he was the pied piper.

It was extra dark with cloud cover hiding the moon that had been so bright the night before, so the ocean was still a dark mass as we found our mats and Bodhi began the session. He led us through some rebirthing visualisation, something I knew The Meditation Queen had on her YouTube channel but I'd avoided it. I hadn't been ready but now I was, and I went to that other place of calm and focus as I followed Bodhi's voice.

Russ must have done something about the baby because there wasn't a sound other than the gentle toing and froing of the ocean. It was nice to take a minute after the whirlwind of the night before to check in with myself and balance all of my thoughts and emotions. Bodhi helped us to let go of old hurts and old emotions and I ended the session feeling fresh and light. Peace flowed through my body, a beautiful, lovely serenity. The lovely quiet was broken by a scream that curdled the blood in my veins and sent chills up my spine.

My eyes popped open and followed Natalie's eyeline. The sun had come up and the gentle waves that had been soothing us throughout the meditation were washing over the body of Russ' lady friend. Her hair hung down her back, matted with salt water and caked with blood from the knife sticking out of her back. Her face lay buried in the sand. She wasn't moving.

Mr Slick sprang into action and went to check Lana's body. One of the Lorna Jane mums pulled out her phone to call for help. As soon as I caught my breath, I went to find Jaz, Jay and Russ while Margaret Packersham soothed Natalie.

Jaz and Jay were on the top floor in their apartment drinking coffee in their pyjamas. Once I'd finished telling them what was going on, Jay showed his military background, his expression changing from jovial to business.

'Jaz, you stay here. Do you hear me, you stay right here,' he commanded. He'd once been her bodyguard, that's how they'd met and she'd run away with him when she was seventeen. Old habits died hard.

She clearly knew better than to argue with that tone. 'Go. I'll be right here,' she assured him. He left to take care of what needed taking care of.

'You okay Jo?' Jaz asked.

'Yeah, I have to go tell Russ.'

She nodded as she reached for her phone. 'Come back if you need a safe space, okay?' she offered.

I hugged her and left to go and tell Russ.

He was standing just inside the door of his room, jigging the baby to keep it quiet.

'Sorry,' he apologised. 'I don't know where the hell Lana is, she's disappeared,' he said, clearly annoyed.

'I know where she is,' I told him.

He looked at me expectantly, his eyes frowning as he waited, taking in my face.

'Her body is down on the beach,' I told him.

'Her body?'

'She's dead, Russ. Well, I think she's dead. She wasn't moving. Her face was in the sand and the waves were washing over her and she didn't move, not even when Natalie screamed like a madwoman, so yeah, I'm sure she's dead. Mr Slick was checking. One of the Lorna Jane mums was calling an ambulance and I just sent Jay down there.'

'Bloody hell, what happened?' he asked, running his hand through his hair.

'I don't know. What do we do?' I begged.

'Breathe, Jo, breathe,' he said, placing a hand on my shoulder. 'It'll be okay,' he insisted. 'Come, sit, we'll have tea.'

'What? No. We can't drink bloody tea. That baby's mumma is dead, Russ. We have to do something.'

'If she's already dead, then there's nothing to be done, Jo.'

'How can you be so calm?'

'Trust me, my brain's going a hundred mile a minute. But I've been trained to handle certain situations, Jo. Right now though, you're my priority. I'll see what I can do for Lana when I know you're okay. Just breathe,' he said, his face doing the same thing Jay's had done, going somewhere else, becoming someone else.

'Russ, what exactly did you do before you were a PI?'

He smiled. 'I couldn't tell you if I wanted to,' he answered, smiling tightly.

He'd never answered the question in the past either. What kind of work had he done that he could never speak of? I suspected highly classified. The sort of work that terrified most of us, but kept us safe. I just wanted to wrap my arms around him at the thought of what he may have seen in that life. Whatever he'd seen, whatever he'd been through, it had left him detached from the death of his lady friend.

'Come on, if it makes you feel better, we'll go down and see what's what,' he said.

The sun was well and truly up when we got downstairs. A waitress was handing out coffee and my fellow guests stood on the patio drinking, clearly unsure what to do with themselves. I took one to keep my hands warm. Russ took one as well and held the baby in the crook of his other arm where he now slept peacefully.

Natalie and Margaret Packersham migrated to us as if in need of the comfort of numbers, of community. The air was eerily silent for so many people that usually filled the space with their chatter.

'Are you okay?' I asked Natalie whose face was still white as bone.

She nodded.

I wrapped my arm around her and brought her in close for comfort.

'Do we know what happened?' I asked.

Margaret Packersham answered. 'Looks like she was stabbed in the back. Can you believe it? I know we didn't like her coming here and interrupting what you had going on with Russ but stabbed in the back? Who would do such a thing?' she asked.

Natalie looked torn between staring at the body that still lay on the sand waiting for the police and turning away. I guess death was like that.

'She was there the whole time we were meditating,' Natalie mumbled absently as though just finally comprehending what had happened.

The police arrived not long after followed by Christian, Ainsley and a lawyer.

The police eyed the threesome warily as they headed towards Jay. Jay led them down to the body as the Harringtons came over to us.

'What the hell's going on?' asked Christian as his sister came over to hug him and relieve Ainsley of the children.

'Russ' lady friend was found dead on the beach this morning.'

'She's not my bloody lady friend,' Russ snapped.

'What am I supposed to call her then? Russ' baby mumma?'

'Lana, just call her that. She has nothing to do with me other than we maybe had a drunken roll in the hay last year.'

'Maybe?' Ainsley asked with her eyebrows raised as though to say, don't you go bullshitting me, I'm a mumma now, I have a special radar.

'I don't remember her, okay?' Russ admitted. 'I wasn't in a good place. She was a casualty.'

'Probably not the right word today,' the lawyer added. 'I'm Michael Wheeler, family lawyer' he said, holding out his hand.

'I'm guessing you're Russell Whittington, my new client?' he asked apprehensively.

'Russ. Yes.'

'Did you say, Russ? Just who I was looking for,' a man in red plaid flannel and cheap sunglasses interrupted, not waiting for Russ to answer. 'Fella down there says you knew the deceased? You have a lawyer already?' he asked.

Russ glared at the man with the buzz cut. 'Family lawyer and you are?'

'Detective Ross. You knew the deceased?'

'Barely.'

Detective Ross nodded at the baby.

'I lived a little... carefree in Vegas the last year or so. Apparently, this is the result,' he said, nodding at the baby. 'I'd forgotten Lana even existed and if I'm honest, I didn't even know her name to begin with. It was one of those nights. I'm not even sure the baby is mine. The lawyer is here with the paternity results and to discuss what happens from here, what my obligations are and how shared custody would work, if the test is positive.'

Everyone looked to Michael the lawyer. I held my breath. 'The test is positive,' he replied.

Russ nodded, taking it in. I stood there a little dumbfounded that Russ would now be a full-time dad.

'Right then, Russ, we're going to have to have a chat, I think,' the detective said.

'Right, well, considering the circumstances, I'll be doing that with a lawyer. Any skills in that area, Michael?'

'I wouldn't rely on me, but I can sit in if you like until someone else can get here.'

Russ nodded. 'I'll call my dad, he'll send someone.'

'I could organise you someone,' offered Christian, clearly feeling bad for Russ having to call his dad. His dad was some big wig in the police department that I knew Russ avoided when he could.

'It's okay, he'll know in about five minutes if they're interviewing me, so it's best it comes from me.'

'How is it exactly your father will have that information?' the suspicious detective asked.

'Because he's your boss. Well, your boss' boss' boss, I suspect.'

The detective just looked at Russ with a scowl on his face.

Russ held out his hand. 'Russell Barclay Whittington the third. You'd know my father, Russell Barclay Whittington the second, also known as Barclay Whittington,' he politely informed the detective.

'Right, then?' he said, trying not to show his fear over interviewing a high-profile suspect.

'Oh god, it's like the Harringtons all over again,' I groaned to Ainsley as I reached for another coffee as the waitress passed.

Ainsley smirked.

Russ walked away from the group to have his heated call with his dad, the detective keeping close watch.

'What a mess,' Ainsley commented. 'He didn't do it though, did he?'

'Of course not,' I defended. 'Come on Ains, this is Russ.'

'I know but she just rocked up here with a baby. I imagine

it's a bit of a shock, one that he'd rather not have. What's Russ even doing in the country?' she asked.

'He had some issues in Vegas. They asked him to leave.'

'What? Why?' she asked suspiciously.

'He got into a fight. He was a bit out of control.'

'That's not going to look good for him,' Michael the family lawyer added.

'No shit,' I said, turning around to check on Russ.

'Does anyone know where he was last night?' Michael the family lawyer asked.

Margaret Packersham and Natalie turned to me with smirks on their faces.

'Jo?' Ainsley asked. When I didn't answer and instead focussed on drinking my coffee, she asked again. 'Jo, where was Russ last night?'

'Argh, fine,' I groaned. 'He was with me.'

She looked at me as though waiting for the rest as though she didn't understand what that implied.

'In my room Ainsley. In my bed. Do I need to spell it out?'

She smiled.

'Now is not the time to gloat Ainsley Harrington, you wipe that grin off your face.'

Russ hung up his call and returned. The detective followed.

'My lawyer will be a couple of hours,' he told the detective as the detective's phone rang.

The detective stepped away to take the call and by the look on his face, I suspected it was Russ' dad with instructions.

'Why is Ainsley looking at me like that?' he asked.

'She knows.'

'Knows what?'

'Where you were last night. She's gloating,' I told him.

'Why is she gloating?'

'Because this was all part of her plan. Not you, but me with someone. Although she and Jaz lined this all up, so who knows how much she knew. Mrs Harrington?' I questioned.

She shrugged.

'You knew Russ was here and you didn't tell me?'

'No, of course not. Well, maybe,' she conceded.

'How? Jaz didn't even know he was our Russ.'

'Our Russ?' he queried.

'Shut up, you know what I mean.'

'I saw a photo she put on the pub's Facebook page. I thought it'd be good for you to see a familiar face other than mine.'

'That's it?'

'And well... You were like two peas in Vegas. If it wasn't for Benny...' she said, leaving the rest unsaid.

I nodded because I'd said the same thing.

Russ nodded because that was the cause of his downward spiral.

The detective returned. 'Okay, so I can't speak to you until your lawyer's here, what about you, you two seem friendly?' he asked me.

'She waits for the lawyer too,' Russ said.

The detective sighed and made do with Margaret Packersham. We knew the detective would have no interest in her or Natalie as they hadn't even spoken to Lana. Christian sent the family lawyer with them though just to make sure. You never knew how these things could play out.

'So who's this, then?' Ainsley asked as Nico woke and began squirming.

'Nico. Apparently, he's my son,' Russ said, turning Nico around to get a good look at him. 'My father's really going to kill me. He's going to chop off my balls and feed them to the bloody sharks,' he told his son who just watched him with wide, curious eyes.

'How old is he?' asked Ainsley.

'Two months. I think. What the hell am I going to do with a baby?' he asked.

'You'll manage,' Christian told him with a smirk and a slap on the back.

The baby became restless and Ainsley took him, working her maternal magic while Russ looked on in awe.

Eventually Jaz came back down, assuring Ainsley one of her most trusted staff was upstairs watching ABC TV with the children and she insisted we all go inside and eat something before all the food went to waste.

No one argued, we just turned and followed her inside. I didn't mind. I was starving. I'd had a wonderful night of shenanigans with Russ and a long, tiring morning. The dead woman on the beach hindered my appetite though. They were still on the beach processing her body. I felt sad for her. For dying. For the knife in her back. For the way she'd been found. For the humiliation of it. The indignity. I didn't want her around but I didn't want her to die.

One by one, people came and went from their meeting with the detective. The day wore on. Lunch came and went. The fancy criminal lawyer arrived from the city. He'd interviewed each of us then sat at a table alone, drinking coffee, waiting for the detective to call us. Michael Wheeler, the family lawyer, was doing all the things that needed doing to sort out Russ' custody. The other guests were getting restless. They moaned about being questioned. They threw daggers at Russ. They scowled at me. As though we'd been the ones to off the poor woman in some twisted conspiracy.

Finally, tired of the looks and suspicion and the bickering, we took a restless Nico up to Russ' room.

'Is this really going to be your life now?' I asked, still trying to comprehend it all as he fed his son.

'It has to be. Keeping him is not the easiest choice but it's the right choice. For me,' he said.

'I know. I know. I'm just struggling to get my head around it,' I told him.

'Me too. It feels so surreal. It changes everything.'

'I guess,' I said, feeling sad about that, that despite the chaos caused by his existence, he'd lost his mumma.

'Not us, Jo. Never us. That's if you'll still have me. I know it's a lot to take on and I'm not asking you to step into Lana's place or anything but still, I know me coming with a child is a lot. I'll understand,' he said. I could hear the shake in his voice. If you didn't know him, you might have missed it, but I knew him too well.

I put my arms around him and sank into him. 'I don't know how this is going to work, Russ. I don't know if I'm even cut out to raise another woman's child. A dead woman's child. I don't even know what that life looks like or how that would work.

But I'm in this, us, and if you come with a child, then so be it. We will figure it out.'

He squeezed me tight but didn't speak and I wondered if he just couldn't, but a knock at the door stopped me from inquiring.

The detective waited on the other side.

'Miss Walsh. Are you ready?'

I nodded. I turned back to kiss Russ. 'Don't worry. I'll be okay,' I assured him and followed the detective down the stairs.

We collected the lawyer from where he was working on his laptop in the T-Bar on the way through and we followed the detective down the hallway to the office he was using.

Jay had offered up his office for the detective to use as an interview room. I guessed it was the one room Jaz hadn't renovated because there was no flair or colour or love. It was masculine with grey walls. I suspected the same grey walls that had been there when they moved in. A simple black desk that also looked inherited was in the middle of the room. There was a very comfortable looking black leather chair on one side of the desk that had Jaz Harrington written all over it. On the other were two serviceable dining room chairs.

There were no windows, just a computer and a single photo frame that I wondered if Jaz had forced upon Jay. Otherwise there was nothing personal in the room. It was purposeful and serviceable. It was very Jay.

'I'm detective Ross, why don't you have a seat?'

I sat on one side of Jay's desk with Russ' lawyer and the detective sat on the other in Jay's big comfortable chair. He took his time organising himself, having a sip of water, opening his notebook to the page he wanted, turning his phone to silent, clicking his pen into action.

'So, Miss Walsh, tell me about last night? Start from the beginning. How do you know Russell Whittington?'

'Three years ago my friend and I were looking for someone in Las Vegas, Russ was a PI there and he helped us find him.'

'And?'

'And what? We found him. He died. We came home.'

'Died, just like that?'

I didn't appreciate his tone or the look on his face and may have scowled at him. 'Henry was an old man living on the streets of Las Vegas,' I told him. 'He died of natural causes. Call the Las Vegas Police, ask them. This is old news.'

He tapped some things into his laptop while we sat there, the silence heavy in the room. I looked at the fancy lawyer who just rolled his eyes, which told me not to worry. The detective took some more time to read whatever he found about Henry Mayberry. As I thought he would, he found more. 'You also had another little incident at a place called Mrs May's I see? Again, a few years ago. All connected?'

'It had nothing to do with me. Ainsley inherited the café from a friend who turned out to be a Madam. Her husband, the man we went to Vegas to find, was a renowned thief. He'd sent his wife, the madam, jewels. One was a brooch that belonged to a Russian family. Someone saw Ainsley wearing it. Ainsley didn't know at the time that the brooch was stolen. But the woman made it her mission to get the jewels back. She followed us all the way to Vegas and was waiting for us in the café when we got back. I just got in the way. We called the police. Told them everything. Gave back all of Henry Mayberry's stolen goods.'

'This Ainsley...' he began.

'Ainsley Harrington,' added Russ' fancy lawyer before the detective could get too carried away. 'Married to Christian Harrington. Yes, THE Christian Harrington, you may have seen all the Harrington's out there on your way in?' he added, once he saw the name had caught the detective's attention.

The detective changed his direction quick enough. I wouldn't want to take on the Harringtons unnecessarily either. 'And you and Mr Whittington were...'

'Friends. My boyfriend had just died. Christian was supposed to go with Ainsley but there was a work emergency. I tagged along with Ainsley at the last minute. I wasn't in a great place. Russ was my friend.'

'How did your boyfriend die?'

'What? What does that have to do with anything?' I asked. When the detective just stared me down, I crumbled and answered. 'It was a car accident on his way to work.'

'And where were you at the time?'

'I was at the café. Ainsley had gone away with Christian for the weekend to visit his parents, they were getting in late in the morning, so I'd come in extra early to open up for her. Benny had been safe and sound in bed when I'd left. Then some police officers came to the café around morning tea time and told me what happened.'

'I'm seeing a pattern of death, Miss Walsh.'

'What? Benny was killed by an ice addict who didn't stop for a red light. And if you think I had anything to do with that woman's death, you've lost your mind. I don't even know her. I didn't even speak to her.'

'I got the impression from the other guests that you and Mr Whittington are no longer just friends?'

'That's true and before you bother asking, he was with me last night.'

'The whole night?'

'I guess.'

'You guess? Why don't you tell me about last night? Start with this campfire barbeque thing.'

I gave him a play by play from when I finished my shower and joined the group, chatting to Margaret Packersham and Natalie to everything and every conversation I could remember from the night, leaving out the creepy foot massage but including everything else I could remember, despite all the martinis.

'So you don't know where Mr Whittington was for part of the night until you found him on the beach?'

'I wasn't paying attention.'

'Why was that?'

'I was cross at him, okay? We had just got together and then this woman shows up with a baby.'

'And what changed?'

'When I found him down the beach, we talked it out. Straightened it all out. That's what changed.'

'How exactly was it all straightened out?' he asked suspiciously.

'He told me that Lana and the baby didn't change anything with us. He said how he'd do the right thing by Nico if he was his but we didn't change. I believed him. We were good. I made peace with it all.'

'Easy as that? You didn't make some plan together to sort out the inconvenience to your budding romance?'

'What? No! Don't be ridiculous. I've known Russ a long time. I know the life he led in Vegas. And more power to him. He had no ties so he was free to sow his oats however he pleased. But quite honestly, I wasn't altogether surprised he had a random woman show up with a baby. All I cared about was us. Him and me. I didn't want to be the one breaking up a family, but once I knew we were good, that that wasn't changing, it was fine, we were fine.'

'You're not worried about his previous lifestyle?' he asked.

'That isn't any of your business. But for the record, no. Like I said, I know Russ. He's a good guy. Just because he played the field for a while doesn't mean a thing.'

He nodded. 'When you found him on the beach, Miss Walsh, had Mr Whittington been drinking?'

'He was drinking a beer when I found him, other than that, I can't say.'

He nodded. 'Thank you, Miss Walsh, that'll be all.'

Chapter 15

The detective followed me back to Russ' room. I had the distinct impression I'd said something wrong but I couldn't figure out what. I'd told him the truth. That was all. I had to trust the fancy lawyer, that he'd have stopped me if anything was going to look bad for Russ.

I felt the detective watching me as he silently climbed the stairs behind me, thinking, making assumptions about me, about Russ, about everything. I just hoped he made the right ones. I knew how it must look but I knew Russ didn't do it. He would never have left that baby alone.

Russ looked at me questioningly when I walked in, to see if I was okay. I nodded. He nodded.

'Mr Whittington?' the detective asked, Russ' lawyer hovering behind him.

Russ looked at baby Nico lying in the middle of the big bed, clearly torn.

'It's okay,' I told him. 'I'll watch the baby. You go and clear all this up.'

He nodded. Kissed me. 'If he needs anything, my credit card's in my wallet,' he said, writing done the pin for me. 'I'll see you soon,' he said, locking his eyes to mine and taking a deep breath before leaving. All too quickly they were gone and it was just Nico and me in the little room.

'Hey, little guy,' I said as he looked up at me with those big eyes. 'What am I going to do with you?' I asked, smiling at him like I used to when Henry was a baby. But he just stared back at me, watching, taking me in. Poor little thing must be so frightened, I thought. His mumma was gone, the only other vaguely familiar face of Russ now gone too and he was stuck with me, a strange lady. But he didn't seem bothered. Maybe he was used to being passed around? Accustomed to strangers?

I looked around the room. It was much smaller than the one I had been staying in, which I supposed I'd have to relinquish now Ainsley and Christian had come with the kids and the lawyer. It was only right they had the Harrington family suite that Jaz had put together for them. And there was more of them than me, they'd need the extra space.

Hopefully Russ wouldn't mind me bunking in with him and Nico. It made sense with all of Nico's things already in Russ' room, anyway, I thought. It was then I realised that there were no things. There was no bed for Nico, no pusher or bag of clothes. Just a carry bag in which I could see a tin of formula, and a couple of nappies. There were a couple of bottles rinsed by the sink in the bathroom, no sanitiser or anything that would work as one.

Just as I was thinking how mortified Ainsley would be by the lack of supplies for Nico, she opened the door and whispered, 'Hey.'

'Oh, hey,' I greeted her. 'What's with the whispering?'

'Sorry, I wasn't sure if the baby would be asleep.'

'Nope, he's just lying there.'

'You okay?'

I shrugged.

She sat on the bed and starting playing with Nico. 'Do you need anything? For you, for the little guy? I can help you get some bottles ready or something. He wasn't being breastfed, was he?' she asked, suddenly horrified that he might be abruptly weened.

'There's formula in the bag and bottles on the sink, so I don't think he was being breastfed. But Ains, I can't see any things. He has no bed. There's no bag of clothes or even anything to sanitise the bottles.'

'What? What do you mean?' she asked as she began pawing through all the bags around the room.

There was a black duffle that was clearly Russ'. She rifled through an oversized tote that must have been Lana's. Stuffed inside were a couple of maxi dresses, a roll of deodorant, a makeup bag and wallet and both their passports. Then there was the bag with the nappies and formula.

'That's it? He has like two nappies left and only one change of clothes. She barely had anything for herself? What was her plan?'

'I don't know. When she got here, she tried to dump the baby and keep going. She clearly hadn't planned to stay. Maybe she was actually staying somewhere else and that's where all their stuff is?'

'That has to be it, otherwise she travelled half way around

the world with nothing. How long could she have survived with all that's here?'

'Not long.'

'I'll get Jaz to do a ring around. Do you know how she got here?'

'Nope, she just arrived in the front bar the other night during dinner. Apparently, she tried to just walk off after dropping off the baby with Russ but he wasn't having it. I don't know if she had a car outside, a taxi, an uber, a friend? I don't know. I wasn't really talking to Russ at the time and we haven't caught up on it yet.'

'Well if she had a car, Jay will know, he'll know every single car in that carpark. They know all the other hotels and the caravan park, so if she was staying somewhere else, they'll figure out where and sort it all out.'

She called down to Jaz who assured her there were no unaccounted-for cars in the carpark and that she'd do a ring around.

In the meantime, Ainsley changed Nico's nappy and made him a bottle. 'I don't like using unsterilized bottles but I'm guessing the little fella's used to it. There's hardly any formula left here,' she confirmed as she measured out the powder with the little scoop inside the tin.

She made do with what we had and by the time Nico had finished his bottle, Jaz called back. Ainsley put her on speakerphone to save having to repeat every word she said.

'Sorry but no one can confirm she'd been staying with them. It's off season, so it's easy enough for everyone around here to account for all of their guests and they're all accounted for. Unless she had an Airbnb somewhere.'

'I didn't find any keys or anything in her bag when I went through it,' Ainsley said.

'Ains, you probably shouldn't touch her stuff, the cops will want to look through it,' Jaz said.

'I know but the baby has nothing, Jaz. Nothing.'

'Who travels halfway around the world with a baby and brings nothing?' Jaz asked.

'We thought the same. I don't know. She must have been a little crazy.'

'I didn't speak to her, so I can't say,' Jaz said.

'No, me either,' I added. 'She tried talking to a few people around the campfire the night of the barbeque but no one was on board. Except Bodhi, they had a long, animated chat but I guess he's just one of those people who welcomes everyone. But I wonder if he knows anything more,' I suggested almost thinking out loud to myself.

Jaz offered to investigate while we took care of the baby who was falling asleep in Ainsley's arms.

'We're going to have to get him some things,' Ainsley said, her face doing that thing it does when she's thinking too fast. 'Russ is going to need things anyway.'

Ainsley checked in with Jaz to make sure she was okay to keep her kids up in her apartment while we took Nico shopping. Assured they were safe and taken care of, we bundled the little guy up with the one wrap he had and headed out.

Ainsley grabbed a spare blanket and the pram from the back

of their car on the way through and we walked to the nearby town centre to pick up what supplies we could.

'If we hadn't brought the kids, you could have used some of Jaz's stuff that she keeps here for them like the cot and whatnot. But we'll just buy a porta cot and Russ can get something more permanent later. He'll probably need to get a car seat installed before he leaves too.'

'I don't even think he brought a car here, I think his parents dumped him.'

'Really?' she asked surprised.

'Don't you look so surprised, Mrs Harrington, didn't you do the same thing to me?'

'Yeah but that was a town car with a driver,' she smirked.

I couldn't help but laugh because it was funny and silly and just what I needed. I'd missed her. I'd missed her perspective and her friendship with all that had been going on.

We bought takeaway coffee and headed for the chemist. 'Coffee's not as good as yours,' smiled Ainsley.

'How's the café been?'

'You've barely been gone. It's the same as when you left.'

'I know, but you know,' I said as we walked into the chemist.

'I know,' she agreed because she did, she had the same attachment to the place that I did. It was nice that we got each other that way.

'How come you didn't call me when all this happened with Russ?' she asked.

'Which bit?' I wondered.

'All of it,' she smiled.

'Well, firstly, it hasn't even been that long. It has been a bloody whirlwind, Ains. But I wasn't sure if it was anything. I thought it might be something but I wasn't sure and I didn't want you gloating down the phone at me. I wanted to wait and see, and then talk to you when I got home.'

'You could have called me when she showed up,' she said.

'I almost did. So many times. I knew you'd come but you had the kids and the café and your own stuff, I didn't want to bother you.'

'Are you serious?' she asked, nudging me.

'I was okay. I had Jaz and my new friends, Natalie and Margaret Packersham, looking out for me.'

'Well, I'm glad you've made new friends, just don't go ditching the old ones, yeah?'

'Are you kidding? Never,' I said, nudging her this time. 'I'm glad you're here now,' I told her.

'Me too,' she smiled.

'How much stuff do we even need?' I asked, standing in front of a tower of nappies, completely unsure how much of anything to buy.

'How long are you and Russ staying?'

'I don't know. As soon as this dead lady friend business is over with, I guess we'll just go home. Seems a bit of poor taste to stay after something like that happens.'

'Okay. What if we bank on you staying until the end of the week. That should be long enough to sort everything out. Oh, and I'll just send a car with a baby seat to come and get you both, and Russ can sort out what he needs when he gets home.'

'That'd be great. How long are you staying?' I asked suddenly not wanting her to leave at all. It was nice having her here, seeing her face, feeling her spirit. We'd become closer than ever over the last few years. I don't know where I'd be without her.

'We'll just stay the night and head back in the morning. I just wanted to see all this Russ having a baby business for myself and make sure you were doing okay.'

I pulled a dramatic sad face that made her laugh.

'Stop it. We have to focus. This baby needs supplies and Christian and I both need to work tomorrow afternoon. We'll get nothing done if you keep that sad face going.'

'Fine,' I whined with a smile. It was because I was here that she was going to have to have to work tomorrow afternoon anyway. She had my shifts covered but there were still things like ordering supplies and some prep work that needed taking care of and that's what she was doing for me.

'Alright. So just in case, we'll get two packets of nappies and two tins of formula. That should definitely see you through the rest of the week and then some and Russ can stock up properly when you all get home.'

I paid for the items with Russ' credit card and we headed down the street to a cute baby shop. It was only small and looking at the price tags, a little overpriced, but we just needed some essentials to get by so it would do. We bought a pram, a porta cot, enough clothes for him to have a couple of changes a day if need be and some onesies to sleep in. We bought some sheets for the porta cot, new bottles because Ainsley didn't like not knowing where the others had come from, a microwave steriliser, a couple of blankets and some toys.

Just as we lugged our bags outside and I was wondering how

we were going to get it all back to the pub, a car pulled up as we hit the sidewalk and Christian jumped out to take our things.

'It's like you two share the same brain,' I laughed.

'Oh God, we're not that in sync,' Ainsley laughed. 'I messaged him when you were loading up the counter, you dope,' she said, nudging me and rolling her eyes.

'Would you ladies like a lift back?' Christian offered.

'I think we might walk some more,' Ainsley said.

Christian nodded, kissed her cheek and off he went with all our things.

'Are you really ready for all of this, Jo?' Ainsley asked as we started our walk back with Nico sleeping peacefully in Anna's pink pram.

'I don't know. Were you?'

'Probably not,' she smiled. 'When is your next appointment with Dr Bailey?'

'End of the month.'

'I'll call Julie in the morning and see if I can get you in earlier,' she said, referring to Dr Bailey's receptionist as though they were best friends.

'Thanks. Doesn't hurt to be safe I suppose.'

'I think it's great though. You and Russ,' she added.

'Really?'

'Yeah. I saw the way he was with you in Vegas, he adored you.'

'I didn't see that at all,' I said, wondering how I'd missed it, if he'd been that obvious.

'Of course not. Benny had just died, you weren't supposed to see much of anything.'

'He said that's what caused his downward spiral that led to him getting kicked out of Vegas.'

'What did?'

'Me.'

'Ah.'

'He said he couldn't find his footing after that.'

She nodded. 'I felt a bit like that when Christian's dad dragged him up north and we had to go to Vegas without him. I wasn't sure when I'd get to see him again. I was confused. It was like the ground was shaking beneath my feet. But I had you and we had a purpose and a mission, so I managed. If he'd been gone for good and I couldn't call him, I don't know what that would have done to me.'

I squeezed her hand because I remembered how dark a place she'd been in before she'd met Christian. She'd tried to commit suicide she'd been that dark. A lot of that was biological and Dr Bailey sorted it out with his magic pills but the fear of it wasn't so easy to get rid of.

She smiled her thanks. 'Is Russ okay now?'

'I think so. He seemed fine. Said everything made sense now we were together.'

'Are you? Together?'

'Yes. I think so. We talked about it before I went down for my interview with the detective. I told him I was in. That whatever this was, I was in, even if he now came with an extra human.'

'Wow, that's fast, Jo.'

'I know. But it's Russ. And he didn't lie, when we were together, it was like everything stood still and was just as it was meant to be. And I think somewhere, deep down, I knew it all started back in Vegas. I know if it hadn't been for Benny, there would have been something then. It's Russ. It's like I've known him my whole life.'

'It was less than a week ago you were saying you couldn't imagine ever doing life with someone other than Benny. How does that change so fast?'

'I don't know. I did some thinking when I got here. Had some realisations on the beach. Maybe it was the healing I got from Bodhi. But I think mostly it's more a case of I couldn't imagine doing life with just anyone. I just couldn't see it. Until I saw Russ. Russ wasn't just anyone. Don't get me wrong. I fought it for a hot minute. And then after the first time we, you know, I completely lost my shit. I felt so darned guilty about it. I felt like I'd disrespected Benny, like I'd robbed him of something. But Russ... Ains, he was perfect. He said it was fine. He told me to take as long as I needed to deal with it, to get my head and heart in the same place. He'd wait as long as he had to but he wasn't going anywhere. I could kick and scream as much as I wanted but he was in for keeps.'

'Russ said that? Our Russ?'

I laughed. 'I know, it kind of blew me away, Ains. He just held me and it was enough. He explained that whatever I had with him, didn't invalidate the life I had with Benny and I realised it was Russ I wanted to have all those things with, all the things you and Christian have and that it would be okay.'

'Was this before or after his lady friend showed up?' she asked.

I smiled. 'Before. I kicked him to the kerb the minute she showed up. He had a family. I wasn't getting in between that.'

'And then?'

'He explained a woman whose name he couldn't remember showing up with a child, didn't make a family. That he'd do whatever he needed to for his son but he wasn't an option for his lady friend and if that's what she was after, she'd be going home empty handed.'

'Is that what she was after? Russ?'

'I don't know. She never did say.'

'Well, she was after something showing up here with nothing. You think it was money?'

'I don't even know if Russ has any?' I told her as we reached the pub.

Upstairs, Christian had already set the porta cot up for Nico and unpacked the pram and put it all together. He'd used Jaz's microwave to put all the bottles through the steriliser and grinned like a proud papa when we walked in. But then his face dropped.

'What?' I asked.

'You might need to sit,' he suggested.

'I don't want to sit. What's going on?' I asked, sitting anyway.

'Christian?' queried Ainsley when he hesitated.

'It's Russ. They've taken him down to the station.'

'What? He's been arrested?' I shouted, jumping off the bed.

The noise woke Nico. Ainsley comforted him while I stomped around the room.

'I don't think so. I think it's just further questioning. He had the most motive.'

'What the hell happened? Did they find something?'

'I'm not exactly sure. They were packing him into the car

when I got back. The lawyer's gone with him. He'll sort it out. He'll take care of him. Russ has his dad as well, don't worry about him, he'll be fine. He'll be back before you know it.'

'What about the baby?' I asked, staring at Nico as he settled comfortably in Ainsley's arms.

'Russ asked if you can make sure Nico's okay until he's back.'

I nodded. Looked at my watch. Would he even make it back tonight?

'Jo, you okay?' Ainsley asked.

'Sure. Sure. I'm fine. I can do that.'

'He might not be back tonight looking at the time,' she pointed out like I hadn't already realised it.

'I've looked after Henry overnight plenty of times.'

'Not when he was this little.'

'I know. But I changed his nappy and dressed him and fed him. Surely that gave me enough skills to get Nico through the night?'

Ainsley laughed. 'You'll be fine. I'll stay with you though, just in case and you never know, Russ may be back before it even matters.'

'You can't do that. You have a husband and two kids.'

'It's fine,' Christian said. 'Henry will probably have a sleep over at Aunty Jaz's anyway and I can take care of Anna. Ains can express some milk and we'll be fine. It'll be some good bonding time for us,' he insisted.

I nodded. 'Thank you. You two are the best, you know.'

'I know,' agreed Ainsley with a big smile.

'Besides,' added Christian. 'I owe Russ for taking care of my girl in Vegas,' he said, pulling her to him for a quick kiss as though to remind himself she was okay.

Chapter 16

Ainsley waited in the room with Nico while I went to the Harrington family suite and packed up my things.

I look at the bed, the covers still mussed from our night together. I smiled, remembering all the wonderful things we'd done in that bed. Waking entwined, our legs and arms twisted together.

I lay down on the bed for just a minute, breathing in the smell of him. He was everywhere, in the sheets, on his pillow, the familiarity of it startled me. I barely knew him really but everything about him, his smell, his spirit, the feel of him, the taste of him, was so familiar. *God, I hope everything is going to be okay,* I thought, closing my eyes and breathing him in.

There was no time for lying about like a lovesick teenager, I thought. I had responsibilities. Russ needed me to step up. I put our beautiful night together out of my mind for now and got on with my task. It didn't take long, I hadn't brought that much nor had I really unpacked. Except for the clothes Russ and I had left on the floor from the night before, I was living out of my little suitcase.

I gave one last look around the room where we had begun.

I could almost hear him groan. Hear his voice thick with need. See that look in his eye and the way his body had moved. Stop it, I told myself and opened the door. Bodhi stood on the other side about to knock.

'Where are you going?' he asked surprised.

'Just moving rooms,' I told him.

'Why? Which room are you moving to?' he asked suspiciously.

I sighed. 'To Russ' room. I'm watching the baby until he gets back so it makes more sense for me to go there. Besides, now that there are Harringtons in town, I need to surrender the Harrington suite.'

'Is that why your room is nicer than the rest?' he asked, trying to peek over my shoulder.

'Jaz had it done up for when her family visit. She was all booked out with people wanting to see you, so she gave me the family suite.'

He nodded. 'Right. So why are you watching the dead woman's kid?'

I stared at him in shock for a moment. For such an enlightened guy, that was pretty insensitive. I recovered from my surprise and reminded him, 'He's Russ' baby too.'

He looked like he was going to grill me the way Ainsley had on my about face with the whole relationship concept but clearly thought better of it.

'Seems my healing worked a treat then,' he said instead, forcing a smile. 'You were booked in for another session this afternoon actually, I was just coming to reschedule it for you.

Under the circumstances, I've cancelled them all for the rest of the week, but I'd be happy to do one for you tomorrow.'

'I appreciate the offer. But I agree, under the circumstances, it doesn't feel right. I'm just going to wait for Russ to come back and then we'll see about going home.'

'Home?' he asked, his voice harsh. 'You can't go home yet.'

'Why not?' I asked, a little unsure why he thought it was any of his business.

'You came here for treatment, to get well, to be able to go on with your life. We're not done yet.'

'I feel great and really, the treatment I had must have done something because I feel like a whole new person.'

'It's not enough. We have more work to do,' he insisted.

'I'll see about that when I get home,' I told him, thinking he couldn't be the only person in the world who did this.

'And you and Russ, you're going home together?'

'Russ and I are going to see what this is. I don't know where his home is but I know where mine is and that's where I'll be going. Let's just leave it at that right now.'

He nodded but I could see he still had some thoughts on the subject. I didn't care. I wasn't interested in his thoughts. I wasn't interested in anyone's thoughts. Except maybe Ainsley or Dr Bailey or of course Russ himself. Anyone else could shove their thoughts. It was my life and I was living it any way that felt right. And this, Russ, it felt right. Nico, I wasn't so sure about yet, but that was okay, there was time to figure that out.

The lady Jaz hired to perform housekeeping duties when they had guests came up behind Bodhi, ready to clean the room and prepare it for the Harringtons.

'Looks like that's our cue to leave,' I told him as I smiled at her.

'Will you come down for evening meditation in a little while?' he asked hopefully as I stepped outside to let the housekeeper in.

'I don't know, probably not, not unless Russ is back anyway,' I told him. When he looked like he didn't understand and was going to try and persuade me, I reminded him, 'I have to look after the baby.'

'What about your friend? She can watch the baby,' he suggested.

'Ainsley has done enough and she has two kids of her own that need looking after,' I told him, trying to keep my manners in check but losing the fight.

'What's one more then?' he asked.

I stared at him confused by his insensitivity and persistence. 'I'm sorry, I won't make it today. I have to go,' I said, forcing my way past him and walking down the hallway as purposefully as possible in the hope he'd leave me be.

He didn't follow and I was relieved.

Ainsley was sitting on the cane chair on the balcony in front of Russ' room when I got there talking on the phone to her mum. I knew it was her mum because she had a certain tone when talking to her. I smiled. I liked Mrs Donovan a lot. With my own mother so far away, Mrs Donovan had taken it upon herself to provide all the motherly services a girl would need and I was so grateful to have her. 'Tell her, hi,' I told Ainsley as I took my bag into the room.

The housekeeper I'd met downstairs had already been

through Russ' room and swapped the sheets and given the place a good clean. Someone had packed away Lana's things and it was like she hadn't been there at all. Except for the fact Nico was sleeping in his new porta cot.

I sorted myself out, not that there was much to sort but I put some toiletries in the bathroom and again, hoped Russ didn't mind me moving in and setting myself up. Being in this relationship or whatever it was, was one thing, moving myself in to his room was another. But I figured we could rearrange in any way we needed to when he came back. If he came back. I put that thought from my mind as Ainsley came inside.

'How's your mum?'

'Fine. Said the café was slow this afternoon so she used your oven and did some baking. I'm thinking you can expect to find a full freezer when you get home,' she smiled.

'I can't complain about that,' I said.

'You all set up?'

'Yeah. I think.'

'Good, because I'm starving. Grab the baby and we'll go down for dinner,' she instructed.

I nodded. Grabbed Nico in one arm and the pram in the other.

'Why don't you just use the baby carrier? I can help you strap it on,' she suggested.

'No. I don't think so.'

'It will be so much easier than lugging that pram down the stairs.'

'Ains, it hasn't even been 24 hours. I can't go strapping a dead woman's baby to my chest as though it's mine. It just doesn't feel right.'

She smiled tightly, understanding, took the pram from me and headed for the door.

We took the internal stairs and at the bottom, Ainsley flipped out the pram like a pro, helped me buckle Nico in and we headed in to the dining room.

There was one big round table in our sectioned off area to the side of the other diners where Margaret Packersham sat with Natalie, the Lorna Jane mums, Bodhi and Karen, the famous author, and her manager slash lover. Jaz was over by the bar talking to a waitress and Christian had a table where he waited with his kids for Ainsley. There was a chair there for me too but I insisted she should enjoy some family time and I went to sit with my fellow seekers of enlightenment, sitting the pram between Margaret Packersham and me.

'How are you doing?' I asked Natalie.

'Better,' she said.

'Did you call Dr Bailey?' I asked. Ainsley had spoken to Julie, Dr Bailey's receptionist for me and asked for a favour and of course, for his star patient, he'd agreed to have a chat with Natalie considering the circumstances.

'I did. He was great. He helped. I have an appointment to see him in person next week as well,' she said. 'After that, Jaz brought me up some tea that helped me sleep. I missed evening meditation but I feel better for the rest.'

'Of course you do,' I told her, squeezing her hand. The shock of seeing Lana's dead body was worse for her because she'd been the first. Her scream had prepared the rest of us for something awful, if you can be prepared for that at all.

It wasn't long after I'd sat down though that Henry was climbing up my leg.

'Hey, little man, how you doing?'

'I'm okay. How are you?' he asked, snuggling in for a cuddle.

I squished him nice and tight. 'I'm always better when you're here.'

He smiled. 'Are these your new friends?'

'Yep, they sure are,' I said, introducing him to Margaret and Natalie.

'Will you come back to the café though?' he asked innocently.

'Of course, I'll be back at the end of the week. This is just a little holiday,' I assured him.

'And will the baby come too?'

'What do you know about him?'

He shrugged. 'I heard Aunty Jaz say you had the baby now,' he told me.

'Did you now? You know he's not mine, right, that I'm looking after him for my friend, Russ?'

'That's what Dad said. So he's really not yours?'

'Nope. But he might be around sometimes, is that okay?'

'Like Anna?'

'Maybe.'

'Will he play with me when he's bigger?'

'I bet he will.'

'Okay then,' he said climbing down as Christian called him back to eat.

Jaz still had us on a prepared menu and helped the waitress bring out bowls of spaghetti.

'Any word about Russ yet?' she asked.

'No, nothing yet.'

'Could mean they've charged him and he has to wait for a hearing,' offered Bodhi from across the table.

'Not helpful,' Jaz, whispered at him in her Harrington voice.

He shrugged as though he didn't care at all.

'It's okay. I'm sure between his dad and the lawyer, he'll be fine,' I told her.

She nodded. 'Of course he will. You let me know if you need anything though. Did Amanda clean the room?'

'She did. Thank you.'

'Of course. I couldn't have you sleeping in the same bed as that woman. Not that it seems to have mattered, you could have almost any room now, nearly everyone's left.'

'I noticed. Is this all that's left?'

'Yep, this is it,' she said as she went to do something else.

'So why did you all stay?' I asked, curiously. I knew why I was there, I was waiting for Russ but they didn't have to stay.

'Are you kidding?' one of the Lorna Jane mums piped up. 'I'm not missing out on kid free time for nothing. I won't get another chance for a year, I'm not cutting this one short.'

'Amen, Stace,' said her friend.

'There's too many eyes around for Karen to leave just yet,' Karen, the famous author's, manager slash lover told us and I remembered I saw a journalist out the front when we'd come back from our shopping trip. Thankfully he hadn't seen Ainsley. We'd come along the beach path while he'd been lurking against a tree in the carpark. Jaz would have shooed him away before too long.

'I'm not really ready to go home yet, I guess,' said Margaret Packersham. 'Besides, I can't leave you here all alone waiting for your man to come back. I'll stay and give you a hand for as long as you need me,' she offered but I suspected she just wasn't healed enough yet to be in her home alone without her husband. I remembered what that was like.

'Natalie, what about you?' I asked.

'I haven't called my folks to come get me yet,' she said. 'I just don't have the heart. They'll be so disappointed.'

'Disappointed? How could they possibly be disappointed? Nothing that happened to you was your fault. None of this is your fault,' I told her.

'I know. But I'm not better yet and they'll be disappointed with that,' she said sadly.

'Are you kidding?' I told her. 'Look at you, you're having conversations, you're making friends, you've had my back through this whole drama. We've gone for walks and eaten ice cream in bed, you've let me cry on your shoulder. Give yourself some credit, you've made incredible progress,' I told her.

'I guess,' she said, taking it in, thinking.

'And I can give you a couple of extra treatments tomorrow, if you like,' Bodhi offered, still trying to ply his wares despite everything and a shiver ran up my spine. 'We'll see if we can't have you better in a day or so and you can call them then. And make sure you come back to meditation. You too, Jo. You need to keep it up,' he insisted and suddenly I didn't want to be anywhere near him and decided I'd be keeping Natalie away from him too. Something wasn't sitting right with his new found disrespect for people's feelings and what was right. A woman had died. Someone had stabbed her in the back and he didn't seem to care a bit.

'Maybe when Russ is back. I need to watch the baby,' I told him again thinking there was something seriously wrong with his hearing.

Bodhi didn't look impressed with my answer. He was taking the whole spiritual healing plan a little too seriously, I thought. A woman had died. There was a baby without his mumma. The police had taken his dad away. And Bodhi was worried about me meditating? I was starting to think his wiring was wrong and I didn't want anything to do with that.

Besides, I was feeling so much better, anyway. I'd come so far this week already. And if I needed more healing, I'd get it in the city. They mightn't be some travelling guru people thought was the next Dalai Lama but I'm sure they could do the trick if Dr Bailey couldn't sort me out from here.

I just smiled nicely at him and let it go. I wasn't arguing with him about it in front of a table full of people. But I would be keeping as far away from him as possible until Russ returned and we could all go home.

Halfway through dinner, Mr Slick joined us. He squished in between me and Karen the famous author's manager slash lover. Jaz brought him over a bowl of spaghetti as he announced he'd be gone first thing in the morning.

'You don't really seem the sort to have tried something like this anyway,' I told him.

'Nah, load of poppycock, if you ask me,' he whispered. 'But

let's just leave it at that, hey?' he smiled as if he realised everyone was watching him.

It was an unexpected comment and I didn't know what to make of it so I did as he asked and left it at that and focussed on my dinner. I was suddenly feeling very uneasy at the thought that Mr Slick wasn't here for the right reasons. Did that mean he could have killed Lana. I made a note to mention his comment to Jay. I realised that any one at that table could have killed her. It didn't feel random. Her showing up out of the blue. Getting stabbed in the back. It was too coincidental to be random. My addiction to crime tv told me there was no such thing as a coincidence.

Who else could have done it? All I knew was it wasn't me and it couldn't have been Russ. Margaret Packersham told us Lana had died in the early hours of the morning. I'd taken Russ to my bed around midnight and he was busy doing delicious things to my body. Someone had killed her though, but who?

Chapter 17

One by one everyone left as they finished their dinner, heading up to the safety of their rooms. I suspected everyone had come to the same conclusion as I had and no one was comfortable with the idea that one of us had killed Lana. It could have been anyone at the table.

I joined the Harringtons, Ainsley, Christian, Jaz and Jay in a booth in the T-bar when we'd all finished dinner. Jaz's most trusted waitress again took Henry upstairs to Jaz and Jay's apartment to settle him down ready for bed but we kept Anna. I swapped babies with Ainsley so I could get in some snuggle time with Anna while she had her bottle and fell asleep. Ainsley was adept at expressing for occasions like this. Christian might not work for the family business anymore but they were still Harringtons and if a photograph of Ainsley feeding her child hit the magazines, Christian's mother would die. Where the risk was low, she threw caution to the wind because she herself thought it was perfectly fine and natural but with so much going on at the pub, Ainsley figured it was a small courtesy to appease Christian's very prim, socialite mother.

'So,' Jaz began. 'We know it wasn't you and it wasn't Russ who killed that woman, who else could have done it? Why would anyone else have done it?' she asked curiously.

'Who even knew her?' I asked.

'No one. Not even Russ actually knew her. Not really. Maybe that's why she was really here? Maybe it had nothing to do with needing money or wanting Russ, maybe she was running from trouble, she was stashing her kid somewhere safe but the trouble followed her here,' she suggested.

'We haven't been able to find out anything that would suggest that,' Jay said. 'She was close to broke, but not so bad she wouldn't bounce back with a few weeks' work.'

'She'd been in Vegas last year. Could it have been gambling debt?'

'It could. Anything's possible. But we didn't find anything in her history that would suggest she'd been hitting the tables too hard. Her own accounts would look worse before she went to loan sharks.'

'Where'd they even get a knife? It's not like someone walks around carrying a butcher's knife in case they might want to plunge it into someone?' I suggested.

'It was chefs,' Jaz said. 'They must have picked it up from the barbeque area. Chef had been using it earlier and it was in the tub under the bench for cleaning.'

'So someone had thought about it. They'd seen her, or something had happened and they thought, oh I'll just grab that knife and sort that out,' suggested Ainsley.

'Something like that,' smirked Jay at her logic.

'So it still could be anyone,' I said. 'Who's even strong enough to plunge a knife in someone's back?' I asked.

'You don't actually need any strength to do that. You just need the mental fortitude,' Jay said.

'Or be just plain assed crazy,' offered Jaz.

'Or be plain assed crazy,' he agreed. 'Margaret Packersham could have done it. Anyone could have. Maybe not Natalie. I saw the angle it had gone in on and you'd have to have been a certain height and she's the only one who's definitely too short,' he added.

A shiver ran up my spine. It really could have been anyone, I thought. 'What about Mr Slick? I don't know why he's really here but he said something tonight that made me think it wasn't for healing or spiritual enlightenment,' I said, telling them about Mr Slick's weird comment at dinner.

'I'll mention it when I speak to the detective and see what I can dig up on him,' Jay said.

'You haven't heard anything about Russ, have you?' I asked, hopefully.

'Not a thing, I'm sorry.'

'Michael, the family lawyer, has been keeping in touch with the Joe, Russ' lawyer and he says it's still just questioning, they're waiting for his dad to get there before they start, so that's good,' Christian added.

'Where is the family lawyer?' I asked.

'He had his dinner sent up to his room,' Jaz said.

'He's not a really social guy,' smiled Ainsley.

'Well, as long as he's keeping tabs on Russ and is getting

things all sorted for the little guy, I don't care where he eats or who he hangs with,' I told them.

We finished the night off with decadent hot chocolates, then Ainsley went with Christian to put Anna to bed and then went up to Jaz's apartment to tuck Henry in. Jay helped me take the pram upstairs then left Nico and me to our own devices.

'Just you and me again, little guy,' I told him as I changed his nappy and put him in one of the onesies Ainsley had gotten Jaz to wash and dry. Well, not Jaz herself. But they were fresh and soft and fluffy and no longer smelt of ink and shop. I dressed him and wrapped him and gave him a little cuddle before putting him into the porta cot and turning on the musical superhero mobile we'd bought him.

I watched his little face as he lay there staring up at the mobile. His little face was round and he had big eyes and a serious mouth. Other than the eyes, I could totally see Russ in him, the eyes though, they were all his mumma. His dead mumma, I reminded myself.

'I'm sorry you have to go through all this, kiddo,' I told him. 'Your dad's going to take really good care of you though.'

Ainsley came in then with two glasses of Baileys with ice. We went out to the balcony to drink them with a blanket off the bed so Nico could sleep.

'He all good?' she asked.

'Yep.'

'Well done. I knew you could do it.'

I laughed. 'Ains, I love you but you wouldn't be sitting here if you thought I could do it.'

'Moral support, I swear,' she smiled.

'You're the best, you know,' I said, snuggling in to her. 'I'm so glad you're here.'

'Me too. And Russ will be okay, you know.'

'Thanks.'

'So, now we're alone and the baby's asleep, you can tell me all about you and Russ. How'd you hook up?' she asked.

I smiled. 'Are you living vicariously through me now you're an old married woman?'

'Maybe,' she smiled. 'But what kind of best friend would I be if I didn't ask for all the juicy details.'

'Oh, you want the juicy details?' I asked.

'Okay, no, not the juicy details. I still have to look Russ in the eye and I remember the stories he told us in Vegas. I can't know he did any of that with you.'

I laughed. 'Well, I think we were pretty tame in comparison to those stories,' I told her. Then I went on to tell her the rest. All the details she needed to know anyway. I told her how sweet he was, how all that experience he'd accumulated had paid off and about how sad he was the night I'd found him on the beach.

'You had sex with him on the beach? What about all the sand?' she asked screwing her face up.

'I had a blanket from when I was by the fire.'

'Ah, ever the girl scout, huh?'

'It's not like I'd planned to make love to Russ in the moonlight on the beach you know, I was just cold and wandering aimlessly,' I told her, leaving out how mad and disgusted I was with Bodhi after that creepy foot massage.

'You make it all sound like an old-fashioned romance novel and that doesn't sound like the Russ I know at all,' she said.

'I know, it's ridiculous but it feels like one too. I think that's what I struggled with the most, the fact that it all feels so perfect and so right. Is that how you felt with Christian? Is that how you knew he was it?'

'Yeah, it was just something went still inside, like the searching was over and I just felt so at peace when I was with him. I don't think I'm saying it right, that doesn't sound very romantic at all.'

'No, I get what you mean. All the anxiety, all the stuff just stops when you're together because none of it matters and you feel like everything is going to be okay because you have each other. Like two halves. Argh, now that sounds like a bad rom-com line.'

We both laughed as we finished our drinks.

'Am I crazy though, Ains?'

'I saw you two together today and no, I don't think so. Everyone thought I was crazy and moving too fast with Christian, remember? But you saw it, him and me. You saw we could be something and I wouldn't even have gone on a date with him if it wasn't for you, remember?'

'I remember,' I said, smiling at the memory. Christian hadn't been as charming as we knew him to be now but he'd stepped in and come to Ainsley's rescue when the Russian was accosting her over the stolen brooch in the café one day. When he asked her to dinner afterwards, I told her she had to go to say thank you and the rest was history. They had a crazy, fabulous, beautiful whirlwind romance that resulted in the most amazing

Vegas wedding and two beautiful babies, so I'd clearly been right to encourage that first date.

'So you just follow your heart and if your heart says Russ, then go with it, Jo. We have seen how short life can be, how precious every minute is. We're not always guaranteed tomorrow so you can't waste it, not love. It's too rare to get the real deal.'

'Do I really get to have it twice?'

'I don't think God or the Universe or the Angels or whatever is up there puts a limit on our happiness. We limit ourselves when we're not brave enough to wait for the right one or to jump when we find it. And you wouldn't be who you are without Benny, without losing Benny and Russ wouldn't be who he is without whatever the hell it is he did in Vegas,' she smiled. 'There are no limits but if love comes your way, Jo, you grab hold with both hands and don't let go.'

I nodded, a tear in my eye and then hugged her hard.

'Come on, you're probably going to want to get some sleep because I bet that little fella will be up in the middle of the night.'

'Oh god, you think?'

She laughed. 'Yeah, I think. Come on.'

We went inside and got ready for bed. 'It's like old times,' I told her.

'Yeah, but this time we're both mentally stable,' she joked.

'So say we,' I laughed.

Nico and I made it through the night with just one wake up for a feed and change and I didn't even need to wake Ainsley for it. I was glad I'd managed without her because it was probably the first full night's sleep she'd had in a while. I was pretty pleased with myself when I woke and Nico was still peacefully sleeping in his porta cot, happy as a clam. It was just before sunrise and I knew before I rolled over that Ainsley was gone. She'd left a note on the pillow. 'You did great. Gone to snuggle with my husband. See you at breakfast.'

I smiled, she'd probably only pretended to be asleep while I'd tended to Nico in the middle of the night. She wanted me to succeed on my own. I was smiling at how good a friend she was, then scowled as there was a knock at the door? Who the hell was knocking this early? Then as Nico woke and grizzled, I remembered where I was. I scooped him up before he woke up our neighbours and went to open the door. I opened the door to Bodhi with a strangely alert Nico on my hip. How do kids wake so perky?

'You ready?' Bodhi asked with an expectant look on his face.

'Um... no, I have to watch the baby, remember?' I told him as though he couldn't see the baby on my hip. I'd lost count of how many times I'd told him no, he just wasn't listening and I was losing my patience. He looked from me to Nico with a distinct look of distaste on his face. I got it, not everyone could be baby people. He was a young, transient guy with no ties and the world at his feet. I don't imagine he'd understand a life of responsibility. But I guess this was my life now. The life of Jo had taken a dramatic turn but I looked at Nico and despite the circumstances, I wasn't sure I minded.

Bodhi waited a moment more, hoping I'd change my mind, maybe, who knows, but then he huffed and he was gone.

'What was that all about, hey?' I asked Nico as I went to warm his bottle.

These rooms were simple, just a bed, a chair and a small ensuite. No kitchenettes or fancy furnishings. It was a pub, not a hotel and the majority of the time these rooms weren't even used with any regularity and when they were, it was mostly surf bums passing through in need of a bed for a night or two. So I had to do things the old fashioned way and ran the bathroom tap until it was hot and filled a jug Jaz had loaned us from the kitchen with water and put the bottle of formula in it to warm while I changed Nico and got him ready for the day.

While Nico drank his bottle, I checked my phone and saw there was a message from Russ. My heart jumped a little as I opened it. *I'm okay. Waiting for my dad. Don't worry.* It had come through close to midnight so I guessed he may no longer be available, I tried calling him anyway but it went straight to voice mail. So I messaged him a heart emoji and returned my attention to Nico who'd finished his bottle.

'You ready for a little nap?' I asked. He didn't protest, so I put him back into his porta cot so I could get ready. I showered and got myself ready for the day and we headed down for breakfast. Natalie caught me before I reached the stairs.

'Here, let me grab that,' she insisted, taking the pram from me because I still wasn't comfortable strapping a dead woman's baby to my chest.

'Thanks. How you doing?'

'I think I'm okay,' she said.

She did look good. Almost like the shock of seeing a dead

woman on the beach had shaken her free of all the pain she'd been holding on to.

'How were snuggles?' I asked Ainsley as we joined her at the table for breakfast.

She smiled guiltily.

'That good, huh?' I asked nudging her.

She giggled. I shook my head and went to get food while Nico slept in his pram.

'So who do you think did it, anyway?' asked one of the Lorna Jane mums as they joined us at the table with their eggs.

'Shhhh... not in front of the baby, he just lost his mumma,' I told her, even though we'd happily talked about it the night before but it hadn't crossed my mind then.

'Honey, I don't think he understands,' Ainsley smiled.

'I know, but I feel bad for him. But all I know is it wasn't me and it wasn't Russ.'

'You sure? He's been gone a long time, they must have something?' one of the mums said.

'He was waiting on someone for most of the night. He sent a message last night, he wasn't worried so I'm not. I don't know what they have, but apart from the fact he was with me at the time, I know Russ and he didn't feel enough either way about her to do that. He couldn't do that, it's Russ,' I told them.

'Yeah, but blokes can get a bit crazy when their connections with their women are threatened and he was definitely into you. It would have been the easiest solution,' she said.

'But now he's a full-time dad, do you really think that'd have been his ultimate goal? He'd have known that's what would happen. He didn't seem like he was itching to be a dad at all.

Besides, he has some skills, right?' her friend suggested and I wondered how she knew, I barely knew.

'You're right, he has that air about him, that says he served somewhere, like Jay, he has it too, and if he had skills, no one would ever have known. They probably would never have even found her body. Isn't that what people with skills can do?' the first asked conversationally as though discussing my new man's ability to kill a woman and make her body disappear was normal breakfast conversation.

'Can we just stop?' I said. 'Russ didn't do it, so let's leave it at that.'

They heard my tone and were wise enough to look contrite and focussed on their eggs as Jay walked in with a very serious looking woman in a Kmart suit. Not that I had an aversion to shopping at Kmart but I was surprised. Jay was married to a Harrington, spent his spare time with surf bums, a woman in Kmart workwear said something about the person and to me it said, not friends with Jay or Jaz, but they walked towards us together none the less.

'Jo?' Jay asked as though he didn't know who I was. 'This is Elizabeth North from Family and Child Services.'

'Okay, how can I help you?' I asked her.

She looked at Nico sleeping comfortably in his pram.

'Oh, no, no,' I said.

'I'm sorry,' she said kindly. 'I'm just doing my job. Are you his mother? Someone called to say she'd died.'

'No, I'm not his mother,' I admitted.

'They said the police had taken his father in for questioning, is that right?'

'Yes.'

'The message said there was no one to look after the baby. Honestly, the police usually call me before leaving a child unattended,' she said.

Chapter 18

'Well, whatever you've been told is not quite true,' interjected Ainsley in her best Mrs Harrington voice. It was something she'd developed, not just as a mumma but a mumma of a Harrington, wife of a Harrington. They were a famous family, even though Christian had set up his own business and was no longer a part of the family business, he was still a Harrington. People always wanted something from a Harrington, so she'd developed a voice that clearly said back the hell off or I'll rip your vocal cords from your throat with my mouth. We laughed about it but really, it was quite terrifying. 'Jo is not only an old and trusted friend of the baby's father, but his significant other. Mr Whittington specifically requested the child stay in her care until his return.'

Michael Wheeler, the family lawyer appeared seemingly out of the ether although I suspect Jaz had sent one of her staff up to get him. 'Can I help you?' he asked Elizabeth North.

'And you are?' she asked, without even bothering to properly look at him.

'Michael Wheeler, family lawyer working on behalf of

Russell Whittington III in the case of his child, Nico Whittington.'

'That's his name on the birth certificate?' I asked surprised. I'd assumed his mumma had given him her name. Can you even do that without the father's signature? You can't here but I didn't know the American rules.

Michael Wheeler gave me a look that said shut up, so I shut up.

'Mr Whittington has asked that Miss Walsh care for his child in his absence. I actually have the paperwork here for her to sign.'

'Really?' I asked, wondering what paperwork or why he was being so official when Russ was not really gone. He'd be back. He had to come back.

He gave me that look again so I sipped my coffee to keep my mouth busy.

'Everything is in order, Ms North,' he assured her.

'Then why was I called? Something must be off if I was called,' she said, certain of herself.

Bodhi walked in at that moment and I looked up and caught his eye and the looks of guilt and pride and accomplishment all ran across his lovely, childlike, androgynous face.

'Are you kidding me?' I mumbled.

Ainsley nudged me.

'Sorry, not you Ms North,' I said, looking back to Bodhi but he'd disappeared.

'Well, I've been burnt before Mr Wheeler, so I'm going to need to see that paperwork and have some conversations,' she said, holding out her hand.

'Why don't you have a seat over there and I'll bring them over and you can have all the conversations you like,' he said.

Ainsley waved over a waitress and instructed her to get Elizabeth North settled with coffee and food and anything else she needed and to charge it back to her. 'Keep her fed and happy and distracted,' Ainsley insisted.

'Absolutely,' the waitress agreed.

'Jo,' Michael Wheeler said, bringing my attention back to him. 'Please sign the papers,' he said, shoving them at me with a pen.

'They're just standard right? No surprises?' Ainsley asked Michael Wheeler.

'Absolutely,' he agreed.

'You can trust him, he wouldn't work for us otherwise, so just sign them, there's no time to read them,' Ainsley said as I hesitated.

'Russ has already signed them,' I said as I saw his signature. 'You've seen him?' I asked.

'He signed them before they questioned him, just in case,' he told me.

I nodded absently. This is what Russ wanted and I knew Ainsley would never steer me wrong, so for Russ, I signed them and Michael Wheeler disappeared while Elizabeth North was distracted by the waitress and he went to send a copy to his office, so they could do whatever official things needed doing and he returned before her coffee had even arrived with the signed, official papers confirming Russ' wishes.

She wasn't happy but there wasn't a lot she could do about

it. She stood her ground anyway and insisted on a conversation with me.

We humoured her and for the rest of the morning, I suffered through a million questions on where I lived, where I grew up, my family, my friends, my work, how I knew Russ and the details of our relationship.

I left a lot out because Michael Wheeler told me to. I didn't lie exactly, I just left out the bits about my dead boyfriend and our search for Henry Mayberry. I told her I looked after Ainsley's Henry all the time and had sleepovers with him and right on cue, the little fella came over for a hug before Aunty Jaz led him away for breakfast.

Elizabeth North nodded after each of my answers, made some notes, but didn't say too much. When she ran out of questions, Nico was awake so she insisted on checking him over and making sure he was okay. Then she wanted to see where we were staying and I was very glad we'd bought him the porta cot and things so he looked loved and cared for.

'Alright Miss Walsh, everything seems to be in order,' she said, handing Nico back to me. 'I will be in touch in a couple of days, just to make sure everything is going okay and to check how things are going with Mr Whittington. We may need to do a home visit to your residence if Mr Whittington is officially detained and that's where you and the baby go.'

I nodded. 'That's fine, I'm an open book,' I assured her.

'I'm glad this seems to be a misunderstanding. I can't tell you how often that's not the case. We've had a couple in the department lately that seemed to be false alarms but, well, I'll spare you the details. Thank you for taking the time with me today.'

'You really must have the hardest job. I appreciate you acting so quickly in Nico's interest. It's comforting to know people like you are doing the job.'

'Well, thank you. It is a wonder why anyone would have made the call in the first place though,' she said.

'Indeed,' I told her. 'Probably a concerned bystander not aware of my relationship with Russ, is all,' I told her. There was no point adding Bodhi into the mix, I wanted this over and done with and I was sure with all the Harringtons around and Russ coming back soon, we'd be able to take care of Bodhi and get him to back off.

'You okay?' Ainsley asked when she came into my room to find me lying on the bed staring at the ceiling.

I'd seen the Family and Child Services lady to the door and Michael Wheeler, the family lawyer, had seen her the rest of the way out. I'd laid on the bed once they were gone and had been unable to move.

'Ains, what the fuck am I doing? It's all a mess,' I told her.

'It's fine now, it's over. She's gone.'

'Is it? Russ isn't back. I just signed some papers taking I don't know what, guardianship, custody, I don't even know, for some other woman's child. What the hell am I doing taking care of a child? I can barely take care of myself.'

'You're doing fine.'

'Yeah, today. We survived a night. But for how long am I going to look after him? What if they arrest Russ? What if I'm raising this child until the end of time?'

'Then that's what you do. You've got this and I've got you,' she insisted, squeezing my hand.

'Thanks. But you have to go home, you have your own family and you and Christian both have work to do.'

'No, Mum rearranged some stuff and she'll watch the café this afternoon. She and Vivi will figure out what needs ordering. We may end up with enough ham to feed the homeless for a while but they'll figure it out. I'm not leaving until I know you're okay,' she told me.

'You're the best. You really are. But I'll be fine. There's nothing you can do anyway. If I get stuck, there's people who can help me. Jaz and Margaret Packersham and the Lorna Jane mums,' I told her.

She climbed on the bed anyway and lay next to me staring at the ceiling. She reached over and held my hand. 'I'm staying as long as you need me.'

I squeezed her hand because having her there made everything better. But this wasn't her journey, it wasn't her path, she had other things to do and other places to be. 'I'm okay. I promise.'

'I got a hold of Julie and you have an appointment with Dr Bailey on Monday,' she told me.

'Thank you.'

'And you can call Dr Bailey whenever you want, Julie promised to put you through if you need him.'

'Thanks. Now go. There's no point in both of us just lying here staring at the ceiling. The others will help me with the baby if I need them. They're not you, but we'll manage,' I told her.

She nodded but didn't move. 'You want to see Henry before we go?' she asked.

'No, that'll make me sad and I might squish all the air out of him. Tell him I'll see him soon and I love him.'

'I will. Jay is here and when Russ gets back, they'll figure out what Bodhi's deal is. I suspect he might just have a little crush but when Russ is back, he'll put that to rest and they'll figure out who killed Russ' lady friend. Then when all that's done, a car is coming to bring you all home on Sunday. K?'

'K.'

She rolled over and wrapped her arms around me. 'You need me to come back, you just say so and I'll be here.'

'Thanks. I love you.'

'I love you, too.'

'And Russ will be back before you know it, you just wait and see.'

'I hope so, Ains, I hope so.'

She squeezed me tight and then she was gone.

I stared at the ceiling a while longer, closed my eyes and focussed on my breathing. The peace was easier to tap into these days and I tapped and the panic eased. But Nico started fussing, so I got up.

I fed and changed the baby and let him lie with me on the bed while I wondered what the hell had happened to my world? A week ago, I'd had it all sorted. I knew who I was, what life held for me and now it was all upside down. I didn't know what to do with that. I missed my quiet, predictable life. For just a moment, anyway. Then I remembered what it was like to wake up wrapped in Russ' arms and decided it was all worth it.

Natalie brought me food a little after sunset, nice hot, thick vegetable soup with fresh rolls, and told me how miserable Bodhi was being.

'He was going to knock on your door again for evening meditation but I told him not to. I thought The Lorna Jane mums were about to rip his arm off if he did but he didn't. He just sighed and walked off. The meditation was awful. He was miserable and there was no light in it. Lucky Margaret didn't bother to come, she'd have been most upset.'

'What is going on with Bodhi? Me doing or not doing a meditation cannot mean that much to him. My spiritual journey cannot be than important to him.'

'I don't think it is, Jo, I think it's you. I think he fancies you.'

'Ainsley suggested the same thing. Does he even swing that way?' I asked, even as the foot massage incident by the campfire flashed behind my eyes.

'I don't know which way he swings but he seems very focussed on what you do and don't do and where you are, and I swear it was him that called that awful woman to come and take Nico.'

'Oh, I'm sure it was him. I saw his face and it had guilt written all over it but I just can't figure out why he would do that? It's just so... mean.'

'Because you stopped eating with him and coming to meditation. Russ was gone but you still skipped out to look after Nico. Bodhi wasn't happy about it, kept saying how Russ and Nico were holding you back, that they were compromising your wellbeing.'

'You really think he called Family and Child Services to take away Nico just so I'd meditate with him?'

'Maybe he was hoping you would do something more with him?' she suggested.

I shivered at the thought of Bodhi lusting after me. After all the things I'd told him in my healing session, things I'd only ever told Dr Bailey, I felt sick to my stomach.

'Natalie, he didn't, you know, he hasn't been inappropriate with you has he? Because I'll kill him if he has,' I told her.

'No, he's been fine with me. He was working really hard to help me because he knew how important it was to me to make my parents happy. He wanted that for me, and did some extra sessions when he could. He even came to my room a couple of times for coaching and healing but I swear, I was awake and coherent the whole time and he was never once inappropriate in any way. He really was the sweetest. Margaret and the mums say the same, but the mums have noticed how he changes when you say no.'

'Everyone's noticed?'

She nodded.

'God, that's so weird. I think I'm just going to stay locked in here until Russ comes home. You'll bring me food, won't you?'

'Absolutely. Like clockwork,' she agreed with a smile before leaving me to eat my dinner.

Once I'd eaten, I went back to bed, left another voicemail for Russ, curled up and slept because sometimes there's nothing else you can do but sleep and hope the new day is better, or at least that when the new day came, Russ would return.

Chapter 19

The sound of a cooing Nico woke me from a deep sleep. Not again, I whined to myself. I'd already been up once with him, fed him, changed him, spent twenty minutes rocking him until he finally went back to sleep. I rolled over, saw the shadow of a man in the middle of the room and I bolted upright.

'Oh, hey,' Russ whispered as though him being there wasn't a big thing.

'You're back?' I asked, barely able to believe he was there.

He smiled, put Nico into his porta cot and crawled across the bed, his mouth finding mine in a long, slow, languid kiss that curled my toes. 'I'm back,' he whispered.

'It's the middle of the night?'

'I know. They were done with me and were going to drive me back in the morning but I didn't want to be away from you for another second.'

'Are you okay?' I asked, holding his face still in front of me so I could see him.

'I am now,' he smiled.

'What happened?'

'Shhh... later,' he said before slowly taking his fill of me.

Afterwards, I curled into him, needing to be close to him, needing to feel him, hear his heart beating.

I held on tight as though he might disappear like a magical genie but he didn't. I held on anyway.

'Are you okay?' I asked him again.

'I'm okay,' he assured me. 'It's all over now,' he said, trying to pull me closer.

'Is it? How?'

'Because I didn't do it,' he said a little harshly.

'I know that. But they didn't seem to.'

'Sorry, I know,' he said, on a sigh. 'They asked a million questions a million different ways but because I didn't do it, the answers never changed.' They weren't happy. I was clearly the obvious choice.

'You were gone a long time.'

'We had to wait for my father to come up from the city.'

'He took a long time?'

'That's my father for you. Everything is done on his schedule and everyone else can just wait until he gets to them.'

'You were in gaol.'

'I was held for questioning. But yes, I slept on a bed in a tiny cell while waiting for him but it wasn't locked, that's just where the beds are,' he said, pulling me tighter.

I moved away, 'You have cop shop cooties on you still?' I asked.

He laughed. 'The last time we had cop shop cooties, we got rid of them with premium vodka.' He leaned down and kissed me slow and good. 'I like this way better,' he smiled.

'Me too. But you should probably shower,' I told him.

'Only if you come with.'

'Nope, my bones are liquid, I can't move.'

He pouted.

'It's your own fault. Go, then come back here.'

He smiled and went to shower. I watched his beautifully naked body walking away but I was asleep before he came back to bed.

In the morning, I filled Russ in on all that had happened while he'd been gone and had to straddle him with my naked body to stop him from going after Bodhi.

'It's fine, it's just a stupid, little crush. He'll get over it.'

'He tried to have my son put in a foster home,' he grumbled.

'That would never have happened. Michael Wheeler, the family lawyer, was here. Jay was here and if anything, she would have just taken him to your parent's house. He'd have been fine with your mum.'

'I wanted him here with you. How dare he try to separate you from him just to what... hit on you? Who does that?'

'It didn't work, so it doesn't matter,' I told him.

'If he's that intent on getting near you, I bet he had something to do with them taking me in for questioning as well.'

'Why do you say that?'

'Because they had this whole story they were working to that wasn't true but they'd clearly gotten it from somewhere. That's what took so long, convincing them the information they had wasn't true. We went around in circles for hours.'

'You think Bodhi might have made something up so they'd arrest you and I'd be here alone?'

'It sounds like it. My father was not impressed about it either, I can tell you.'

'Where is he now? Your father?'

'Back in the city.'

'He didn't want to meet his grandson?' I asked, thinking that was strange.

'My father had business to attend to and had already been away from the office for too long. He'll meet his grandson when he can fit it into his schedule.'

'Well isn't he all warm and fuzzy?'

Russ laughed. 'Lucky I take after my mother then,' he smiled as he began lavishing my body with his mouth.

Nico woke before he got too far. With a groan and a smile Russ got out of bed to tend to his son.

I hadn't really seen them together. He'd spent his time in here with Nico with Lana. But he was sweet with him, held him carefully but surely as he looked at him in wonder and Nico looked up at him with those big curious eyes. They looked like two peas. Two handsome, mischievous little peas. And they were both mine, I realised.

Russ brought Nico to the bed, laid him between us, cuddled him as a bottle warmed on the bedside. Suddenly, I had it all, the beautiful, attentive man who adored me, who adored his son, a beautiful baby who was just going with the flow despite everything that had happened to him. He wasn't mine but he came as a package deal with Russ and he needed as many people to love him as he could get. I could do that. Love him.

I could maybe even love him like he was my own. He deserved that, didn't he?

I showered and got ready for the day while Russ tended to the baby. When I came out, I stood in the doorway a moment watching them on the bed. There was a children's program on the television and they sat on the bed, side by side, watching the colours flicker across the screen. He smiled when he saw me and my heart melted just a little more.

'Where'd all his stuff come from anyway? Lana came with almost nothing,' he said.

'I noticed. Ainsley wasn't having it. We went shopping.'

'Did my credit card survive Ainsley Harrington?' he asked with a smile.

'Well and truly, she was very restrained. I think it was mostly due to the lack of options though, so be grateful we weren't in the city,' I told him with a smirk. 'Came in handy though when that woman from Family and Child Services came. I don't think we'd have been so lucky if all we'd had was what Lana had brought with her. What was with that, anyway? Who travels halfway around the world with a baby and brings nothing?'

'I don't know. I asked her. She said she was broke.'

'But she had airfare? And bus fare to get out here and resources to find you but she couldn't pack nappies and more than one change of clothes or any toys for her kid?'

'I know, I don't know what else to say.'

'You told the police all of this, didn't you? She sounds very sketchy.'

'Sketchy?' he asked with a smile.

'Yes, sketchy,' I said with conviction.

'Yes, I told the police every little detail I could think of.'

'But you still don't know what she wanted?'

'Nope. I have no idea. She could have just dumped the baby in the US if that's all she wanted to do. She could have left a note with him, they would have found me.'

'But you're a smart guy and a PI, surely you had an impression, an idea or something about what she was after?'

'I don't know. I couldn't get a read on her. Once I caught up with her and begged her to come back and figure it out, she came on strong. I made it clear that was not why I'd dragged her back. I think she was just going to stay the one night to appease me but then something changed her mind. She got this look in her eye, lost interest in me but she wouldn't say what was going on. But I'm going to sit down with Jay and the lawyer this morning and we're going to see what we can dig up about her.'

'Harrington resources?' I asked.

'They have access to the best technology, to information the cops can't easily access, so yep, I'll take any help I can get. It won't change anything but my son should be able to get answers when he asks the questions and just maybe we can figure out who killed her.'

'Good, because I want to get all this sorted and go home. I'm done with all of it now and I just want to go home.'

'Home? And where might that be?'

'What do you mean? I live above the café,' I told him.

He smiled indulgently at me. 'I guess I'm more asking who you might be taking with you? I don't want to be moving too fast but after the last couple of days, I don't like the idea of spending a single night without you.'

I stared at him, not really sure what to say. I'd been thinking the same thing but it had been an airy fairy thought. I didn't think he'd be on the same page, not now there was Nico and as I sat there, the realities of what he was suggesting dawned on me. My parents. My home. Our lives. His family. A baby! Could a baby even live in Mrs May's old apartment? She'd run a brothel on the third floor for goodness sake. Sure, we'd cleaned it all up but still, this was a little baby.

'If it's too quick, it's fine, I can stay with my folks for now,' he offered.

'No, I don't want to be without you either, I was just thinking about logistics.'

He smiled. 'Of course you were, and what exactly were you thinking?'

I told him.

'Nico will be fine. We'll figure it out. There's a lot we'll have to figure out. I have to do something about a job and fixing the mess I've made of my life and getting everything back on track. For you, for me, for Nico. I want us to be a family.'

'I don't even know what that means and under the circumstances, it's just a little weird. How about we just crash together and see where it leads. For now.'

'If that's what will make you feel better, then absolutely,' he smiled. 'But right now, I think I might die if I don't eat something.'

We gathered Nico and all of his accompanying needs and off we went for breakfast, like a family, whether I liked it or not. I couldn't help smiling though because being with Russ felt good, having Nico in my arms while Russ carried the pram down the stairs felt right. *Sorry Lana,* I thought.

'This would have been us even if she was still alive,' Russ said. 'I swear she'd have left the baby anyway. Or we'd be here whenever I had visitation. Don't feel guilty that it feels good,' he told me. The fact he understood what I was feeling and wasn't frightened by it, had me fall just a little a more.

'Hey, Russ, you good?' asked Jay who'd come over to us after we'd finished breakfast.

'Yeah,' he told Jay. 'Are you alright with the baby while we go and see what we can dig up?' he asked me.

'Of course, go, get this shit sorted.'

'I'll do my best,' he said, leaning down to kiss me, before kissing his son and then he disappeared with Jay and the fancy lawyer in tow.

Everyone else was keeping to themselves. They'd eaten after morning meditation and disappeared into their rooms with the doors locked. I didn't much fancy wandering around on my own, so I did the same.

'I think we're getting the hang of this, little fella,' I told Nico as he watched me get his bottle ready. 'So why are you so happy now when you cried so much for your mumma, huh?' I asked, not really thinking about what I was saying but realising it was true once I said it. He'd cried a lot. Russ had complained that Lana couldn't quieten him. He wailed all the time. But he'd stopped. He almost seemed happy, if babies could be happy.

Just as I thought it though, he started to get fussy and I could see his little face was working its way up to a wail. His bottle wasn't ready yet but I scooped him up anyway and snuggled him right up against me and he appeared to snuggle back, almost getting sleepy.

'Did your mumma not snuggle enough with you, huh?' I asked as I tested his bottle. He watched me as though he understood my words and I couldn't help smiling. 'Here you go,' I said, giving him the bottle. He sucked like there was no tomorrow and I wondered if she'd been feeding him enough with the scraps of formula that we'd found in the tin.

Then just as I thought of the formula, I wondered how she'd gotten onto the plane with an open can of formula. She couldn't have. Not exiting America. You were almost strip searched just to get through security, no way were they letting an open tin partly filled with powder on board. She had to have been in the country longer than she said. Something wasn't adding up.

I messaged my thoughts to Russ.

'I thought that too,' he replied. 'Oh, and Mr Slick is just a douchebag, nothing in what he said,' he added.

That was a relief. One more person to tick off the list. I left the rest of the investigating and theorising to Russ and Jay to figure out, there was no point me adding anything further, not that I had anything to add.

'Jo, you in there?' called Natalie from outside my door.

I let her and Margaret Packersham in. 'We need some air so we're going for a walk, would you like to come?' Margaret asked.

'If you don't mind a tag along,' I said, indicating Nico.

Margaret Packersham hesitated to answer but Natalie was all for it.

'You okay?' I asked Margaret.

'Of course. It's just, I thought you weren't going to get too attached,' she said. 'Where's his dad?' she asked.

'He's with Jay,' I told her.

'Well, it's a little unfair of him to dump his kid on you now he's back, don't you think?' she said.

I shrugged. 'When you're in, you're in, I suppose,' I told her. 'And Russ is off with Jay trying to figure out who killed the little guy's mumma.'

'Right, so I suppose they'll be occupied for most of the day,' she grumbled. She must have noticed my face because she quickly added, 'They should have it figured out in no time. Lucky you have us to keep you company, then,' she smiled.

'Well, if there's anything to find, they'll find it,' I told her as I gathered my things.

'You sound very sure,' she said.

'They are very good at what they do, they're highly trained in secret business and they have all The Harrington resources at their disposal.'

'Do they now? Well, that's lucky then,' she said. 'Come on, the day's getting away from us,' she said and off we all went.

We walked into town and stopped at the little bakery for lunch.

'Oh, it is nice to be out,' I told them as we ate our freshly baked pies and pasties.

Afterwards, Margaret dragged us into an arts and crafts shop. We wandered for a bit, looking at the souvenirs and things but Nico was getting restless and I didn't bring any bottles because I'd thought we were just going for a little walk, not an afternoon shopping trip.

'I'm sorry, ladies, but I'm going to have to head back, I think,' I told them.

'No worries, we can come back with you,' Natalie said.

'Noooo,' begged Margaret. 'There's a little art gallery I wanted you to see, it's just around the corner. We can squeeze one more stop in, can't we?' she pleaded.

I gave Nico his dummy and he seemed to settle back down as we started moving again so I thought maybe we could stay out a little longer. It was nice to be out after everything that had happened. To be doing something else.

'Come on then, just for a bit,' I agreed.

Margaret led us into the gallery, which had bright paintings, charcoal drawings and sculptures of sea life.

'That's pretty,' Natalie commented absently as though looking for something nice in the strange array of art as we stopped in front of a bronzed dolphin. She checked the price and her pretty green eyeballs nearly fell out of their sockets.

'It's a nice enough gallery but not in my price range,' Natalie whispered.

'Not really my style either,' I whispered back as Margaret wandered on seemingly unaware.

I was grateful when Nico started to fuss again and was this time allowed to leave and we all walked back to the pub. Nico was better with the rocking and rolling of his pram but I sensed it wouldn't last long and was glad when we finally arrived.

'Well, thank you for the walk and the company, ladies,' I

told them. I scooped Nico out of his pram, left the pram at the bottom of the stairs for Russ to fetch later, and left Natalie and Margaret to go and have an afternoon cocktail.

'Oh shit,' I whispered as I opened the door to find the room in complete disarray. Bedding had been thrown around the room. My suitcase upended. Russ' duffle bag emptied and clothes strewn amongst the bedding. Nico's clothes and toys were all over the place, baby formula scattered like snow. Either Russ had come back and thrown one hell of a hissy fit while we were out or someone else had been in here. Russ was a lot of things but a tantrum throwing teenage girl was not one of them.

I closed the door and headed straight for Jaz and Jay's apartment.

'Jo?' Russ asked, looking up surprised when I burst in. 'What's wrong?'

'Someone's been through my room. Our room.'

'Are you sure?' Jay asked.

'Unless Russ threw a hissy fit while I was out and destroyed it himself, then yes, I'm sure.'

Russ smiled.

So did Jay. 'You and Nico stay in here, we'll go have a look,' Jay said. 'Make yourself at home.'

Russ and Jay went downstairs and I sat there with a hungry, whingey Nico, bobbing him up and down on my knee.

It wasn't long before they returned. Russ brought with him the nappy bag with nappies, formula and clean bottles. 'We've called the police.'

'You can hang out up here as long as you like,' Jay offered. 'Or go downstairs, you might need a cocktail,' he offered.

'Come on, we can have tea,' offered Russ.

'I don't want tea, Russ. I want to know who went through our stuff.'

'Tea always makes one feel better after a shock and we'll figure it out.'

I huffed all the way down, but he was right. It was something to do and the tea calmed me.

'What's going on, Russ?' I asked.

'I don't know but we'll figure it out.'

'Are we even safe here anymore?'

'You're safe with me.'

'Russ, someone broke into our room and went through our stuff. I think it's time we just packed up and went home,' I told him.

'We'll be fine. We'll figure this out Jo and we'll go home soon enough, I promise,' he said, reaching for my hand.

The waitress brought over some cake and I asked her where Natalie and Margaret Packersham were because they'd gone to have cocktails but they weren't there.

'Natalie's folks called, so she went upstairs and I don't know what happened to Margaret. She was here,' she said, before leaving.

We ate our cake and waited. Finally, someone came down to tell us we could go back to our room. They'd found nothing.

'What do you think they were looking for?' I asked Russ as we began putting everything back in order.

'I'm not sure. Maybe they weren't searching for anything and just wanted to frighten us.'

'You don't exactly look like the easily frightened type,' I told him.

'No, but perhaps they think you are. Perhaps if you're unsettled enough, we'll all leave and Jay and I will stop poking our nose in things.'

'Really? You think someone is worried about what the two of you will find?'

'My guess is someone's worried about something.'

'I just can't guess who. Who would care enough about her being here to kill her. I just don't get it,' I said.

'Me either. You definitely locked the door before you went out though?'

'Absolutely. I remember juggling the baby and my handbag to do it.'

'So someone had to have access to a key.'

'Or they just have some skills?'

'Maybe. I'll speak to Jay about how secure the locks are.'

'Knowing Jay though, those locks would be as secure as anything.'

'You'd think so.'

'So if they have skills, they're excellent skills to get past anything Jay has installed,' I suggested.

He nodded. 'So where'd you all get to today, anyway?' he asked changing the subject.

I told him about our outing and laughed about the ugly overpriced art while we put the room back together.

Once Nico was happily napping and everything was in order,

Russ asked, 'Are you going to be okay if I pop up and speak to Jay?'

'Yeah. I think so. I'll lock the door. No one will try and break in while I'm here, will they?'

'Unlikely,' he agreed, leaning down to kiss me. 'You sure you'll be alright?'

'Yes, go. I want to know what he knows too.'

I double-checked the lock after Russ was gone and then I laid down to read one of the library books I'd brought with me. It was quiet with Nico sleeping. The musical mobile had stopped. Russ was gone. It wasn't the same, relaxing space it had been. The room felt dirty now, knowing someone had been poking about in our things felt creepy. I looked down at the selection of books I'd laid out and they were all too close to home. Suddenly I was wishing for some Austen, something funny to distract me from having had my personal space invaded. Mine and Russ' and that poor baby. Hadn't Nico been through enough?

Something clanked against the balcony railing outside and I sat upright, my skin prickling as I listened but there was nothing. 'It was just a bird or nut from a tree or something,' I told myself. I lay back on the pillows and laughed at myself. I was losing my mind.

I was about to get up and make a cup of tea when something tapped on the window. 'Shit,' I said, near jumping out of my skin. I went over to the window and pulled back the curtain but there was no one there.

'You think it's your mumma coming to haunt me?' I asked Nico as I took him out of his bed and snuggled on my bed with him. 'I wouldn't blame her, you know, despite what your dad says.' Nico didn't wake but I felt better having him with me. If something happened and I had to make a run for it, I wanted him close.

I shook my head at myself. I was getting paranoid now. I wasn't going to have to make a run for it. From who? Russ was just upstairs, a phone call away. Who would even want to hurt me? The break in, that had to be something else. I don't know what, but Russ would figure it out.

To get myself back on track, I called Julie at Dr Bailey's. I had so much to talk to him about and maybe if I spoke to him about the guilt of bonding with Nico, I'd be less jumpy. I couldn't have Nico suffering for it. Thankfully Dr Bailey was doing paperwork between patients so Julie put me straight through.

I filled Dr Bailey in on all that had happened since I'd arrived even though I suspected Ainsley had already given him the highlights when she'd prepared him for my call.

'Well, you girls certainly know how to turn things on their head, don't you?' he chuckled on the other end of the line.

'It's not funny, Dr Bailey. This poor woman was murdered and here I am taking care of her son as though he's mine. I'm sleeping with his dad as though she didn't even exist and now, she's at my window tapping her disapproval, saying, *I'm watching you lady.*'

He stifled another chuckle and I imagined him trying to keep his serious face on as he often had to when faced with the trials of our lives. 'Jo, she and Russ were never a couple, so let's be clear about that. As for the child, he needs someone to care for him. Did you kill her?'

'Of course not,' I said, horrified he could even ask.

'Then the situation is not your fault and you can't feel responsible for it. The child needed someone and you are Russ' someone so it's right that you step in.'

'You make it all sound so simple.'

'The poor woman is dead. There's no undoing that, Jo. It is what it is now. Tragic and sad, of course, but you need to do what needs doing for the baby. The baby doesn't know any different, he still needs food and love. Would you rather walk away from Russ and let him do it alone?'

'Of course not.'

'Then so be it. I'm sure the poor woman is grateful someone is caring for her son.'

'Not if she wanted Russ for herself and now she's going to come and haunt me,' I said.

'She's not going to haunt you, Jo. It's just your imagination.'

'Then maybe it's Benny. Pissed I'm sleeping with a new man and not only that, I've gone and got myself an instant family. The family he always wanted us to have. What would he think of that? He's probably devastated.'

'Benny wouldn't have wanted you to be alone forever. He loved you. He was a good guy, wasn't he?'

'Yes.'

'Then he would have wanted good things for you. He'd have wanted you to be loved and adored and all those things.'

'I suppose.'

'Stop fighting it, Jo. Stop punishing yourself because he died and you lived. You get to be happy.'

'Thanks, Dr Bailey.'

'You're welcome. Are you okay now?'

'For the minute. I'm still coming to see you Monday.'

'Good. And Julie has kept your appointment for the end of the month, alright?'

'Yes, thank you,' I said and we said our goodbyes and I made a note in my phone to pick up the Haigh's chocolates Julie liked before my appointment to say thank you. When you met Julie, with her over-coiffed hair and her red rimmed glasses perched halfway down her nose so she looked over them to analyse you, you would never expect her to come through the way she did, but every time, she came through.

Chapter 20

I t was late when Russ came back to the room. I'd felt better after my chat with Dr Bailey, and Nico and I had enjoyed an afternoon nap.

'I have food,' Russ taunted as he woke me.

As he said it, my stomach rumbled.

Jaz had sent up cake and soup in a big thermos with crusty rolls and two cups of coffee.

We were just finishing the cake and the coffee and Russ was telling me how he and Jay had gone around in circles with theories, while they were waiting for some background searches to come back from the Harrington's security team, when Bodhi knocked on the door.

'What the hell does he want?' Russ spat, knowing exactly who it would be at that time of day.

'Shhhh... It won't do anyone any good if you go losing your shit at Bodhi. Let me handle it.'

'He called Family and Child Services on my son, Jo. That's not okay.'

'I know. I'm handling it. Let me before you get yourself into trouble. Nico needs you, I need you,' I told him.

He nodded and let me answer the door.

The sun was setting behind Bodhi and he had his usual trail of disciples. 'You coming to meditation?' Bodhi asked.

'No, I don't think so,' I told him, annoyed and surprised that after everything he still wouldn't let it go. Did he really think that after calling Family and Child Services on us, threatening to have Nico taken away and telling whatever stories he'd told the detective about Russ, that I'd want anything to do with him or his meditations? I'd find another practitioner when we got home but I wasn't doing it with him.

'But Russ is back now, the baby is being cared for,' he said as though all the rest hadn't happened.

I stepped outside so as not to wake the baby and infuriate Russ any more than he already was but didn't fully close the door. 'You're kidding, right? After all you've done, you think I want anything to do with you?'

'All what?' he asked innocently.

'I know it was you who called Family and Child Services, Bodhi, I just don't know why. And what exactly did you say to the detective about Russ?' The Lorna Jane mums looked horrified, like they were about to have a piece of him. Margaret Packersham and Natalie stood awkwardly to the side watching the scene play out. I was surprised they were still taking his help but each person had their own journey, I supposed, and he hadn't done anything to them.

At the mere whisper of controversy, Karen the famous author's manager slash lover led Karen away.

'Me? No, no,' he defended but he wasn't the least bit convincing.

'You're an idiot and a liar then, that's even worse,' I told him.

'Fine. I just, it wasn't fair that you were stuck with the baby. It's not your baby. It wasn't your responsibility. You have to focus on you, on your journey, on getting better,' he admitted as one of the Lorna Jane mums stopped the other from punching him in the face and they led each other away.

'It is a person and my wellbeing is no longer any of your business. Thank you for your help, your healing treatment, the lovely meditations, I'm grateful, I am. But you had no business interfering with me and Russ, and that innocent baby. He lost his mumma. Russ was being questioned. He needed someone looking out for him. Where was your empathy, Bodhi?'

'I'm sorry. I'm embarrassed. It was selfish. Please Jo, please forgive me. I'm sorry. Please come and meditate and I will prove I am so sorry,' he begged.

'No, thank you,' I said, leaving him standing there with Margaret Packersham and Natalie on the balcony and going inside, and closing and locking the door.

'You handled him like a pro,' Russ said proudly from where he sat on the edge of the bed.

'I'm so bloody mad, I just wanted to rip his head off.'

He laughed. 'You sound like Ainsley. And for the record, I wouldn't have stopped you from ripping his head off.'

I laughed. 'Maybe you don't have to actually give birth to get that fierce protective gene.'

He stood up and came to me, kissed me on the head. 'I think it's called being a compassionate human,' he smiled.

'Maybe. I guess I haven't had to fight for anyone before. It feels good to have a purpose.'

'Good. Because Nico and I don't plan on going anywhere anytime soon.'

'What are we going to do Russ? When this is all over?'

'I was talking to Jay before. I think I'm going to set up my own firm in the city. Maybe I could buy us a house. If you want. We can stay in the apartment if you prefer but it's only one bedroom, right? I know it's a lot, a lot of changes, an unexpected package deal.'

'You're good at what you do. You should set up your own firm. And someday, a house would be nice.'

'We'll get used to all of this first though,' he said. 'Nico won't need his own space just yet.'

'The Family and Child Services lady will want to check on him. We're on her radar now, even if it's not official.'

'Let her check. We'll be fine,' he said as my brain was already running through all the changes I could make to Mrs May's to accommodate Nico. We could move some things out of the living room and make some space for him for a little while. That would work. Then if we were all still happy, we could get that house Russ was talking about. Russ was right. We needed to get used to us for a minute first. To being a family. Make sure everyone's happy, everything works. We could move forward after that. It hadn't even been a week yet, we needed some time.

So I let it all go for now and after dinner, we snuggled up in front of the little television, and watched an old movie.

Come morning, Russ and Nico were gone, a note left in their place. 'Gone to Jay's for an update. Taken Nico with me. Hope you slept well xR.'

He must have gotten up to the baby during the night as well, as I'd slept all the way through for the first night in days. It was relief that he was picking up his share of the responsibilities as soon as he'd returned.

I took my time showering and getting ready for the day. I checked in with Ainsley to let her know I was alright. Tidied up a little then headed down for breakfast.

There were only a few tourists and locals left. If Karen, the famous author, and her manager slash lover or the Lorna Jane mums had eaten, then they'd gone. Bodhi was nowhere to be seen either. Natalie and Margaret Packersham were at a table in the corner finishing their coffee, so I waved as I went to get eggs before joining them.

I felt Bodhi come up behind me as I stood at the buffet scooping scrambled eggs onto my plate. My skin crawled and a shiver ran down my spine before he even spoke. 'Please, will you ever forgive me?' Bodhi whispered in my ear.

His voice and proximity startled me and I took a sideways step for personal space as I turned around.

'Let's just leave it. I don't have the energy for you, Bodhi. I'd rather we just go our separate ways,' I told him.

'No, I can't live with that ending, Jo. I just can't,' he insisted.

'Well, I'm afraid you're going to have to.'

'What about your healing? Your journey?' he asked.

'Thank you for all you've done. I'm grateful for the experience and maybe I'll find another healing practitioner someday. But I'm doing great. I feel better than I have in a really long time. So I'm good. I have achieved what I came here for and now it is time for us to part ways. I am moving on and feeling more like myself than I have in a long while.'

'But there's so much more we could do, so much more life you could live,' he said. 'I had plans for us.'

'What kind of plans?' I asked, as a chill ran through my body. What was he doing making plans for us? What us?

'There is a whole world out there, Jo, you should be in it. I can give that to you. The world, the adventure, the healing, all of it,' he said, reaching for my hand.

I was too slow. He'd caught me off guard and had me in his grip before I could tear my hand away.

I looked around for someone to help me. Anyone. Natalie and Margaret Packersham were engrossed in their own conversation. No one else was paying us any attention.

'This path you're on, this life, the man, the baby, it's not for you,' Bodhi told me. 'It's the wrong life. It's someone else's life. Come with me and I'll show you where you're meant to be.'

I was finally able to yank my hand away from him. 'I don't know who you think you are, or what you think you know about me, but you're way off base and this is highly inappropriate. I appreciate what you have done for me. I don't entirely understand what you do, but I appreciate it. But there is no reality where I leave my life and go anywhere with you. With or without Russ, I have no intention of leaving my friends, my family, my job,' I told him. 'And let me make this very clear,' I added. 'I have no intention now or at any time in the future of having any kind of relationship with you, professional, medical, personal or otherwise. Do you understand?' I told him, not sure I could be any clearer.

He reached for me again, clearly not so easily deterred.

'Jo?' called Russ, his face furious, Jay's hand on his shoulder seemingly holding him back.

'We are done, Bodhi. No more. Do not speak to me again,' I told Bodhi as I went over to see Russ, putting my eggs on Natalie and Margaret Packersham's table as I passed.

'Everything okay?' Russ asked.

'Dandy. You?'

'Fine. Jay and I are just heading out for a bit to follow some things up.'

'No news then?'

'Not yet. Maybe a lead. Someone she spent a night with when she arrived in the country. Not sure what it means yet, but we'll figure it out,' he assured me. 'You sure you're okay?' he asked, glancing over my shoulder at Bodhi who was watching us from the breakfast buffet.

'Yep. Just clearing some things up with Bodhi,' I smiled. 'We're on the same page now though.'

'You weren't?'

'He was worried I was neglecting my treatments. But I'm good for now. I'll see Dr Bailey next week and work on some meditation when I get home.'

'Good,' he smiled, leaning down to kiss me. 'I'll join you in those medis, yeah?'

'I look forward to it,' I told him.

'Alright, Nico's upstairs with Jaz. He's sleeping and she's working. She said don't worry about him. I'll be back as soon as I can,' he said and he left with a smile.

Natalie and Margaret Packersham didn't seem to have seen

what had happened with Bodhi. They were wrapped up watching Brene Brown videos on YouTube when I sat down. I didn't want to make a fuss, it was over now, he was gone, so I smiled and let it go and focussed on my eggs.

I was more unsettled by the altercation than I'd realised though. It was creepy. The way he kept harassing me. The way he looked at me and grabbed at me. I couldn't wait to go home. I thought about telling Natalie. After all she'd been through, she should know. But she'd insisted he had been the perfect practitioner with her. I figured with treatments suspended, she was safe enough. I didn't want to frighten her. Not after all she'd been through, and the trust issues she already had, she didn't need to be questioning Bodhi as well. It had the potential to destroy the new life she had planned and it was a good life, she deserved to live it.

Chapter 21

'Well I don't know about you girls, but I need to take some time out. There's a spa not far from here, anyone want to come for a massage?' Margaret asked.

'No, I'm just going to hang out here, I think. I'll go upstairs soon and relieve Jaz,' I said.

'I'm not really a massage kind of person,' Natalie said.

'Alright then, I'll see you soon,' she said and left us.

The room was empty. Just Natalie and me. The staff had cleared away the food and were serving tea.

'A pot of New York Breakfast tea?' offered the waitress.

'Thank you.'

'I'm sorry,' Natalie said, once the waitress had left.

'For what?'

'For still going to meditation with Bodhi after what he did and the things he said.'

I smiled tightly, trying to be understanding.

'I just can't go home if I'm not better. So I had to go. I really didn't want to. To be honest, he was a little frightening. I just didn't know what else to do,' she said.

'I understand. It's okay,' I said, squeezing her hand. 'But for the record, always listen to your intuition. It will never lead you astray. If you don't want to go somewhere or you don't want to do something, or you change your mind, that's okay. You do what feels right for you. Promise me,' I told her, thinking of all the awful people who'd taken advantage of her. I didn't want her to ever be back there again. I'd seen so many beautiful people doing things to please others and losing themselves in the process. At the end of the day, it made no difference to anyone but them, and then they had to live with it.

She nodded. 'I promise.'

'Okay, how about we have a look at what you need for uni?' I suggested. 'What course do you think you might like to start with?'

We started scrolling through different courses, psychology, counselling, even looking at non-traditional study options for naturopathy and yoga.

'I think counselling or something would be a good place to start,' she said.

As we were googling requirements on the university website for a psychology degree and discussing the possibility of her being able to squeeze in for the mid-year intake, two police officers walked in with grim, serious looks. They looked around the room as though we weren't the only ones in there and headed for us.

My body broke out into an involuntary sweat as the memory of two other officers coming to Mrs May's in the middle of the morning to tell me Benny had died flashed through my mind. Breathe, Jo, breathe, I told myself, trying to hold myself together.

'Miss Walsh?' the older of the two officers asked.

I reached for Natalie's hand as I stood and nodded, unconsciously holding my breath.

'We need to talk to you about Russell Whittington.'

Instantly that day in the café came flooding back. The uniformed officers telling me Benny was dead. The devastation, the way my heart felt like it had stopped and my body went into some kind of suspended animation as what they said filtered into my brain. I felt it all again as though it were real, felt the loss, the heartbreak, the unending heartbreak I thought I'd never overcome. I fell back onto the seat, tears streaming from my eyes without my consent, my breath caught in my chest. I couldn't breathe.

'Miss Walsh, are you okay?' the officer asked.

'What's going on?' Natalie asked. I'm not sure to whom exactly.

The older officer answered. 'We just wanted to know where he was. We've had some information come through about Lana Barrett that we need to follow up on and he and Jay aren't answering their phones.'

'What?' I asked, softly. I reached for Natalie's hand as I pulled out my phone and tried calling him. It went to voicemail and suddenly, I couldn't breathe. I'd tried Benny after the police had left. For hours, days, I'd tried calling him, sure they were wrong, not Benny, it couldn't have been Benny, then eventually the number was out of service. His phone disconnected.

I heard Natalie speak to one of the staff but I didn't hear what she said. Moments later, Jaz was squatting in front of me. 'Jo, what's happened?'

'Have you heard from Jay?' Natalie asked.

'Yeah, I just spoke to him, he and Russ are just finishing up, they'll be back soon,' she said. 'Why? What's going on?' she asked, looking from me to the police officers standing by.

'They're okay? Russ is okay?' I asked on a whisper, feeling very far away.

'Yes, as far as I know,' she added. 'Why? What's going on?'

'I'm sorry,' I said, wiping my eyes and waving away her concern, reminding myself Russ was okay. This time.

'Can you get Russell to call us when he's returns?' the officer asked, looking very confused.

I nodded, they thanked us and left looking perplexed.

'You okay?' Natalie asked when I'd caught my breath.

'I can't do this,' I whispered.

'Do what?' Jaz asked.

'Tell Russ, I'm sorry,' I asked as I walked away and out the patio doors before they could reply.

I wasn't ready for this. I wasn't ready to love someone again, to lose someone again. He was okay this time. But what about next time. What about tomorrow or next week or next year? What if the next time they come to me, he's not okay? I couldn't bare it a second time. I'd gotten carried away. Thought I was okay, that I was ready. Thought Bodhi's hocus pocus had cured me. But it hadn't. There was nothing that could cure this, this fear, the constant possibility that I could lose everything all over again.

These last few blissful days had been nothing but a dream

bubble. I'd thought for a minute that maybe I could have everything Ainsley had, the adoring husband, the children, the family, a life that really, truly mattered. But I was fooling myself. I was fooling Russ and that wasn't fair.

I had been right all along, that other life wasn't for me. I'd always be this broken fragment of a person. There was no amount of meditation or hocus pocus or mind-blowing sex that was going to change that. A piece of me was gone and there was no getting it back. Once you knew what I knew, lived with just how fragile life could be and felt the pain I'd felt, there was no going back to before, there was no unknowing that.

Being alone wasn't so bad, I told myself. No one fought me for the remote, no one questioned what I ate for dinner or how many hours of House Hunters I watched. Being alone was better than never knowing if someone was coming home, never knowing if that knock on the door was going to be the news that tore that person from you, tore you from the life you'd built, the hopes and dreams you shared. I couldn't live like that. Russ would understand. He'd have to.

I threw what I could in my tote and left. I needed space to think. I needed to go home. I'd get the bus, call Ainsley to send the car, something. But I couldn't stay here. I couldn't look Russ in the eye and tell him I wasn't brave enough, that I wasn't strong enough to risk losing him. Ainsley would understand.

I walked along the beach, breathing in the fresh sea air, enjoying the sunshine on my face. This was the right thing to do. Especially now there was Nico. It was better I leave now while everyone was still intact, while everyone could move on.

I sat on a bench hidden from the bustling square of the town centre by the sand dunes to catch my breath, hidden from the world. I was better when I was alone. I knew how to do that now, I thought as I watched the waves coming and going.

I took out my phone. I had to call Ainsley, I needed a ride. I scrolled for her name on my call list.

'It's fine, don't worry about it,' someone said in the quiet.

The voice made me jump. I'd thought I was alone. I looked around, but I couldn't see anyone.

I listened for a second before realising it was a familiar voice coming from somewhere in the dunes. Bodhi. Uncomfortable with the prospect of encountering Bodhi here where it was so quiet, where I was so alone, I looked for a place to disappear into. He'd given me the creeps earlier and I wasn't in the mood for another altercation. Then he spoke again.

'For a Harrington she was an easy mark but it's time to move on. I just need another day to wait for the heat on this Lana drama to go away and then I'm out of here, so be ready to make arrangements for the next stop,' he said. I realised he was on the phone.

There was a break while the person on the other end of his phone call spoke.

'Of course no one suspects I killed Lana. Why would they? No one even knows I knew her. I still can't believe that bitch was going to blackmail us. Us for goodness sake. After all we did for her. Stupid, ungrateful woman. She should have known better. But desperate people do stupid, desperate things. It was her own fault for threatening everything we've built.'

My phone dinged with a message and I jumped. I'd forgotten I was holding it, gripping it like it was a weapon. Bodhi stepped out of the dunes before I could hide. He looked at me, our eyes locking, recognition dawning in his, that I'd heard everything he'd said, and I ran.

My legs burned as I ran up the sand. Then I hit the lawned area families picnicked on and ran for the main street, never so glad for the accidental fitness that came from working in a café.

I could hear Bodhi behind me, his feet hitting the ground. 'Jo, wait,' he called, over and over.

He'd killed Lana. He was a con artist. He'd fleeced Jaz Harrington. And I'd heard everything.

I looked back, he was gaining ground. I was never going to make it to the main road and instead blended with a busload of disembarking tourists on the main street, following them into a café and headed straight for the ladies' room.

I sat in a cubicle and caught my breath. Come on Jo, what now?

I read Ainsley's message, which was just a cute picture of the kids cuddling. I turned the sound off before it got me in any more trouble.

I sent Russ a quick text, *'Bodhi killed Lana.'*

I sent another to Ainsley. *'In trouble. Send car. Pin dropped.'*

I dropped a pin on google maps so she could find me, grateful for modern technology because I wasn't even sure where I was but when I turned on my location, google maps knew exactly where I was. Then I breathed until someone knocked on my toilet door and asked if I was okay.

I'd been here too long. I had to leave and hope Bodhi had moved on. I couldn't see him when I came out. I bought a coffee at the counter and went to find a corner to hide in but the busload of tourists had filled the room.

'There's space outside,' offered the friendly waitress.

I looked outside and there was one table in open view of the world overlooking the grassy park. I looked in the other direction to the front door and saw Bodhi walk in from the street but he hadn't seen me. So, I calmly walked out but I couldn't sit out there where he could see me clear as day. Ainsley's driver would have to find me. He'd be a couple of hours anyway, so maybe I could just find somewhere safer to hide while I waited and double back later.

I disappeared as inconspicuously as possible around the back of the building and headed towards the beach. I could follow it up the bluff and hide out in the national park or follow it as far as the next town. I didn't know how far it was, but if I got a good enough head start, I could do it. If Bodhi was looking in the café, he'd be looking in all the populated spaces for the next little bit so I had time. I took the opportunity and went in the opposite direction in the hope of buying some time.

If I could just get to the police station, they would let Ainsley know where I was and help keep me safe and out of sight until the Harrington driver got here. I pulled out my phone to see if I could find the police station on my map. *Shit, shit, shit.* I had three missed calls from Ainsley, two from Russ and only 9% charge. I hadn't charged it before going down to breakfast. It was never going to last the one hour and forty-five minutes left before the driver got here.

A message came through from Ainsley. 'Driver is on his way. Are you okay? Call me. Please,' she begged and then my phone died. It was gone. Silent. I was all alone. How would they find me without the pin, the location, the find my friends app?

I walked along the beach until I saw the big white building with the red and yellow flags flying on top of it. The surf lifesaving club. They would help me.

The leftovers from their morning training were still under the verandah, some kayaks, the red flotation devices. Water dripped from them like someone had just squirted them down with the nearby hose.

I climbed the metal stairs, the cold ocean wind swirling around me and I was glad to go into the warmth of the building. There were a few men over at the pool table, one behind the bar and a few patrons already getting ready for lunch. I went up to the bar and ordered a coke, paid with my credit card knowing every breadcrumb would help and asked to use the phone.

'I need to call Detective Ross from the police station,' I told the handsome, jovial guy behind the bar.

'You alright?' he asked.

'Not really,' I told him.

'That's alright, I know Dave's number,' he said, dialling it in for me and handing me the phone. 'You just sit tight, alright? We got you.'

I sighed with relief as I listened to the phone ringing. Detective Ross' voicemail picked up and I was partway through leaving my message, telling him Bodhi was Lana's killer and where I was and that I was in trouble, when Bodhi walked in.

He looked at me, hesitated with surprise for half a second and made a beeline.

'That your trouble?' the bartender asked.

'Yeah,' I told him.

He nodded to the guys playing pool and, in a moment, they'd surrounded Bodhi. It was going to be okay, I told myself. I was going to get through this. As I was mentally promising all the money in my account to the lifesaving club's fundraising efforts, Bodhi pulled out a gun.

'Whoa, man,' the guys surrounding him backed up a few steps with their hands in the air.

The chef, a big burly guy, came out from the kitchen in his whites and quietly led the few early lunch patrons into a room I couldn't see.

'Come on now, Jo, you don't want me to hurt all these people, do you?' Bodhi asked.

'Bodhi, come on, this is crazy,' I told him.

'What's crazy is you listening in on people's private conversations.'

'I didn't mean to. I'm sorry. Let's just pretend I heard nothing. I'll just sit here and get some lunch and give you all the time you need to disappear,' I told him.

'While you make a phone call?' he asked.

'My phone's dead,' I told him.

'And how many other phones are in this room?' he asked and I was relieved that he didn't seem to have noticed I'd just made a call using their landline, which the bartender had already put back behind the bar.

I just had to delay him long enough for Detective Ross to come, I told myself. But I'd left a message. I hadn't actually spoken to him. It could be hours before he checked his messages.

The bartender put his hand on mine, letting me know everything was going to be okay. But Bodhi had a look in his eye, a wild, desperate look.

The burly looking chef began edging his way over to where we stood but Bodhi saw him and grabbed the young lifesaver on his left and put the gun to his head.

'Now, now,' the bartender said.

'No. Jo. Let's go,' Bodhi told me.

I saw the fear in the lifesaver's eyes. He must have only been eighteen or nineteen. The same age as Natalie. This wasn't his fight. It wasn't his problem.

'Okay, okay,' I finally agreed.

'Jo, you don't have to, just stay. Dave will be here soon enough,' he said.

'I only got his voicemail,' I told the bartender. 'It's fine. Call Jay at the Colonel and tell him what happened. He'll know what to do,' I told the bartender.

He nodded and as I slipped off the stall, he was already reaching for his phone.

Bodhi moved the gun from the young lifesaver's head, pointed it at my stomach and slowly backed himself towards the door. I shook the adrenaline out of my hands as I walked, focussed, one foot in front of the other. *It's okay, Jo, Jay will be back by now, he will come,* I told myself.

Chapter 22

We walked down the metal steps with Bodhi behind me holding the gun firmly into the small of my back. I looked around as I walked, taking stock of where we were and what was around. On the beach, there was just one small family building sandcastles but there was nowhere to run if I went that way. The stairs led to the lawn behind the surf lifesaving club. The grass was full of families. Despite the wind and the cold, they picnicked and threw Frisbees, they barbequed and kicked their soccer balls. Dogs and toddlers chased the seagulls and parents relaxed on picnic blankets. Too many people. Too many children who could get hurt.

Bodhi led me through them all, one arm across my shoulders holding me tight, the other pressing the gun into my side, hidden by my tote bag.

As we exited the park area, I did another stocktake, looking for where the road was, where the shops were, where I could disappear into a crowd or where I could get up some pace. I was fit. I was on my feet, moving all day. Bodhi was muscle strong but was he fit enough to catch me if I got a head start? Was

I fast enough to put some distance between us? Would he do something stupid if I made a run for it?

'Keep that up and my next stop is that fucking kid,' he ground out in my ear.

Nico!

But could he get close enough? Not after this. Russ wouldn't let it happen.

'Don't think I won't. Don't think I don't have someone in just the right spot to take care of business,' he said, his breath hot and slimy in my ear.

He wasn't working alone. He had someone, someone who was in the pub, close enough to hurt Nico without anyone being suspicious. But who? The Lorna Jane mums? Natalie? Margaret Packersham? Karen, the famous author, and her manager slash lover? It could be anyone. It could be any one of the patrons in the front bar. It mightn't even be someone staying there. It could be one of the staff, a passer-by.

I stopped looking around, stopped struggling. I kicked off a shoe as we walked, waited a while and kicked off another. I knocked the eftpos card I'd used at the surf lifesaving club out of my pocket and hoped no one stole it before someone could follow my breadcrumbs.

'Where are you taking me?' I asked, not that I was sure the details were of any use to me, but I asked anyway.

'We're getting out of here.'

'And going where?'

'Somewhere not here.'

'And how do you think you're getting me out of here?' I asked.

'I'll make it happen,' he insisted.

He dragged me to the other side of the main street. We were heading towards the main road that went all the way around the peninsula. Up ahead was a bus shelter. *The bus.* It would take us to the city. There were a lot of stops between here and the city, he could choose to stop anywhere. How would anyone find me in that haystack? Bodhi bought two tickets from the vending machine and checked his watch. I saw the bus stuck at traffic lights a couple hundred metres up the road. I didn't have long.

Bodhi's phone rang. He took the call, turning his head away from me but keeping the gun pointed at me. He spat some words at the caller about not having time to talk, telling whoever was on the other end to watch the kid until they got a message from him. I knew I only had moments to do something. I took a lipstick out of my bag and wrote on the wooden seat by my leg opposite to where Bodhi sat. Jo Walsh was here. Call 000. It was all I could think of.

Bodhi turned then, just as the bus crossed the intersection ahead and pulled into the stop.

'Do not make a fuss getting on this bus. I will kill you and then I will have that kid killed and Natalie, maybe she'll be next,' he declared. As my face paled, he added. 'See, I know where to hurt you so don't push me.'

I climbed on the bus and let him push me with his hand at the small of my back to my seat, where he wedged me against the window. As the bus drove off, I looked out the window to see Russ staring at me. He'd almost made it. But he was too late. Our eyes locked as the bus drove away. I put my hand to the window as a tear fell but there was nothing either of us could do.

People came and went from the bus and I sat there like a fool, shoeless with a gun in my side and no one noticed. How often had I done the same thing? Had I been somewhere completely unaware of someone else's turmoil? The odds were good I had and who would have ever known? No one noticed me sitting here holding on to my bladder with all I had, trying not to cry like a baby to protect Nico and Natalie.

'Was any of it even real?' I asked Bodhi. I felt sick thinking about all the things I'd told him. I was stupid for thinking I'd been healed. That it could be so easy. That Benny had been there to help me. That I believed he wished for me to move on. That he had other work to do. I knew it wasn't true. I knew it but I'd wanted to believe it. Needed to believe it.

'The healings?' he asked as though he wasn't sure what I was referring to. 'What I can do is real, yes. That's why people all over the world are begging to have me visit them. Was it your dead boyfriend who came to your healing? That I can't be sure of but there was a spirit there but I can't see form, no one can see form like that, it's just an essence.'

I nodded. At least that was something. Hopefully, it meant the stuff with Benny could be real too. I still wanted to believe that spirit had been Benny and like Dr Bailey and everyone else kept saying, he loved me and wanted me to move on but would stay for me if I needed him and hopefully Benny hadn't left me yet. I sent up a prayer to whoever might be listening, to Benny if he could hear me. *Please*, I begged. *Don't let me die.* A few years ago, I'd have been happy to. I'd have joined Benny in a heartbeat but now... I didn't want to die. I didn't know what I wanted. I knew I couldn't be with Russ. I couldn't bear that threat of losing him hovering over us every day. I loved him, I think. I did. But I couldn't risk it. I wasn't strong enough. But still... I wanted to live.

'Why me?' I asked, wondering why he'd chosen me as the object of his misguided affections.

'I saw something of myself in you. I see a future where we could change the world together.'

'I've never wanted to change the world,' I told him.

'I'll do the world changing and you'll be by my side, keeping everything running, keeping everyone happy, keeping me happy and centred.'

'It all comes back to sex, doesn't it,' I said, disappointed.

'I must say, that aspect was far more appealing when you'd been celibate for so long.'

'What?'

'You hadn't had sex since your boyfriend died, the first time back would have felt like the first time and oh,' he said, groaning at whatever he was thinking. 'To have been the one to bring you back.' He closed his eyes and my stomach turned at the serene look on his face. I had to turn to the window and focus on the houses whizzing by so as to not vomit in the middle of the bus.

He reached for my hand. 'You are a beautiful, powerful woman, Jo, in here,' he said, putting his hand on my solar plexus. Your energy and power is concentrated when you climax. To feel that, to be in the presence of that after it had been building for so long, I imagine it had to be extraordinary.'

'Yeah, well, it's going to be pretty tough for you to make any of that happen without my consent.'

'You forget the foot massage?' he asked.

'I'm trying too. You know you disgust me, right?'

He chuckled. 'Jo,' he said, twirling a lock of my hair around his finger. 'I can do things that no other man could even imagine. I could make you come with just a single touch. You experience that and there'll be no going back. Nothing will ever measure up after that.'

'You sound very sure of yourself.'

'I'm not new at this,' he said.

'What? Kidnapping women and forcing yourself on them?'

His face reddened with anger. 'I will not have to force myself on you, I guarantee you. You will be begging me to make you come. You'll see,' he growled into my ear.

I huffed and turned to the window. There was no reasoning with a madman. I instead tried running through my options. Did this bus go all the way into the city? If it did, that was close to home, I could work with that, I knew the city like the back of my hand. But it was the weekend, sometimes buses stopped halfway, changed to another bus. Or what if we got off at a stop somewhere else? What stops were along the way? I wondered. I tried to think about which way the bus was going. Maybe the beach. Maybe Marion shopping centre. It was big and busy. Lots of ways to get separated there. Lots of places to hide. Lots of exits to disappear out of. Noarlunga would be harder but possible too. Would there even be a chance to escape? To disappear on the way to a bathroom? Out a backdoor? I planned ideas in my head, so I had an option at the ready should something present itself.

Bodhi read a text on his phone then pressed the stop button on the bus. Shit, it meant we weren't going to any of those places, I thought as the bus pulled into the next stop.

'Come,' he said, grabbing my arm and lifting me up.

I tried catching the eyes of people we passed so when my face was on the news someone might remember me and be able to say where we got off, so someone would be able to piece together the puzzle of my disappearance. But no one even looked at me, too intent on staring out the window, playing games on their phone or reading a book.

We stepped off the bus in a random middle of suburbia stop. I'd been trying to pay attention, focus on where we were, landmarks, something. But out this way, there wasn't a lot that deciphered it from one place or another.

'Where are we?' I asked.

'Doesn't matter. Sit,' he told me, indicating the seat in the bus shelter.

I sat and waited for further instructions, taking in my surroundings, trying to figure out what was next. Were we walking somewhere? What was his plan? I looked around and there was nothing. Houses that were middle of the day, working class quiet. No pedestrians or cyclists, barely any passing motorists. Bodhi could kill me right here and no one would even notice, I thought, a chill racing up my spine.

A red sedan that had seen better days pulled up to the kerb.

'Come on,' Bodhi instructed.

'No,' I whispered as it dawned on me that if I got in that

car, that was it, it was all over. I'd never see Ainsley and Henry and Anna again. I'd never see Russ or Nico. Any version of the future I'd spent the last week fighting for would be gone.

'Are you really going to push me?' he asked, glancing at the car.

I just had to hope that by now the Harringtons had battened down the hatches and Nico and Natalie were safe within the walls of the pub, and that whoever was driving the car was his accomplice. It was time to save me and I was not getting in that car.

Bodhi leaned into the passenger window to talk to his companion and I ran. I just had to hope I could get far enough ahead before he noticed so that I had a chance. I just needed a chance and a house where someone was actually home.

A hundred metres down the road, I heard music wafting out of a window and turned into their driveway and ran up to their door, bashing as loud as I could. A dog barked from the back but no one came.

'Hello! Please!' I shouted as I bashed.

I kept shouting and calling for help until Bodhi caught up to me.

'You stupid bitch,' he shouted at me. 'What the hell do you think you're doing?'

'Let me go,' I begged. 'Come on, please, let me go. You can go, find someone else, do whatever, just please, let me go,' I cried.

'You don't get it. It doesn't even matter what I want anymore. I can't let you go. You know too much. Come with me or die, they are your only choices now, do you understand?'

Ignoring him, I kicked and screamed and called for help as he tried dragging me away but still, no one came.

A car pulled into the driveway and relief washed through me until I realised it was the red sedan. Bodhi dragged me kicking and screaming like a toddler to the car. As he threw me into the back seat and slammed the door. I knew it was over. I'd lost.

Chapter 23

I looked up at the driver. 'Margaret Packersham?' I asked, my heart doing a sad little flip of disappointment.

'Hello dear,' she greeted me.

'That's it?'

'What did you want?' she asked innocently.

'Um, maybe an explanation?'

'For what?'

'Are you serious? Why are you here? Why are you helping Bodhi kidnap me? Do you help him con people as well? Is Margaret Packersham even your name?'

'That's a lot of questions, Jo.'

'Can you answer them?'

She considered the questions for a moment before replying. 'No, that is not my name. I am here because Bodhi is my son. I am helping him because I love him. And no, we don't *con* people, Jo, we provide a service for which we are duly compensated.'

'If you don't con people then why do you pretend you don't know Bodhi and you tell that whole bullshit story about your dead husband and having a daughter in London.'

'I do have a daughter in London and my husband did die. I just left out the part about having a son. You're very nosey, dear. But we don't want to make people feel uncomfortable having Bodhi's mother around, so it makes everyone more comfortable if I'm a visiting grieving widow with a daughter far away. People tend to be far more generous if they think he's all alone and just going where the wind blows him.'

'Generous how?'

'When Bodhi heals people, they are grateful. People like to show Bodhi their gratitude. Either it's the host offering him free room and board while he's there. Or the ladies, they like to offer up things no mother needs to know about. Others are so grateful, they want to compensate him for all he's done. Financially. Don't you feel grateful to be healed?' she asked innocently.

'Is that why Bodhi was hitting on me, so I'd be grateful?'

'I suggested he focus on Natalie. Her parents would be very grateful if she came home healed after all she's been through, but then you came along with your dead boyfriend and rent free living, which on its own says tidy little nest egg with which to show your gratitude. Then you add in that you're friends with the Harringtons, and we could only imagine how grateful they'd be if we could get them to come for treatment. We already had Jaz, but she was just testing the waters. We needed more. We've seen them in the magazines, they need healing probably more than anyone.'

'You know Jaz is going to move mountains to ruin you. That is the downside of messing with powerful people. She might seem like sprinkles and sandcastles, but I promise you, she's not. They're not. They have more power than you can comprehend and she'll use it. Without even blinking.'

'Well, we'll see about that,' she smirked. 'You're not the only one who told their secrets in your first session,' she added.

'You're disgusting, you know that?'

'Jo, dear, please. It was never meant to go so awry. I knew Bodhi was getting attached. He wanted you to come with us but I told him it was too much, just stick to the plan and then came Russ and I knew there was no way you'd leave him and the baby. He wouldn't let it go, so I tried to just get you to leave. I tried frightening you but even that didn't work. Then you overheard things you weren't supposed to hear so we couldn't leave you behind,' she said, as though it all made sense.

'Why did you kill Lana?' I asked Bodhi, relieved in some way the break in to our room was just a misguided attempt to spook me.

'Lana...' Margaret Packersham said on a sigh. 'She was going to ruin everything.'

'I knew Lana from a retreat I did a couple of years ago in Missouri,' Bodhi admitted. 'We... well, we had some fun. Unlike you, she enjoyed her foot massage and she was very grateful for the healing she received and when it was time, we went our separate ways.'

'Yet a year ago she was having one-night stands with strangers in Vegas and seemingly showed up here broke.'

'I told you, she was very grateful. It's not my business if people give more than they should,' Bodhi said. 'And... before I healed her, she didn't have the confidence to sleep with anyone.'

'You think her whoring around Vegas was a win?'

'Of course,' Margaret Packersham interjected. 'Not everyone wants the same thing, Jo. If she wanted to become comfortable with her body and her sexuality, then isn't that her business?'

'I suppose,' I conceded but not believing that was all there was to it. 'But she ended up broke and alone with a baby,' I added.

'You're assuming she was broke and alone. What if she just wanted Russ?'

'She came with nothing.'

'She travelled light under the assumption Russ would take care of everything.'

'Is that true?'

'It could be.'

'You don't know for sure? You didn't ask?'

'No, we didn't know each other, Jo. Are you following along at all?'

'I spoke to her,' Bodhi added. 'She didn't want the kid. She wanted to be an actress. She was just going to dump him with Russ and keep moving. Her flight home wasn't for a few days, so when he begged her to stay. She thought she'd see what else he might have to offer, then she saw me and thought she could get her money back.'

'Why would she want her money back if she was a happily healed customer?'

'People can sometimes regret their generosity and gratitude down the track when times are tough,' Margaret Packersham said as though she were my wise counsel.

'I think you take advantage of people during their times of

weakness and they realise it when they get home but it's done, they're embarrassed and you didn't technically break any laws, so they don't actually have any course of action to take.'

They both shrugged as though doing so was no big deal.

'So if you killed Lana for threatening to spill your secrets, why haven't you killed me for knowing too much yet?'

'Because I suspect you already gave away what my son did and you are worth more alive than you are dead. We need you to get out of the country.'

'What my mother means is, in return for your life, the Harringtons need to fly us out of the country.'

'I think you're overestimating my value to the Harringtons,' I told them.

'I don't think so and you'd better hope not. Your life literally depends on it,' Margaret Packersham said as she pulled into a roadhouse.

We were about an hour away now from where we had started with nothing but open fields all around the roadhouse. 'What are we doing?' I asked, trying to keep the conversation going in the hope of garnering as much information as possible. Knowledge was power right? I had to hope that I could figure something out. I couldn't do that if they kept me in the dark.

'We need petrol and I need a bathroom break,' Margaret Packersham announced.

'Good, I'm starving. I need something to eat,' Bodhi said.

We pulled up to a bowser and I looked around. There were options. There was a semi in the car park. A family with a caravan. Margaret got out and put the bowser into the tank. Bodhi checked the child locks were in place before locking me in the car and going into the roadhouse. Margaret Packersham followed him a minute later.

Shit, I thought, leaning back in the car. How was anyone going to find me? I knew the Harringtons wouldn't pay for me. I wouldn't want them to and I doubted Bodhi and Margaret Packersham were aware that Jaz and Christian had parted ways professionally from the family company that their brother Tom now ran, so I suspected any request they sent through official channels would get lost or fall into a confused person's inbox.

I looked around the car for something that might help me escape and I saw one of them had left their phone down the side of their seat. It was a new Samsung, the same as mine, which meant it had power sharing capabilities. I quickly placed my phone against theirs and pressed the on button until my phone had just enough charge to come to life.

Bodhi came out of the roadhouse with a bag of food and I quickly sat back and threw my phone back in my handbag at my feet. My phone hadn't charged enough to make a call or send a message but if Russ was doing his thing, then it'd have been just enough to ping my location. It was the only hope I had.

While we waited for Margaret Packersham to return, Bodhi turned to look at me and said, 'You know, I might be able to save your life if you change your mind about being with me.'

'What?'

'My mother sounds tough but if I ask her to keep you, she will. She doesn't like to say no to me. I can make that happen.'

'She's going to kill me anyway, isn't she?'

He shrugged as though it were no big deal.

'But if I agree to be with you, she won't?'

'We could do amazing things together, you know? Travel the world, see amazing places.'

'While conning people out of their money under the guise of gratitude?'

'We never ever ask for anything. They offer.'

'Right.'

'If you want me to save you, you have to say so, before my mother comes back,' he told me.

I saw her walk out of the roadhouse with a cup of coffee in hand. I had seconds. But I couldn't do it, not even to save my life.

'I could heal you, anything you needed to be okay with it,' he offered, begged.

'No,' I whispered.

'What? Why? You have too,' he stomped like toddler throwing a tantrum. 'You'd really rather die than be with me?' he asked with surprise. His emotions meant nothing to me. He turned them on and off like a tap. Like a psychotic narcissist.

'Yes, I'd rather die. You are disgusting. Your mother is disgusting and I'd rather die than be with you,' I said clearly so there was no mistake.

Bodhi steamed as his mother climbed back into the car.

'What took you so long?' he spat at her, that tantrum clearly continuing.

'What was going on in here?' she demanded.

'Nothing,' he said. 'We'll need to find a quiet spot in the woods when we get to them though and get rid of that dead weight back there,' he spat.

'That dead weight is our only way out of the country, so stop pouting. We'll take care of her when we have that plane.'

'Is it sorted?' Bodhi asked her.

'Not yet. I tried calling Harrington Enterprises and no one knows who I'm talking about.'

'I told you I wasn't that important to the Harringtons,' I reminded them.

'You better hope you are and that the message I left makes it through to someone who knows who the hell you are.'

'My friends don't even work for Harrington Enterprises, you know that, right?'

'Of course they do. It's the family business,' she said but I heard the waver in her voice. She didn't know.

I chuckled to myself. I wasn't going to enlighten her to the name of Christian's company. I wasn't having him or his company dragged through my business, not after all he'd done to build it, how much work he'd put in to make it successful. He'd gone up against his father's company with nothing and was now his number one competitor. His father no longer ran Harrington Enterprises. He'd handed the reigns over to Tom who enjoyed the brotherly competition. But I'd only met Tom once when he'd passed through town and Ainsley had dragged me out to dinner but I'd met his wife, Alex, a few times but I doubted either would remember me nor care enough to take the ransom seriously. Maybe they'd pass it on to their security team who would know Jay was working on something, he'd been using their resources to dig up information on Lana, but that could take days.

'What are we going to do?' Bodhi asked innocently.

'Well, we don't have time to sit here arguing, we're going to keep heading towards Melbourne where they keep their helicopters and planes and Jo, you better hope that by the time we get there, someone has figured their shit out or they'll be finding you on the side of the highway with the roadkill,' she explained.

I sat back in the chair, quietly analysing them both. If I left my bag, I'd be faster if I ran for it. It didn't work last time because I'd gone to the house. I wasn't prepared that time, I was winging it. But this time, if I was prepared for him, if I had a plan, maybe I could do something. I carried cartons of coffee and supplies downstairs and upstairs and moved them around. I wasn't a lightweight. If I separated them, maybe I had a shot.

I could definitely take Margaret Packersham in a fight. But she wouldn't chase me if I ran, he would. So I had to be sure I had enough to take him on. There'd be adrenaline to help me and I'd have the desperate need to survive on my side. I watched how he drank the coffee his mother had brought him. That would be it. We were in the middle of nowhere. The caffeine from his coffee would have to hit his bladder in about twenty minutes, I calculated. Margaret Packersham would have to pull over so he could pee. I just had to figure out the child locks on my door.

The minutes ticked by. The scenery went from arid farmland to forest. I was counting the minutes down. I took off my seatbelt in readiness. A kangaroo hopped into the cover of trees as we passed. The forest ahead seemed to part for us as the road wound through it and as we exited the bend, Margaret swore.

I looked ahead and a big, black Harrington Industries helicopter blocked the road. Standing in front of the helicopter, Jay and Russ flanked the detective still in his red flannel flapping in the breeze with his gun pointed at the car.

Margaret slammed on the brakes, adjusted her gears and I could see she was going to take a u turn and go back the way we came. We were turning too fast for me to put on a seatbelt so I gripped the seat with my hands, bracing myself. Halfway into the turn there was a gunshot. Plan B. Shoot out a tyre. The car spun and spun, I lost my grip on the seat and screamed as the car hit the guardrail.

I tried to grab a hold of a headrest but I missed and flew across the car, landing against the door. For a moment everything was black, but then Margaret Packersham wailed, a sound that chilled my blood.

My arm was numb. My head spun and my ears rang. As Margaret's wail brought me around, I looked up to see Bodhi with a piece of guardrail where his legs should be. I couldn't see his face as his head hung forward, resting on his chest but the wail from his mother said I didn't need to see.

Glass shattered on the opposite window. It took a moment to comprehend but I looked up. I couldn't move, I felt stuck but my head moved and I saw Russ, saw his mouth moving but couldn't hear his words.

I finally caught the end of his sentence. 'Help is coming. Hang on, baby, hang on.'

I heard another helicopter land somewhere but I couldn't focus, I couldn't stay awake. I heard the noise of them in the dark fog, as though muffled through layers of stuffing. But then

I felt the cold air on my skin, felt the touch of people and heard the sound of Russ' voice in my ear before the cold went away and the sound of the helicopter filled my ears again.

Chapter 24

I woke to shouts and what felt like wind on my skin. I opened my eyes, just a little. The light was bright, flickering past in a whirr as people shouted instructions at each other. The bed i was on stopped moving.

'On three,' a man said. He counted down. I was moved from one bed to another.

'There you are, Jo,' a kind man said as I opened my eyes. 'Can you tell me where it hurts?' he asked.

I tried to speak but nothing came out. My mouth and throat were as dry as a desert. I tried making saliva but it didn't work.

'Can we have some water?' the kind man called and someone shoved a straw in my mouth. 'Just a sip,' he instructed.

The sip was all I needed to make things work. 'My arm,' I told them. 'My head.'

He nodded. 'That's okay, we'll take care of them. You have a little sleep now, okay?'

They must have given me something because it wasn't like before when I could hear things through the fog. This time there was nothing.

I woke in a small quiet room, cords in my arm, a beeping

noise soft in the background. I blinked into the dark until my eyes adjusted and I found him. The new hospital had built bench seats under the windows, big enough to curl up on or lie down on, depending how tall you were. Russ was too tall for the bench, too broad. He'd squished himself on there anyway. Stubble covered his peaceful, sleeping face and I don't think I'd ever seen anything so perfect.

'Hey,' he said, waking to see me, watching him. 'You okay?'

'I don't know yet,' I told him as I tried to take stock. My arm was in plaster, the whole side of my body hurt and I had the headache from hell.

'Let me get a nurse,' he said, pressing the call button.

'You're lucky, Jo,' the nurse told me. 'Nothing too serious, how do you feel?'

She was right, I was lucky. A broken arm and a concussion would heal, the bruising would fade. I would be okay. I slept some more in a morphine induced slumber and woke to a quiet conversation.

'Hey,' I whispered when I saw Ainsley's face.

'Jo Jo, I'm so sorry,' she begged, rushing over to my bedside. 'I'll never make you go anywhere ever again, I swear it,' she promised.

'Hey, hey,' I soothed her as she cried all her tears. 'I'm going to be okay,' I promised her.

She tried smiling.

'I might need another appointment with Dr Bailey though,' I joked.

She nodded, laughed. 'I've already spoken to Julie and they're coordinating with your doctors.'

'Of course they are,' I smiled. 'Where's Henry, you didn't bring him, did you,' I panicked, sitting up, suddenly afraid he'd have seen me broken like this.

'No, no, he's at the house with Jaz. She's so sorry she brought Bodhi into everyone's life. She's mad as a cut snake and she feels just awful,' she promised.

'It's not her fault,' I assured her. 'What about Nico?' I asked, looking around.

'Jaz has him too. Natalie's there giving her a hand,' she promised.

'They brought Natalie back?'

'Jaz couldn't just leave her there to wait for her folks and she knew she'd want to see you.'

'I'm so glad,' I told her and I was. I didn't want her to be alone, not sure what had happened. I nodded and laid back on a sigh. 'What happened to them? To Bodhi and Margaret?'

Russ replaced Ainsley who went out to make some calls and update people.

'Margaret broke her hip, but unlike you, she was wearing a seatbelt,' he chastised. 'Bodhi lost his legs, but it looks like he's going to be okay.'

'Bloody hell,' I said, nodding, taking it all in.

'Why weren't you wearing a seatbelt Jo, this could have ended so much worse?'

'I was planning to run. I was counting down to when he'd need to pee. I wanted to be ready.'

'Oh baby,' he said, leaning down to kiss my head. 'Did you have any idea she was involved?' Russ asked.

'No. I was as shocked as you,' I told him. 'I didn't even know they knew each other until she pulled up next to us in the middle of nowhere driving the car. But they knew, Lana. She'd given Bodhi her life savings in gratitude for being healed. When she saw him, she thought he was her key to getting her money back. But he didn't like being blackmailed.'

He shook his head, 'So he stabbed the poor woman in the back?' he asked, still trying to comprehend it. 'You told Natalie to tell me you were sorry? Sorry for what? What's going on, Jo?' he asked.

'I was being a coward, Russ. You deserve so much better than me,' I told him, my hand on his lovely face.

'What does that mean?'

'It means we need to move on, go back to our own lives.'

'What do you mean go back to our own lives?'

'Your life. My life.'

'What about our life?'

'There can't be an *our* life. There can't be a we, or an our,' I said, my eyes overflowing with tears.

'Jo, why? What the hell happened?' he begged, his eyes welling.

I leant back against the pile of pillows and suddenly all the emotion flowed out. I shook as I cried, my breath getting stuck in amongst it all and Russ just pulled me to his chest and let me cry it out.

When I stopped shaking, stopped crying, he asked, 'Tell me what's going on in that pretty head of yours? Please.'

'You were gone. The detective came. I can't go through that again Russ, I can't. I couldn't breathe. I nearly lost it.'

'What did he say?' he asked. His eyes burned with anger and I was glad there was nothing he could do.

'He just wanted to know where you were, had some new information he wanted to run past you.'

'That's all?'

'That's all? A couple of cops walk in, in the middle of the morning and say they need to talk to you about this person you care about and it all comes rushing back. I can't go through that again, Russ. I can't lose someone again. Every second of every day could be the last one, could be the moment someone comes to tell me you're gone. I can't lose you so no, I can't do this. Before we go any further, I'm done. We have to be done,' I said, closing my eyes because I couldn't look at his beautiful face.

When I opened my eyes, he was gone.

'Are you going to tell me what's going on?' Ainsley asked when she came in a little while later with a thermos of tea.

'What do you mean?'

'You and Russ. You don't mean it, do you?'

'You saw him?' I asked.

'He's inconsolable, Jo. You can't mean it.'

'Yes, I mean it. It's better this way for everyone. That kid doesn't need me being a neurotic mess and I can't go through it all again, Ains, I just can't. I can't live in fear of losing him.'

'Ahuh,' she said, nodding, pouring me some tea. 'You think it's going to be that easy, Jo? You think he's giving up just because you threw a tantrum?' she said.

'A tantrum?'

She smirked and I couldn't get mad at her because I was just about to throw one. I took a deep breath. 'I don't know how else to be,' I told her as there was a knock on the door.

'Well, perhaps it's time you found one,' she said, before leaving as Russ came back in.

'I don't know how else to be,' I told him. 'The fear, it just gripped me and I couldn't breathe. I couldn't bear the thought of anything happening to you and Nico. That's how Bodhi got me to go with him, he said he had someone close enough to hurt Nico.'

'And you sacrificed yourself for him?'

I nodded.

'You can't live in fear,' he told me.

'I can live however I like.'

'Jo, I get it.'

'No, you don't, no one can.'

'Everyone's afraid of something, Jo.'

'What are you afraid of?' I challenged because I knew there was nothing Russ was afraid of.

'Losing you.'

'Yeah, sure.'

'I just about bloody did,' he said, throwing whatever was in his hand on the floor. 'My heart was in my bloody throat and when that car hit the railing... God Jo. Jay tried to hold me back. We didn't know what we'd find but I had to see. I couldn't leave you in there. I fucking love you. Don't you get it? I'm afraid of who I was when you left last time. I'm afraid of the vapid life I lived before I met you. I'm afraid I'll never again know what it's like to sleep with you in my arms because I swear that was the greatest feeling I've ever had.'

'And now imagine someone walks in, in the middle of the day, while you're serving coffee and tells you I'm dead and never coming home. Russ, it rips a hole in you. It tears out a piece of your soul and you can't ever get that back and then you have to live with the fear, every day of your life, wondering who's next? And there's nothing anyone can do or say because the reality is, that at any second, any one of us could be gone.'

He pulled me to him. 'I'd rather die having lived as many seconds with you as possible than die never knowing what it's like to live a life with you.'

'It's better to have loved and lost than to have never loved at all? That's bullshit that people who haven't lost say,' I said, tearing myself away from him and flopping back onto the pillows.

'It was actually written by Lord Tennyson after he unexpectedly lost his best friend, so he knows something about loss. You can't live a half-life, Jo, what's the point in living at all?'

'I don't know, Russ. All I know is I can't stand the thought of losing you, too, and I don't know how else to not live in fear.'

He kindly turned me to face him, softly held my face to his. 'I can't promise you I'll always be okay, but I can promise I will always do my best to come home to you. Right now, my heart is breaking and a little piece of me is dying at the thought of you walking away. And for what? Not because you don't love me. I'd never beg you stay if you didn't love me but for fear? Jo, I'm so bloody afraid you're going to walk out that door and I'll never see you again. I'll do anything you need to help you through this. I'll be patient, I'll wait, anything but please, do not leave me,' he begged, his eyes welling.

It was that, that broke me. Russ is a man, a tough, ballsy, devil may care man that doesn't crumble, that always finds a way but he was crumbling in front of me and I couldn't do that to him. Suddenly, my own heart, my own fears, paled in insignificance to this beautiful man. His happiness meant more. I pulled him to me, savoured his arms around me. 'We'll live every second as if it is our last, because we know,' I said.

'Every second,' he said. 'No regrets.'

Once he was sure I was okay and staying put, he left me to check in with Ainsley, go and make the necessary arrangements for Nico and me at home. I smiled at the thought of him having to get past Vivi. Then I thought about my parents. Had they been? Had they met him? They must be terrified.

I found my phone next to my bed. Someone had charged it. The screen looked like a spiderweb with all the cracks but it worked. There was a message from my mum. 'Sorry we missed you, we're glad you're okay. We'll come on the weekend when Ainsley said you'll be home. Call us.'

My dad was a farmer. He had a property in the north east. Dad raised cattle that he didn't like to leave unattended for too long. Farming wasn't a job, it was a life. I'd learnt that from an early age and it was one of the reasons I'd refused to go home with them when Benny died. I wasn't sure I'd be able to get out twice. But I loved them and they loved the land. I pressed my mum's name on my phone and the photo from her birthday a few years ago, smiling in front of a plate of teacakes sat on my screen while the phone rang.

'Hello?' she asked, always a question as though she was still confused by the telephone and hadn't seen my name come up on her caller ID.

'Hey, Mum.'

'Oh, Jo, are you okay?' she asked, seeming to hold her breath.

'Yeah, I'm sore, but I'm okay.'

'I wanted to stay but your dad... he needed to get home. Hugh's gone away for a few days for footy and we didn't have time to organise for anyone to check on the cows.'

'It's okay, Mum, I understand.'

'And you had so many people there already. Ainsley and that nice man, he wouldn't leave that seat, you know.'

'Yeah, I guessed.'

'I'm glad you might be moving on honey. Are you?'

'Maybe. Yeah. I guess.'

'Well, that is a relief for me, I tell you,' she said. 'Would you like me to come and get you and bring you home? I don't like the idea of you up in that apartment trying to look after yourself with a broken arm,' she said.

'It's fine. Russ is going to help. I'll be okay, Mum. It's just a broken arm. Dad will need you more if Hugh's away.' My brother and I had never been close, not like Ainsley and Shaun or the Harringtons. He was fine enough people, I guess, but he was eight years older than me and happy as a pig on the farm. We just weren't the same people.

'Well, you call me if you change your mind and I'll come down on the weekend to check in on you, alright?'

'Sure, Mum. That will be great.'

'Alright. I love you. I'll see you then.'

'Love you too. Hi to Dad.'

It had been nice to hear her voice, comforting and I sat with that for a few minutes, glad to know she was happy for me and Russ and that she was there if I needed her. It was enough, just to know, sometimes.

'Hey, you up for a visitor?' Natalie asked from the doorway.

'Oh, hey. Of course. Come in. I'm so glad to see you. Are you okay?' I asked her.

She shrugged. 'I just feel... I don't even know what to think or feel. How could they do that? The both of them? I just don't understand,' she said and I was suddenly glad Bodhi had decided on me and left Natalie be.

'If it makes any difference, what Bodhi does, the healings, the meditations, all that was real. He promised me that.'

She shrugged. 'I guess that's something.'

'And now we can all go home and move on and forget about him and bloody Margaret Packersham.'

'Yeah, I guess so,' she said, sadly.

'Are you really okay?' I asked.

'Yeah, just means I have to go back home almost the same as I left. They'll be disappointed,' she said.

'But you're not the same, Natalie. When we met, you were walking around like a shadow. Look at you now, making friends, doing things, taking care of me. You're not the same. But if you need somewhere to stay, I have rooms. Please, come and stay, just for a while or as long as you like,' I said. 'And I'm close to the uni, so you can do your study and live with me and move forward with your life. You deserve a good life, Natalie.'

She smiled. Squeezed my hand. 'Are you sure you don't mind?' she asked.

'Not a bit. The rooms are just sitting there empty and I think after all that's happened, I'll be glad for the company.'

'What about Russ?'

'What about him?'

'Don't you two have plans?'

'Maybe. But what happens with us makes no difference. There's a whole third floor of rooms just sitting there doing nothing. I promise, you're welcome for as long as you like,' I insisted.

'Thank you,' she smiled as Russ came back.

'Natalie's coming to stay upstairs,' I told him so there would be no awkwardness.

'That's fantastic,' he said. 'We'll be like one big family,' he smiled.

Chapter 25

'Alright, let's give you a once over and if we're happy, you can go home today,' the doctor told me on Monday morning.

I was still sore, bruised down one side, on my face and my arm was in an awful, bright pink cast. Ainsley had chosen it while I was sedated. She'd thought it was hilarious. I thought it looked like candy floss and considering I wasn't a twelve-year-old girl, it was hard to look at.

'You'll get used to it,' Russ insisted every time he caught me staring at it with a look of hatred.

It was a small price for all I'd been through though. It was a miracle I'd walked away from the accident with just bruising and a broken arm. It could have been so much worse. I shuddered to think what would have happened if they hadn't gotten to us in time.

I was looking forward to finally being back in my home, my bed, having my own things, the quiet and the peace of the place. I was looking forward to seeing Mrs Donovan and Vivi too. Being a part of the hubbub of the café that was my home, my sanctuary.

Natalie had been sleeping at Ainsley's but she'd been helping out at the café. Trying to keep herself busy. We didn't want her to sleep there alone though. Not yet. She'd been through so much. Ainsley said Natalie had spoken to her parents. I thought they'd have come for her in an instant after everything that had happened. She was only eighteen. But her parents hadn't come. They were relieved she had somewhere else to go. To be done with all 'that business'. It meant Natalie was now a part of my family as much as Nico. I could tell Ainsley felt the same. Between us, she'd have all the family she would need.

Russ came in wearing a suit, brandishing a bag. 'Ainsley sent you some clothes,' he declared. There'd been a small memorial for Lana early that morning, attended by the friend she'd stayed with when she'd arrived in the country, plus Russ, Nico and Natalie. Her remains had been cremated. Her friend was taking them back to Missouri. They'd both planned to go to the states after Lana had dropped Nico off. They wanted to be actresses in Hollywood. Lana wanted to make sure Nico got to Russ first. She didn't want him getting lost in the system. She'd been through the system before she'd found her parents. She didn't want that for Nico. But then she'd seen Bodhi and thought she might as well top up her bank account before she left. That was where Russ and Jay had gone that morning everything had gone awry, they'd found the friend.

'Ah, nice,' I said, gratefully taking the bag from him.

'Where's Natalie?' I asked.

'I dropped her off at the café. She's going to give Ainsley a hand with Anna and Nico and whatever else needs doing. I think she said Kelsey was there helping out as well. Sounded like a full house,' he said.

'Always is,' I smiled.

'How about you, how are you doing?' I asked, pulling him closer, smoothing out his lapel.

'I'm okay. Happy you're coming home,' he said.

'Well, you sure do smell good,' I told him before I kissed him.

He'd been staying at Christian's hotel around the corner from the hospital. Well, staying was probably a bit much, he was using the space to shower and change his clothes. Nico was still at Ainsley's with Natalie, so it would be nice to have everyone come home to where they belong. It was time to move on.

I'd showered with the help of a nurse that morning while Russ was out but I doubted I smelt as good as he did. I was glad there was a bath at Mrs May's because I could manage that on my own. I didn't want Russ having to help me shower. Not yet. Not this soon. It wasn't sexy. We hadn't been together long enough yet for all the non-sexy things. There'd be time for that. Now wasn't it.

I dressed while Russ went down to the chemist to fill my scripts. I signed my papers and farewelled the nice people who'd cared for me.

A car waited in front of the hospital. Russ loaded in the flowers and balloons, then helped me in. We'd have to think about getting a car now we had Nico, I thought. Another thing to add to the list.

It felt almost silly having someone drive us home. It wasn't that far to the café. We could have walked. If I wasn't so broken. The driver pulled up in front of the café and waited for us to leave. It was a no parking zone in the middle of the morning so we exited as quickly as we could before he got a ticket.

'So, this is it, huh? The infamous Mrs May's?' Russ said as we stood on the footpath taking it in. 'You ready?' he asked.

'God, yes,' I smiled.

Everyone was waiting inside the café. Vivi in a bright purple kimono looking ever the glamour queen. Mrs Donovan looked up from behind the register and smiled wide when she saw me. Henry was sitting in a booth with our resident Russian-in-perpetual-mourning and ran over to hug my leg as soon as he saw me. I smiled. I was home.

It took a while to get up the stairs but up there waited Ainsley and Nico. 'Shhhh... he's asleep,' she said.

She'd rearranged the living room just as I'd thought I would do it and she'd put in a cot and a change table and he was all set up as though he'd lived there his whole life. I couldn't resist a little peak inside the cot and he looked peaceful, happy as a clam. Anna slept across the room in a porta cot and I thought life was pretty damn good.

'Why don't you get settled? I'll show Natalie to her room and where everything is.'

I nodded. Pulled her in for a hug. 'Thank you,' I said, tears strangling my voice.

'Oh hey, always,' she promised.

'Always,' I agreed.

My things had found their way home. Russ' things and Nico's bags were on the bed.

'Why don't you let me sort all this out. You go sit down in the living room,' he said.

So I did. I put the television on quietly to not wake the babies and no sooner had I sat than Vivi was coming in with a pot of tea.

'You've had quite an adventure, haven't you?' she smiled as she sat a minute to rest.

I lent my head on her shoulder. 'I'm glad to be home, Vivi.'

'Well, we're very glad to have you home and in one piece, my love. Now, tell me about Mr Handsome,' she chuckled.

So I did. I told her all about that amazing man who refused to let me walk away.

'I'm so happy for you. You deserve to be loved again.'

'So do you, Vivi,' I told her. She had her lovely life and her naughty misadventures with lots of lovely men, but she'd cut herself off from love for a long time too.

'Oh, you hush now,' she said, patting my hand but I could feel her smiling and I knew she had a story to tell. But she disappeared before I could ask her as Mrs Donovan hollered for her from the bottom of the stairs but she left me with a smile and my pot of tea.

I went downstairs later and sat in a booth with Russ. Ainsley had given Russ' credit card a workout in preparation for our homecoming, and among the many purchases had picked up a baby monitor so we put it on the table to keep an eye on the babies and Mrs Donovan brought us tea. We watched the people coming and going. Russ brought the babies down when they woke and Mrs Donovan sat for a while with Anna.

The rush died off and Vivi left. Mrs Donovan soon after. Natalie had a handle of the machines so Ainsley sat for a while, did some paperwork with Anna on her knee.

'Go home, we've got it,' I told her.

'No, no, we're fine,' she insisted as Anna fussed.

'Look at Natalie, she's a pro, we got it, Ains, go be with your family.'

She hesitated but at Russ' nod she gave in and left.

Russ took Nico upstairs for a feed and I sat, flipping through a discarded magazine while Natalie took care of things. I walked upstairs with her after we locked up.

'Alright, good night,' she said at the landing.

'No, wait a second. You have to eat something.'

'Oh I can just Uber Eats something,' she said.

'Natalie, you're family now and families eat together,' I told her. 'I bet Mrs Donovan has stashed some food in my freezer,' I suggested.

When Natalie eventually agreed, I led us down the hallway and into the kitchen.

I was right, there was a lasagne in the fridge ready and waiting for us so Russ put it in the oven to heat and I made us all some tea while we waited.

We sat around the table, Russ jigging Nico on his knee, Natalie and me. It was a family, a strange, crazy, beautiful little family.

'You all set up?' I asked Natalie.

'Yeah, thanks.'

'I know there's not much up there. You can turn one of the other rooms into a living room if you want to and you can come down here to the kitchen any time. I want you to think of this as your place too. You're never intruding, okay,' I told her.

'Thank you,' she said and I could see that meant more to her than she was letting on.

After we ate, Natalie called it a night and went upstairs and I led Russ to my bed. I sat on the edge trying to take off my shoes and he knelt on the floor in front of me.

'What are you doing?' I asked, thinking surely I could manage. It might take a while but I would manage.

'You know how we were saying no regrets, live every second like it's our last?' he asked as though I might have forgotten.

'Yes,' I answered anyway.

'Well, this is me living every second like it might be our last and if I were to die, I wouldn't want to die without having asked you to marry me.'

'What? You've lost your bloody mind,' I told him.

He laughed. 'I know, it's crazy and it makes no sense. But we know how fragile life is. Look at Benny. Look at what happened to Lana and what almost happened to you. I almost lost you. I can't even think what would have happened if I hadn't gotten to you in time.

'I want to build a life with you, Jo, and I don't want to wait for a societally acceptable period of time to do so. I want to do it now, this second. I want to build a life with you as my wife. Whatever it is we decide to do with our lives, I want us to do it together, to raise Nico together and maybe have more babies. And when it is my time, I want my headstone to read, beloved husband of Joanne Walsh.'

'Beloved, huh?' I laughed, trying to process it all.

'Besides, we've known each other for more than three years, we've been through stuff, more stuff than most people go through in a lifetime and marrying you would be the most right thing I've ever done in my life.'

I smiled because it did feel right and whatever happened, if he were to die, I'd want it on his headstone that I loved him and I wanted my headstone to say that I was the beloved wife of Russell Whittington III. So I nodded and I grinned and he swept me into his arms.

I'd very much have liked to do wonderfully wicked things with him on Mrs May's floor but he wasn't having any of it. He scooped me up and laid me on the bed. He unbuttoned my shirt but then stopped, running his fingers over my bruised side, his other hand cupping my broken arm.

'I don't want to hurt you,' he told me.

With my good hand, I gently pulled his mouth to mine, kissing him long and slow. 'It's okay. I know none of this is sexy. We have the rest of our lives,' I told him.

He stroked one of the bruises on the side of my face. 'There is nothing you could do that would make you not sexy,' he insisted.

'And that is why I'm going to marry you,' I told him before he gently, ever so gently proved how sexy he thought I was.

Epilogue

We settled into life in the weeks that followed our return home. My bruises slowly healed and it wasn't long before the ones on my face had gone altogether. I wasn't much use to anyone until the cast came off of my arm but it meant I got to spend a lot of time with Nico.

I'd always thought about having children. Benny and I had talked about it now and again. I'd wondered some more when I saw Henry and Anna, what it would be like. I'd never imagined what it would be like to raise someone else's child though. It had never crossed my mind.

When I'd come home from the hospital and the reality of Nico being in my life for the rest of our lives hit, I wondered if I could love him enough, if I could love him as much as he deserved. Because he did deserve that. All children did. But I wasn't his mumma. I hadn't birthed him and I didn't know. I knew I could adore him, because I adored Henry and Anna, but would it be the same as a Mumma's love?

It was hard work. Even though Russ was doing a lot of the physical stuff because my arm was in a cast, but every day, I loved that little boy more. My heart near burst every time he looked at me, every time he searched for me in a room. And when he smiled at me for the first time...my heart almost stopped.

Michael Wheeler, the family lawyer, had already begun processing the paperwork for me to adopt Nico. I didn't want to replace his mumma but he needed one. We'd contacted Lana's parents and they'd sent us a beautiful photo of her from before she'd met Bodhi and a nice photo of them so we could frame them for Nico and we sent them regular updates. As he got bigger, we'd add in some face time so they could know him. They were lovely people who were heartbroken by what had happened to Lana after she'd met Bodhi. They'd thought he'd be the answer to her shyness, to help her be brave after her less than perfect early years. They'd never expected someone would do that to a nice girl who just wanted to be like everyone else. It made me wonder what he did in some of his sessions. I'd found a new healer out north, a nice lady with a special gift and I'd asked her how things could have gone so awry.

She thought when people napped, he was adding subliminal messaging to his repertoire. It was sneaky and cruel. But we all had to move on. He wouldn't be fleecing any more unsuspecting women. There was nothing else to do.

Dr Bailey was happy with my progress. He'd moved my appointments to bi monthly. If the next couple of sessions went well, he'd move them to quarterly, then every six months. Before I knew it, he'd just be a man I used to know.

He was pleased with how I was going, but it was all Russ. Somewhere deep inside my brain and my heart, I'd known all along that he would come. And he'd changed everything. I panicked now and then, worried over Benny but I had to believe there was truth in what Bodhi did and that Benny had other work to do. My other healer didn't see him when we'd had our few sessions but she saw someone, something, that brought light. I liked to think it was Lana, now at peace and grateful her son was okay, that he was getting the childhood she'd always wished for.

The day my cast came off, Ainsley helped me pick out a pretty, flowing, beige dress from David Jones, something pretty for Natalie, and then we walked across town to St Francis' where Russ and Nico waited with Christian. I didn't want a fancy frock. I'd thought I would once. I once thought I'd want the whole circus. Hundreds of people watching on, music playing as I followed four bridesmaids down the aisle. A big, over the top soiree somewhere with a ballroom full of peonies with a three course sit-down dinner, and lots of champagne and toasts, and silly speeches from a best man and my dad.

But it turned out, I didn't want any of it. Russ had offered it to me. Ainsley offered to organise the whole thing. But I just wanted to marry Russ with our two best friends, Natalie, and our son beside us, our family. I didn't want all those people and all that pomp and ceremony. The six am start for hair and makeup and this and that. I just wanted to go to the church that had been my safe place to rest, and marry Russ.

I still wasn't sure what I thought about God and religion and churches. But I believed in something. I believed in something divine, something guided and ordained and so I wanted to go to where all that accumulated, and have Father John do his official pronouncing. I guess he'd gotten me after all.

Russ had indulged me since we'd returned and the four of us continued my routine of walking to church before going over to Ainsley and Christian's for brunch on Sunday's. Father John had been surprised to see me with my instant family and when I'd asked him to marry us, he'd insisted on a sit down. He'd been watching me all those Sundays, keeping an eye on me, praying for me. He just wanted to meet Russ and make sure everything was okay. He tried again to get me to come to the later session, bring a plate, join the community, but I'd smiled and thanked him and promised him we'd christen Nico there instead. It was something we wanted to do when the adoption came through, a way to celebrate our family.

Father John stood in the grand archway in his regal looking robes with a big smile on his face and welcomed me with an engulfing hug. We all walked down the aisle together without any pomp, the empty mahogany pews on either side, the grand altar in front of us, the beautiful stained-glass windows above, and it was more perfect than I'd imagined.

It was a simple ceremony just as I'd wanted it to be. Just us. No elaborate vows, just the predetermined I-dos. We exchanged simple gold bands and Father John did his pronouncing with a big smile.

I walked back up the aisle looking at the band on my finger, it was simple but beautiful because of what it represented. My love for Russ. Our commitment to each other. Until death do us part. It was simple and clean and perfect. I'd refused an engagement ring, insisting Russ put the money towards the house we wanted to buy, despite him telling me he had more than enough money for both. We needed somewhere for Nico.

We needed a car and we couldn't keep one at the café. I didn't need an engagement ring.

We began the walk back. Stopped at my Sunday morning café for coffee, then kept walking. I smiled the whole way. The sun was shining. Spring was finally here. People had a little more pep in their step and I had everything.

A few months ago, everyone had been so worried about me, worried I wasn't moving on, worried I was wasting away up there in that apartment. Maybe I had been. I don't know. I'd felt fine. I'd felt okay. I'd gotten up every day and I enjoyed the work I did and the people I met. But I had been afraid. I'd been afraid to let go. Afraid of what letting go meant. But Benny would always be in my heart. He made me who I was. We shared something special, something beautiful and I'd never forget him, never stop loving him. I couldn't imagine now though, living the rest of my life without Russ, without Nico and Natalie. We were a family.

I was glad Ainsley had sent me to the pub, glad she'd seen Russ on the pub's Facebook page and weaved her magic with Jaz. So much had happened, so many awful things but I'd always be grateful. Grateful for the beach and the space to think, grateful for Jaz and her kindness and her wisdom. Grateful for Natalie and her friendship. Grateful for the healing and the chance to meditate. Grateful for the chance to let go.

Now I had the very best friends a girl could have in Ainsley and Christian, walking next to me. Russ' arm draped across my shoulder. Natalie pushing Nico's pram as though she were his loving big sister. I laid my head on Russ' shoulder and thought

I might have been the luckiest girl in the world. I'd wondered when Ainsley had had Anna how a person could feel that much joy. Now I knew.

Not everyone had been thrilled with the idea of me marrying a man I'd seemingly just met. I understood, I did. One minute I was a hermit refusing to let go of Benny, two weeks later I'm announcing my engagement to a man they'd never heard of. I would have sounded insane.

My parents thought I'd lost my mind but on Mum's first visit after I'd returned home, she was begging Russ to never leave me because she couldn't believe how much I'd changed. She saw how he adored me and what mother wouldn't want that for their child?

A few days after she'd returned back to the farm, gifts started arriving for Nico. A stuffed cow. Cow onesies and cow rattles. I had no idea where she was finding it all but I didn't care, and Nico looked adorable. Every time something arrived, I sent her photos of him and she was every bit the proud Grandma.

Russ' very practical cop Dad nearly lost his mind until he saw us together, saw how much better Russ was. Mrs Whittington couldn't have cared about anything we did as long as she had Nico in front of her. It was love at first sight for them both and he'd been just what she needed after she'd been so worried about Russ. So we eventually got their blessing.

Poor Mrs Donovan had to sit down and have a cup of tea. But Ainsley and Christian were thrilled. Vivi and Natalie were thrilled.

They were all there waiting for us in the café when we returned, even my brother had taken a night away from the beloved farm to come and wish me well. Mrs Donovan had been minding baby Anna and Henry for the day. Henry ran through the crowd to us when we came in as though we'd been trekking for days. He gave us all lovely hugs and was already running around in his lovely little suit calling Russ, Uncle Russ as though he'd known him his whole life.

Our resident Russian-in-perpetual-morning stayed and stole baby Nico and sat in her booth cooing to him and nodding her approval at our soiree. She tapped her foot to the music and smiled. I wondered what she really thought of it all?

Once, Mrs May had held the most magnificent parties in the café. Vivi had told us all about them. She'd gone to one, by accident. The ladies had worn the fanciest dresses and were dripping with diamonds. The men had worn lovely suits, smoked cigars and drank vodka while playing cards. The ladies drank champagne and Mrs May would provide special ladies for when the gentleman needed to let off some steam. But her parties had always been a who's who of the underworld, Vivi said. It was hard to imagine now but I hoped we were doing her proud. Despite the lack of extra-curricular offerings, people were swilling fancy sparkling wine and eating lovely canapes cooked by the chef from Christian's fancy new hotel.

When she'd had her fill of excitement and it was time for her to leave, our resident Russian-in-perpetual-mourning came over, reached up with both hands, held my face and kissed each of my cheeks. 'You be happy. You deserve happy,' she said, tapped my face and left, her comfortable black shoes squelching as she went. She'd become a part of our lives, our family. Someday we'd get to know more about her.

Russ and I were still living above the café. I'd helped him set up a private investigation business. Christian rented him an office in the building he used as his home base, but I loved working at the café too much to give it up altogether.

Natalie was still living in one of the rooms upstairs. She was a part of our family. Even though she wasn't that much younger than me. We'd have adopted her if we could and she knew how much she meant to us. She'd be starting a degree in psychology at the next uni intake and I was glad everything that had happened with Bodhi hadn't stolen that from her.

In the meantime, she'd been working full time in the café so Ainsley could spend time with her kids until I was back to full strength. She'd stay on part time while she was studying so I could help raise Nico and Russ could go full steam ahead with his business. He'd been waiting until I was well enough, treating me like a china doll and doing most of the Nico work himself. But I was well now and we could all start living our lives.

We'd found a house we loved and were waiting to see if our offer would be accepted. But we weren't in a hurry, we had time. If it wasn't that house, it would be another. The right one for our family would come when the time was right. And when we did move, we'd hand Mrs May's apartment over to Natalie but for now, Natalie was better for having us there.

I looked over to where she was dancing with Henry. Her hair was in a ponytail. She wore a pretty sky-blue dress with a cardigan but the pain of her past had eased. You could see it in the way she smiled and the way she laughed with Henry. She was going to be okay.

Time passed, I danced and I laughed, Ainsley, Russ and I had a vodka shot for old times, then she left to dance with her family.

'Well, Mrs Walsh-Whittington, are you ready to go?' Russ asked.

The party was dying down. People were leaving. Henry was asleep on the bench. Russ' parents were bundling up Nico for a much-anticipated sleepover. It was time to go. Christian had given us a room at his hotel for the night as one of their wedding gifts. He'd also organised a week away for our new little family in his very lovely Whitsundays hotel.

'I am indeed, Mr Whittington. I'd very much like to go and do naughty things to my husband,' I said.

He let out a loud belly laugh that made my blood zing with happiness. 'Well, I'm sure your husband would very much like you to do naughty things to him,' he smiled before leaning down to kiss me as though he, himself, had planned for some very naughty marital shenanigans. I think I was going to like living every second like it might be our last.

ALEXANDRA DEEN

A Harrington Family Story

Alexandra DEEN

TAMARA MARTIN

B eside me, the River Seine bubbled like a witch's brew. Fat raindrops soaked my clothes, chilling me right through to the bone. Tears streaked what remained of my make up and I was glad I couldn't see my own face. I'd become a version of myself I no longer recognised. Not just in the last couple of hours, but the last few years if I were honest. If I were brave enough to face the reality of who I'd become, who I'd allowed myself to become because it would be easier. It was expected.

The streets of the most romantic city in the world were

suspiciously quiet, as though it were ashamed it hadn't lived up to the hype. My feet hurt, from the cold, from the wet, from poorly chosen pretty ballet flats. I shivered, unable to stop the quivering of my lip.

A car horn blared, my heart near leapt from my chest.

I stepped back onto the kerb. 'Pay attention, Lexi,' I scolded myself. Billy bloody McCrae certainly wasn't worth getting run down on a dark Parisian street. So my life was officially in the gutter, it wasn't reason enough to die. Or worse, end up in a Parisian hospital all alone and having to call my mother to come and get me.

Catching my breath, I wiped my tear-stained face, checked the street for traffic and trundled across the road towards the music, the laughter, the dry roof of the hostel matching the map on the now bedraggled pamphlet in my hand.

I was angry and sad and so disappointed the weight of it crushed my lungs, stealing my breath as I stood before the big blue doors, the rain falling in sheets around me, my clothes soaked and heavy. I watched a piece of peeling paint flapping in the breeze, resisting the urge to pull at it and wondered if I should I knock on the door or should I just walk in? I'd never stayed in such a place before, somewhere without a doorman to direct me. Was there an etiquette I should have been aware of? The paint chipped doors suggested etiquette didn't rule this little corner of Paris.

Looking for guidance, for something, I spotted a girl with wild black curls sitting on the balustrade of a small verandah heaving with jovial young people, drinking beer from bottles, unaware the world was full of misery and cheating bastard boyfriends. She laughed, her whole body shaking from the happiness. I wondered if it would feel as good as it looked, to laugh that way, to be that happy. I wondered if I'd ever been that happy. If I'd ever laughed that freely. I couldn't remember.

The girl looked over her sun-kissed shoulder, smiled and nodded towards the door. I turned away, embarrassed. What was wrong with me? I don't stand on streets in the middle of the night, lurking, staring at strangers. I was losing my bloody mind.

I sucked in a deep, fortifying breath. It wasn't a palatial hotel with marble floors, but it would do until I could get the hell out of Paris, I reminded myself and pulled open the door.

The foyer was sparse but clean and dry. A worn timber chair sat beneath a phone attached to the wall. A staircase opposite wound its way up into the hidden heart of the hostel. The well-worn reception desk was directly in front. Behind the desk, sat a girl with red hair so bright it almost glowed, framing a face as perfect as porcelain. The girl chuckled at something Homer Simpson said in French on the television beside her, completely oblivious or perhaps purposely ignoring the fact that I'd just stumbled in and was dripping all over the streaked timber floor.

I walked towards the desk, my shoes squelching loudly in the quiet, my insides cringing from embarrassment. She finally looked up from the television as I reached the counter, raising her eyebrows, trying not to smile at the makeup streaked all over my face and hair stuck to my head like paint and dripping all over her counter.

'Dorm or single, hon?' she asked with a poetic French accent.

'Whatever's cheapest?' I stammered, tears choking my vocal chords as I pulled scrunched, damp euros from my handbag.

'Dorm it is, then. Room two, bunk three.' She put a key attached to a block of wood atop a pile of linen and a towel and handed the pile over the counter as though I were an army recruit reporting for duty. She sent me up the stairs with no further question, as though I'd stood before her in a sundress in the middle of the afternoon instead of a drowned, miserable version of a person in the middle of the night. But maybe that's what happened in places like this? Vagrants, society's misfits and those spat out by the world, appeared at all hours so often, it was accepted as the norm?

Four bunk beds had been crammed into the room she sent me to, each flanked at the foot with a metal locker. Flimsy curtains covered the long, short, rectangular windows that were too high up to see out of. The dull light from the bulb hidden under the white plastic shade on the ceiling wasn't dull enough to hide the worn timber floor covered with the debris of the room's missing inhabitants; a discarded towel, a pair of thongs, backpacks, socks and a navy blue hoodie.

They had squeezed the tiniest bathroom I'd ever seen into the far corner, just big enough for a toilet, basin and shower. It was a far cry from the fancy hotel I'd woken in with its giant bathtub and shiny white tiles and luxury complimentary bath products, but it didn't matter. Not much mattered right now other than getting through the night and thinking about tomorrow when tomorrow showed up.

As I organised my things, my mind flashed to the morning when I'd strolled the streets of Paris, the bridges that arched over the Seine, hand in hand, happy, in love. I'd seen the Eiffel Tower rising above the trees in the distance, wondered if it would be there that Billy would sink to one knee on the grass and ask me to be his wife. I'd have said yes, too. I'd been a fool. Of course I'd been a fool. I'd been a fool for years. Now I had to find the strength to go home and face my family, my friends. What friends? They'd all known, I'd seen it on their faces in the fancy Parisian restaurant where we were dining, when my life had unravelled at my feet. They'd eaten dinner in my home, eaten my food and drunk my wine laughing in my face, laughing behind my back.

No, they were Billy's friends and he could keep them. I didn't want them. Friends don't allow you to be blindsided in foreign countries. Friends save you, they protect you, they look out for you. They don't just sit back and watch your life crumble. No, I had no friends. I didn't have much of anything now. Perhaps just the scrap of dignity I'd held onto when I'd told Billy to go to hell and walked out of the fancy restaurant where he'd sat with that woman draped across his lap and the revelations had unfolded, piece by piece in seconds but what had felt like hours. I'd walked out with nothing, no friends, no savings, nowhere to go, nothing.

I dug around in my suitcase for something to wear to bed but almost everything was damp. I knew I should have bought the one with the hard shell case, I thought to myself as I began pulling things out. After hanging my wet clothes over the edges of my bed, over my suitcase, from the open locker door, I squeezed between the bunks to the bathroom. The cubicle was small but the water was hot and I thawed, movement returning to my fingertips and toes. I leant on the wall, letting the hot water beat on my body, glad to be feeling something other than devastation or misery or self hatred.

Careful not to overuse the hot water, I reluctantly stepped out of the shower, my bones finally warmed, my skin red, raw, and shiny new. I threw on an almost dry t-shirt and undies, already imagining the sweet perfection of the warm bed and the desperate bout of indulgent wallowing that waited.

With my towel and wet clothes gathered in my arms, I squeezed between the bunks and found the girl with the wild black curls sitting on my bed, absently picking at a hang nail and swinging her leg as though to a tune only she could hear.

She looked up as I dropped my loot onto my suitcase.

'Hey,' she said in an Australian accent, holding out a bottle of beer.

'Hello,' I replied as though in question, but taking the beer she offered anyway.

'You alright?' she asked.

I shrugged.

'Wanna talk about it?' she asked.

'Not really.'

'That means you really should. It'd be better than wallowing or letting it eat you up all night. It might help you sleep at least,' she offered.

I shrugged. She had some good points and really, what did I have to lose? Pride? I couldn't lose much more and maybe once I hit bottom I could start building myself back up. Somehow.

'I got duped, that's all. Utterly blindsided. The man I loved wasn't who I thought he was. My friends let me down, let me fall. I just, I don't know, my head's still spinning.'

'Are there actual details in there? Come on, sit, spit them out, otherwise you'll keep seeing them every time you close your eyes.'

'I sure as hell don't need that,' I laughed, surprising myself. 'We came for a wedding. We were at dinner with some of our friends. I went to the toilet, stopped to take a phone call from mum. I'd called her earlier but forgot the time difference. Anyway, we only talked for a few minutes. When I came back into the restaurant, there was this girl, I'd seen her a couple of times at the footy, never paid her any attention, knew she knew some of our friends but had no idea her and Billy knew each other as anything more than passing acquaintances. I'll never forget her, tall, lanky, all arms and legs, Kardashian hair and a laugh like a strangled hyena. She was draped all over my boyfriend. His hands were all over her and his face was buried in her hair. I don't know what he was doing, kissing her neck, whispering something. I don't know. I just froze and when he saw me he just laughed. He was drunk I guess, just enough to not care what I saw or what he said. Suggested a ménage a trois. Said it'd be very French of us.'

'What did your friends do?'

'They just sat there. Fuckers,' I laughed, taking a long sip of cold beer.

'Fuckers,' agreed my new friend, tapping her bottle to mine.

'She wasn't the only one. She laughed when I thought she was. Then it all began falling into place, the late nights, the 2am showers, the unanswered calls and I asked the questions. Turns out he's been all over the place with anyone who'd take him for years. None of it was real. We weren't real and I just don't know who I am now without him. Everything has been him. Everything I'd planned for the rest of my life had been with him. Now it's just me and I don't know what to do. He chose everything, decided everything and I let him because he was usually right and it was easier than hearing I told you so. So I let him and now I feel so stupid and lost.'

'Did you notice you never said you loved him or that your heart was broken? You've just been humiliated and horribly inconvenienced,' she smiled.

'Really? Huh,' I mumbled, realising she was exactly right. I was pissed off. I was annoyed. I was afraid and utterly humiliated. But I wasn't sad. I wasn't brokenhearted. How was that possible? I'd loved him, didn't I? We shared a home, a bed, a future. I'd planned babies and old age with him. I had to have loved him. But this bringer of beer and kind shoulders was right, my heart didn't feel broken. I wanted to wallow but I didn't feel the need to cry for him. I'd cried from the surprise, the devastation, for who I'd become, but the thought of never seeing Billy again, never having to listen to his obnoxious lectures or be bossed around, left me with nothing but relief.

As I finished my beer, my new friend said, 'Come on, plenty more of those downstairs. Your new life starts now. A new life where you're in charge,' she smiled.

I liked the sound of that.

'We'll be gentle, I promise,' she offered, holding her hand out to me.

I took her hand and let her pull me up.

'I'm Lydia,' she said, finally introducing herself.

'Alexandra.'

'Come on Alex, let's go see if you're in there somewhere.'

I laughed, forgiving her for the choice of nickname. I hated Alex, it was a boy's name. My friends and family call me Lexi, but for one night, what did it matter? For one night I could be anyone and at that moment I was pretty done with Lexi the lovely doormat.

I followed Lydia onto the verandah and into the throng of people still enjoying the night and thanked my beer buzz when she called everyone to attention, commanding the spotlight.

'Alex, this is everyone. Everyone, this is Alex. She needs beer and kindness and it's our duty as fellow travelers, to provide her with both,' she insisted as I tried smiling.

Mumbles of agreement followed sympathetic nods. Beers were passed forward through the crowd of people with words of sympathy and welcome. Lydia draped a kind, friendly, comforting arm around me and led me to the balustrade she'd occupied earlier.

'What a bastard. Forget him,' Lydia said. 'Everything will be better now you've left him, you'll see. You'll pick yourself back up and find a new way now you've found the strength to stand up for yourself.'

'He has to be a real asshole to bring you all this way and then do that,' claimed a bright, bubbly girl with blonde dreadlocks when Lydia told her my boyfriend had turned out to be an ass. She was another Aussie. In fact, they mostly seemed to be Aussies, like the hostel was a magnet for lost Aussie souls, although I seemed to be the only one truly lost.

'Thanks,' I said, taking deep breaths, waiting for the tears welling in my eyes to evaporate. It would take some getting used to, figuring out who I was without him, thinking of how I would move forward alone, it had all happened so suddenly it was a lot to comprehend. Six years with the same man was a long time. He's all I knew, we'd been together my entire adult life.

A few beers in and I couldn't believe the world I'd landed in. These people spoke of adventures and places that sounded too good to be true, surfing in places I'd never heard of, finding treasure in small European towns where no one spoke English, cycling along the coastline in remote villages, the sun kissing their skin, falling in love, eating incredible food. They laughed loud, they wore simple cotton summer dresses and crazy board shorts, the men with permanent five o'clock shadows, living in a world so far removed from my grey cubicle and suburban life back home that I could hardly comprehend any of it and now here they were, welcoming me into their fold, commiserating with me over beers as though we were old friends.

I leant on the balustrade, looking out over the dark road, slick and wet under the moon's bright rays now the clouds had moved on. Had I really stood out there on the footpath in the rain? Now I was dry and warm and comforted, sipping cold beer amongst the laughter and camaraderie, I couldn't believe that had been me. Who was that person? In fact, who was that person I'd become over the last six years? Not someone I recognised. Not someone I particularly liked and I hadn't even realised it was happening. Somewhere it'd just been easier to give me up and go with the flow, abide by everyone else's expectations, my boss, my mother, Billy. I didn't even know which bits were me and which were Billy. All I knew was Lydia was right. It was time to find out who I was.

'What's with all the thinking?' asked Lydia, twisting the top off another beer.

'Oh, nothing,' I half smiled. 'Just thinking how different the day's ended to how I'd expected.'

'Yeah, life does that,' she smiled.

'I've been here one bloody day and my life's been turned upside down. How does that even happen? This trip was not supposed to go this way.'

'Maybe it was and you just didn't realise it. The universe has a way of kicking us up the behind when we don't pay attention.'

I laughed a huffy laugh because she was probably right. 'It was easy to ignore it all.'

'Isn't it always,' she grinned. 'Until the kicking comes and you have no choice.'

'So, what are your plans from here?' a man asked, joining us at the balustrade.

I turned away from the rain soaked street, looked up and our eyes locked. It was him. My knight, my saviour who'd given me the pamphlet that had led me here. The waiter with the sun bleached shaggy hair, broad shoulders, wide smile and laughing grey green eyes that knew things, that loved things, that loved life. He wore a loose fitting, faded yellow tank top with bright, multi-coloured board shorts and blue thongs on his sun drenched feet.

The sun had soaked his body, from his biceps to his beautiful broad shoulders. I tried not to look but my eyes wanted to linger, to drink him in. Where did men that beautiful even come from? What was I even doing noticing? I was supposed to be crying into my beer not admiring handsome strangers that help damsels in distress find refuge. But for just one second, everything stood still and my breath caught in my chest.

'You?' I asked softly.

He smiled.

'You know each other?' Lydia asked.

I wanted to laugh, as if I know men that look like him. Billy was alright, handsome enough, a good catch even, so everyone kept telling me, but Billy had nothing on this bloke. This bloke was tall, slightly rugged, his strong jaw covered lightly in stubble, everything about him was strong, then there was his lovely mouth and puppy dog eyes that smiled without trying. I mentally shook my head clear to stop from staring.

'It was my restaurant she was at earlier,' he told Lydia. 'Well not mine,' he said to me, 'the one where I was working. Just filling in actually, not really my thing waiting tables, prefer pouring beers, but a mate needed a favour, they were short and needed a hand.'

'Well, thanks,' I said. 'I've no idea where I'd have gone without the pamphlet you gave me.'

'Oh a regular knight, huh,' joked Lydia.

'I'm Tom by the way,' he smiled, his whole face lighting up as though lit from the inside by his own personal sun. Then, his right bicep flexed beautifully as he stretched his arm around Lydia's shoulders, draping it there casually, as though he'd done it a thousand times. I felt my heart sink all the way down to my toes.

Don't be ridiculous, I told myself. Of course he has a girlfriend. What was wrong with me? What was wrong with my brain? I'd just left Billy, the supposed love of my life, the man I'd shared intimate moments with, cared for when he was sick, gone to birthday parties with, hosted barbeques with, told all my deepest secrets and wishes to, the man I'd expected a bloody proposal from under the Eiffel Tower. My head was still spinning with everything that had happened, where I'd ended up, what lay ahead. I couldn't fancy someone else already. My traumatised brain was just confused, that was all.

'Um, I'll see if I can get a flight home in the morning, I suppose,' I said, answering Tom's question

'Home? No!' cried Lydia. 'You're in Paris, Alex. You've only been here a day. You can't go yet. This is one of the most beautiful cities you'll ever see.'

I shrugged. She was right. But I was short on funds now I had a life to rebuild and really, no inclination to wander the streets alone.

'You know what you should do,' Tom said, looking at Lydia as though he'd solved the most intricate puzzles of the universe.

'Absolutely!' she cried, reading his mind.

I watched them, waiting for an explanation.

'Come down the coast with us, Alex. Oh you have to. It's just what you need, a bit of sun and sand, the ocean will heal all those wounds and you'll be good as new in no time. France is incredible, you can't miss out now that you're here. Please.

Please say oui,' Lydia begged, gripping my arm in anticipation.

'What? No, no. We just met. You don't want me imposing on your trip,' I insisted, despite how nice the prospect of forgetting my life and laying on a beach in a foreign country sounded.

'Don't be ridiculous, the more the merrier. We'd love you to come with us. I promise, we're relatively normal, non murdering types, you have to come and balance out all the testosterone,' she insisted with a smile that left me both nervous and more excited than I could remember ever being.

'We have a car,' Tom added proudly.

'That's so nice, really it is but I don't think my failing funds will allow me to stay much longer than tonight anyway, I'm afraid. This was Billy's trip. He paid for the flights, the accommodation. I've just got a little spending money for bits and bobs, souvenirs, snacks, maybe a dinner or two, that sort of thing,' I admitted sadly.

'That doesn't matter,' Lydia said, waving my worries away. 'None of us have any money, but we get by, that's half the fun.'

'Really?' I couldn't believe it. They were all so happy. They didn't look hungry and the travel stories they'd shared in the last hour were so mind blowing they didn't even seem real; how could they all have no money? Living the life they lived cost money, surely? Billy and I had spent nights planning and budgeting for this trip. But what if all this time I'd had it backwards? 'But how?' I had to ask.

'Ah, you have to come for us to share all our secrets,' Lydia winked, laughing.

'C'mon, Alex, it'll be fun. You need some fun. We leave first thing tomorrow and it's just for a few days. It will cost next to nothing, I promise. We have a spare bed in the villa, and I am pretty sure it has your name on it,' Tom insisted.

'You can't go home yet, you have to come,' begged Lydia.

All the usual thoughts ran through my head again as though on repeat. Blah, blah, blah. What I really wanted to do was blow off my life and go to the bloody beach with this group of the coolest, most amazing people I'd ever met. To have the much needed fun Tom spoke of. To lay in the sun and pretend none of it had happened, that I hadn't been so humiliated I was afraid to look people in the eye. Forget it all and laugh. It'd been so long since I'd just let go and laughed, I'd forgotten what it felt like. These people were reminding me and I wasn't ready to let it go, to go back.

So, after taking a long sip of beer for courage, I ignored that annoying voice in my head, the one that had led me down this path in the first place. 'Fine, fine, okay, *oui*,' I agreed, panicking as soon as the words were out despite my newfound courage and resolution.

I couldn't drive to some French coast with these people. I'd just met them. It was crazy. Lydia was crazy. Tom was crazy. They were all crazy. But it did seem silly to waste the airfare Billy had paid for and they were right, I was in Paris, anything was possible in Paris, right? – **buy your copy now to keep reading.**

B eside me, the River Seine bubbled like a witch's brew. Fat raindrops soaked my clothes, chilling me right through to the bone. Tears streaked what remained of my make up and I was glad I couldn't see my own face. I'd become a version of myself I no longer recognised. Not just in the last couple of hours, but the last few years if I were honest. If I were brave enough to face the reality of who I'd become, who I'd allowed myself to become because it would be easier. It was expected.

The streets of the most romantic city in the world were suspiciously quiet, as though it were ashamed it hadn't lived up to the hype. My feet hurt, from the cold, from the wet, from poorly chosen pretty ballet flats. I shivered, unable to stop the quivering of my lip.

A car horn blared, my heart near leapt from my chest.

I stepped back onto the kerb. 'Pay attention, Lexi,' I scolded myself. Billy bloody McCrae certainly wasn't worth getting run down on a dark Parisian street. So my life was officially in the gutter, it wasn't reason enough to die. Or worse, end up in a Parisian hospital all alone and having to call my mother to come and get me.

Catching my breath, I wiped my tear-stained face, checked the street for traffic and trundled across the road towards the music, the laughter, the dry roof of the hostel matching the map on the now bedraggled pamphlet in my hand.

I was angry and sad and so disappointed the weight of it crushed my lungs, stealing my breath as I stood before the big blue doors, the rain falling in sheets around me, my clothes soaked and heavy. I watched a piece of peeling paint flapping in the breeze, resisting the urge to pull at it and wondered if I should I knock on the door or should I just walk in? I'd never stayed in such a place before, somewhere without a doorman to direct me. Was there an etiquette I should have been aware of? The paint chipped doors suggested etiquette didn't rule this little corner of Paris.

Looking for guidance, for something, I spotted a girl with

wild black curls sitting on the balustrade of a small verandah heaving with jovial young people, drinking beer from bottles, unaware the world was full of misery and cheating bastard boyfriends. She laughed, her whole body shaking from the happiness. I wondered if it would feel as good as it looked, to laugh that way, to be that happy. I wondered if I'd ever been that happy. If I'd ever laughed that freely. I couldn't remember.

The girl looked over her sun-kissed shoulder, smiled and nodded towards the door. I turned away, embarrassed. What was wrong with me? I don't stand on streets in the middle of the night, lurking, staring at strangers. I was losing my bloody mind.

I sucked in a deep, fortifying breath. It wasn't a palatial hotel with marble floors, but it would do until I could get the hell out of Paris, I reminded myself and pulled open the door.

The foyer was sparse but clean and dry. A worn timber chair sat beneath a phone attached to the wall. A staircase opposite wound its way up into the hidden heart of the hostel. The well-worn reception desk was directly in front. Behind the desk, sat a girl with red hair so bright it almost glowed, framing a face as perfect as porcelain. The girl chuckled at something Homer Simpson said in French on the television beside her, completely oblivious or perhaps purposely ignoring the fact that I'd just stumbled in and was dripping all over the streaked timber floor.

I walked towards the desk, my shoes squelching loudly in the quiet, my insides cringing from embarrassment. She finally looked up from the television as I reached the counter, raising her eyebrows, trying not to smile at the makeup streaked all over my face and hair stuck to my head like paint and dripping all over her counter.

'Dorm or single, hon?' she asked with a poetic French accent.

'Whatever's cheapest?' I stammered, tears choking my vocal chords as I pulled scrunched, damp euros from my handbag.

'Dorm it is, then. Room two, bunk three.' She put a key attached to a block of wood atop a pile of linen and a towel and handed the pile over the counter as though I were an army recruit reporting for duty. She sent me up the stairs with no further question, as though I'd stood before her in a sundress in the middle of the afternoon instead of a drowned, miserable version of a person in the middle of the night. But maybe that's what happened in places like this? Vagrants, society's misfits and those spat out by the world, appeared at all hours so often, it was accepted as the norm?

Four bunk beds had been crammed into the room she sent me to, each flanked at the foot with a metal locker. Flimsy curtains covered the long, short, rectangular windows that were too high up to see out of. The dull light from the bulb hidden under the white plastic shade on the ceiling wasn't dull enough to hide the worn timber floor covered with the debris of the room's missing inhabitants; a discarded towel, a pair of thongs, backpacks, socks and a navy blue hoodie.

They had squeezed the tiniest bathroom I'd ever seen into the far corner, just big enough for a toilet, basin and shower. It was a far cry from the fancy hotel I'd woken in with its giant bathtub and shiny white tiles and luxury complimentary bath products, but it didn't matter. Not much mattered right now other than getting through the night and thinking about tomorrow when tomorrow showed up.

As I organised my things, my mind flashed to the morning when I'd strolled the streets of Paris, the bridges that arched over the Seine, hand in hand, happy, in love. I'd seen the Eiffel Tower rising above the trees in the distance, wondered if it would be there that Billy would sink to one knee on the grass and ask me to be his wife. I'd have said yes, too. I'd been a fool. Of course I'd been a fool. I'd been a fool for years. Now I had to find the strength to go home and face my family, my friends. What friends? They'd all known, I'd seen it on their faces in the fancy Parisian restaurant where we were dining, when my life had unravelled at my feet. They'd eaten dinner in my home, eaten my food and drunk my wine laughing in my face, laughing behind my back.

No, they were Billy's friends and he could keep them. I didn't want them. Friends don't allow you to be blindsided in foreign countries. Friends save you, they protect you, they look out for you. They don't just sit back and watch your life crumble. No, I had no friends. I didn't have much of anything now. Perhaps just the scrap of dignity I'd held onto when I'd told Billy to go to hell and walked out of the fancy restaurant where he'd sat with that woman draped across his lap and the revelations had unfolded, piece by piece in seconds but what had felt like hours. I'd walked out with nothing, no friends, no savings, nowhere to go, nothing.

I dug around in my suitcase for something to wear to bed but almost everything was damp. I knew I should have bought the one with the hard shell case, I thought to myself as I began pulling things out. After hanging my wet clothes over the edges of my bed, over my suitcase, from the open locker door, I squeezed between the bunks to the bathroom. The cubicle was small but the water was hot and I thawed, movement returning to my fingertips and toes. I leant on the wall, letting the hot water beat on my body, glad to be feeling something other than devastation or misery or self hatred.

Careful not to overuse the hot water, I reluctantly stepped out of the shower, my bones finally warmed, my skin red, raw, and shiny new. I threw on an almost dry t-shirt and undies, already imagining the sweet perfection of the warm bed and the desperate bout of indulgent wallowing that waited.

With my towel and wet clothes gathered in my arms, I squeezed between the bunks and found the girl with the wild black curls sitting on my bed, absently picking at a hang nail and swinging her leg as though to a tune only she could hear.

She looked up as I dropped my loot onto my suitcase.

'Hey,' she said in an Australian accent, holding out a bottle of beer.

'Hello,' I replied as though in question, but taking the beer she offered anyway.

'You alright?' she asked.

I shrugged.

'Wanna talk about it?' she asked.

'Not really.'

'That means you really should. It'd be better than wallowing or letting it eat you up all night. It might help you sleep at least,' she offered.

I shrugged. She had some good points and really, what did I

have to lose? Pride? I couldn't lose much more and maybe once I hit bottom I could start building myself back up. Somehow.

'I got duped, that's all. Utterly blindsided. The man I loved wasn't who I thought he was. My friends let me down, let me fall. I just, I don't know, my head's still spinning.'

'Are there actual details in there? Come on, sit, spit them out, otherwise you'll keep seeing them every time you close your eyes.'

'I sure as hell don't need that,' I laughed, surprising myself. 'We came for a wedding. We were at dinner with some of our friends. I went to the toilet, stopped to take a phone call from mum. I'd called her earlier but forgot the time difference. Anyway, we only talked for a few minutes. When I came back into the restaurant, there was this girl, I'd seen her a couple of times at the footy, never paid her any attention, knew she knew some of our friends but had no idea her and Billy knew each other as anything more than passing acquaintances. I'll never forget her, tall, lanky, all arms and legs, Kardashian hair and a laugh like a strangled hyena. She was draped all over my boyfriend. His hands were all over her and his face was buried in her hair. I don't know what he was doing, kissing her neck, whispering something. I don't know. I just froze and when he saw me he just laughed. He was drunk I guess, just enough to not care what I saw or what he said. Suggested a ménage a trois. Said it'd be very French of us.'

'What did your friends do?'

'They just sat there. Fuckers,' I laughed, taking a long sip of cold beer.

'Fuckers,' agreed my new friend, tapping her bottle to mine.

'She wasn't the only one. She laughed when I thought she was. Then it all began falling into place, the late nights, the 2am showers, the unanswered calls and I asked the questions. Turns out he's been all over the place with anyone who'd take him for years. None of it was real. We weren't real and I just don't know who I am now without him. Everything has been him. Everything I'd planned for the rest of my life had been with him. Now it's just me and I don't know what to do. He chose everything, decided everything and I let him because he was usually right and it was easier than hearing I told you so. So I let him and now I feel so stupid and lost.'

'Did you notice you never said you loved him or that your heart was broken? You've just been humiliated and horribly inconvenienced,' she smiled.

'Really? Huh,' I mumbled, realising she was exactly right. I was pissed off. I was annoyed. I was afraid and utterly humiliated. But I wasn't sad. I wasn't brokenhearted. How was that possible? I'd loved him, didn't I? We shared a home, a bed, a future. I'd planned babies and old age with him. I had to have loved him. But this bringer of beer and kind shoulders was right, my heart didn't feel broken. I wanted to wallow but I didn't feel the need to cry for him. I'd cried from the surprise, the devastation, for who I'd become, but the thought of never seeing Billy again, never having to listen to his obnoxious lectures or be bossed around, left me with nothing but relief.

As I finished my beer, my new friend said, 'Come on, plenty more of those downstairs. Your new life starts now. A new life where you're in charge,' she smiled.

I liked the sound of that.

'We'll be gentle, I promise,' she offered, holding her hand out to me.

I took her hand and let her pull me up.

'I'm Lydia,' she said, finally introducing herself.

'Alexandra.'

'Come on Alex, let's go see if you're in there somewhere.'

I laughed, forgiving her for the choice of nickname. I hated Alex, it was a boy's name. My friends and family call me Lexi, but for one night, what did it matter? For one night I could be anyone and at that moment I was pretty done with Lexi the lovely doormat.

I followed Lydia onto the verandah and into the throng of people still enjoying the night and thanked my beer buzz when she called everyone to attention, commanding the spotlight.

'Alex, this is everyone. Everyone, this is Alex. She needs beer and kindness and it's our duty as fellow travelers, to provide her with both,' she insisted as I tried smiling.

Mumbles of agreement followed sympathetic nods. Beers were passed forward through the crowd of people with words of sympathy and welcome. Lydia draped a kind, friendly, comforting arm around me and led me to the balustrade she'd occupied earlier.

'What a bastard. Forget him,' Lydia said. 'Everything will be better now you've left him, you'll see. You'll pick yourself back up and find a new way now you've found the strength to stand up for yourself.'

'He has to be a real asshole to bring you all this way and then do that,' claimed a bright, bubbly girl with blonde dreadlocks when Lydia told her my boyfriend had turned out to be an ass. She was another Aussie. In fact, they mostly seemed to be Aussies, like the hostel was a magnet for lost Aussie souls, although I seemed to be the only one truly lost.

'Thanks,' I said, taking deep breaths, waiting for the tears welling in my eyes to evaporate. It would take some getting used to, figuring out who I was without him, thinking of how I would move forward alone, it had all happened so suddenly it was a lot to comprehend. Six years with the same man was a long time. He's all I knew, we'd been together my entire adult life.

A few beers in and I couldn't believe the world I'd landed in. These people spoke of adventures and places that sounded too good to be true, surfing in places I'd never heard of, finding treasure in small European towns where no one spoke English, cycling along the coastline in remote villages, the sun kissing their skin, falling in love, eating incredible food. They laughed loud, they wore simple cotton summer dresses and crazy board shorts, the men with permanent five o'clock shadows, living in a world so far removed from my grey cubicle and suburban life back home that I could hardly comprehend any of it and now here they were, welcoming me into their fold, commiserating with me over beers as though we were old friends.

I leant on the balustrade, looking out over the dark road, slick and wet under the moon's bright rays now the clouds had moved on. Had I really stood out there on the footpath in the rain? Now I was dry and warm and comforted, sipping cold beer amongst the laughter and camaraderie, I couldn't believe that had been me. Who was that person? In fact, who was that person I'd become over the last six years? Not someone I recognised. Not someone I particularly liked and I hadn't even realised it was happening. Somewhere it'd just been easier to give me up and go with the flow, abide by everyone else's expectations, my boss, my mother, Billy. I didn't even know which bits were me and which were Billy. All I knew was Lydia was right. It was time to find out who I was.

'What's with all the thinking?' asked Lydia, twisting the top off another beer.

'Oh, nothing,' I half smiled. 'Just thinking how different the day's ended to how I'd expected.'

'Yeah, life does that,' she smiled.

'I've been here one bloody day and my life's been turned upside down. How does that even happen? This trip was not supposed to go this way.'

'Maybe it was and you just didn't realise it. The universe has a way of kicking us up the behind when we don't pay attention.'

I laughed a huffy laugh because she was probably right. 'It was easy to ignore it all.'

'Isn't it always,' she grinned. 'Until the kicking comes and you have no choice.'

'So, what are your plans from here?' a man asked, joining us at the balustrade.

I turned away from the rain soaked street, looked up and our eyes locked. It was him. My knight, my saviour who'd given me the pamphlet that had led me here. The waiter with the sun bleached shaggy hair, broad shoulders, wide smile and laughing grey green eyes that knew things, that loved things, that loved life. He wore a loose fitting, faded yellow tank top with bright, multi-coloured board shorts and blue thongs on his sun drenched feet.

The sun had soaked his body, from his biceps to his beautiful broad shoulders. I tried not to look but my eyes wanted to linger, to drink him in. Where did men that beautiful even come from? What was I even doing noticing? I was supposed to be crying into my beer not admiring handsome strangers that help damsels in distress find refuge. But for just one second, everything stood still and my breath caught in my chest.

'You?' I asked softly.

He smiled.

'You know each other?' Lydia asked.

I wanted to laugh, as if I know men that look like him. Billy was alright, handsome enough, a good catch even, so everyone kept telling me, but Billy had nothing on this bloke. This bloke was tall, slightly rugged, his strong jaw covered lightly in stubble, everything about him was strong, then there was his lovely mouth and puppy dog eyes that smiled without trying. I mentally shook my head clear to stop from staring.

'It was my restaurant she was at earlier,' he told Lydia. 'Well not mine,' he said to me, 'the one where I was working. Just filling in actually, not really my thing waiting tables, prefer pouring beers, but a mate needed a favour, they were short and needed a hand.'

'Well, thanks,' I said. 'I've no idea where I'd have gone without the pamphlet you gave me.'

'Oh a regular knight, huh,' joked Lydia.

'I'm Tom by the way,' he smiled, his whole face lighting up as though lit from the inside by his own personal sun. Then, his right bicep flexed beautifully as he stretched his arm around Lydia's shoulders, draping it there casually, as though he'd done it a thousand times. I felt my heart sink all the way down to my toes.

Don't be ridiculous, I told myself. Of course he has a girlfriend. What was wrong with me? What was wrong with my brain? I'd just left Billy, the supposed love of my life, the man I'd shared intimate moments with, cared for when he was sick, gone to birthday parties with, hosted barbeques with, told all my deepest secrets and wishes to, the man I'd expected a bloody proposal from under the Eiffel Tower. My head was still spinning with everything that had happened, where I'd ended up, what lay ahead. I couldn't fancy someone else already. My traumatised brain was just confused, that was all.

'Um, I'll see if I can get a flight home in the morning, I suppose,' I said, answering Tom's question

'Home? No!' cried Lydia. 'You're in Paris, Alex. You've only been here a day. You can't go yet. This is one of the most beautiful cities you'll ever see.'

I shrugged. She was right. But I was short on funds now I had a life to rebuild and really, no inclination to wander the streets alone.

'You know what you should do,' Tom said, looking at Lydia as though he'd solved the most intricate puzzles of the universe.

'Absolutely!' she cried, reading his mind.

I watched them, waiting for an explanation.

'Come down the coast with us, Alex. Oh you have to. It's just what you need, a bit of sun and sand, the ocean will heal all those wounds and you'll be good as new in no time. France is incredible, you can't miss out now that you're here. Please. Please say *oui*,' Lydia begged, gripping my arm in anticipation.

'What? No, no. We just met. You don't want me imposing on your trip,' I insisted, despite how nice the prospect of forgetting my life and laying on a beach in a foreign country sounded.

'Don't be ridiculous, the more the merrier. We'd love you to come with us. I promise, we're relatively normal, non murdering types, you have to come and balance out all the testosterone,' she insisted with a smile that left me both nervous and more excited than I could remember ever being.

'We have a car,' Tom added proudly.

'That's so nice, really it is but I don't think my failing funds will allow me to stay much longer than tonight anyway, I'm afraid. This was Billy's trip. He paid for the flights, the accommodation. I've just got a little spending money for bits and bobs, souvenirs, snacks, maybe a dinner or two, that sort of thing,' I admitted sadly.

'That doesn't matter,' Lydia said, waving my worries away. 'None of us have any money, but we get by, that's half the fun.'

'Really?' I couldn't believe it. They were all so happy. They didn't look hungry and the travel stories they'd shared in the last hour were so mind blowing they didn't even seem real; how could they all have no money? Living the life they lived cost money, surely? Billy and I had spent nights planning and budgeting for this trip. But what if all this time I'd had it backwards? 'But how?' I had to ask.

'Ah, you have to come for us to share all our secrets,' Lydia winked, laughing.

'C'mon, Alex, it'll be fun. You need some fun. We leave first thing tomorrow and it's just for a few days. It will cost next to nothing, I promise. We have a spare bed in the villa, and I am pretty sure it has your name on it,' Tom insisted.

'You can't go home yet, you have to come,' begged Lydia.

All the usual thoughts ran through my head again as though on repeat. Blah, blah, blah. What I really wanted to do was blow off my life and go to the bloody beach with this group of the coolest, most amazing people I'd ever met. To have the much needed fun Tom spoke of. To lay in the sun and pretend none of it had happened, that I hadn't been so humiliated I was afraid to look people in the eye. Forget it all and laugh. It'd been so long since I'd just let go and laughed, I'd forgotten what it felt like. These people were reminding me and I wasn't ready to let it go, to go back.

So, after taking a long sip of beer for courage, I ignored that annoying voice in my head, the one that had led me down this path in the first place. 'Fine, fine, okay, oui,' I agreed, panicking as soon as the words were out despite my newfound courage and resolution.

I couldn't drive to some French coast with these people. I'd just met them. It was crazy. Lydia was crazy. Tom was crazy. They were all crazy. But it did seem silly to waste the airfare Billy had paid for and they were right, I was in Paris, anything was possible in Paris, right? *To keep reading, buy your copy now at www.amazon.com*

If you loved The Life of Jo, I'd love to read your review.

If you'd like to read something else, here are my other titles, or you can head to my website www.tamaramartinauthor.com to join my newsletter or subscribe to my blog, My Favourite Things.

Also by Tamara Martin

Alexandra Deen – A Harrington Family Story
Mrs May's Tea and Toast – A Harrington Family Story
The Rise of Jaz – A Harrington Family Christmas
The Fall of Jaz – A Harrington Family Story

Almost Perfect – A Dystopian Love Story

Running From Me

About the Author

Writer, hiker, food lover, book nerd and TV addict, Tamara is a multi award nominated author fuelled by Doritos, chocolate sultanas and Barossa Valley Shiraz. Tamara lives in the Adelaide suburbs of South Australia and can often be found on her days off wandering the Barossa or McLaren Vale or eating noodles on Rundle Street. She loves to travel and many of the places She sees and the stories she collects end up somewhere in her novels. She loves John Hughes movies, Outlander, Thor and is a sucker for cheesy Christmas movies.

In 2018 her Novella, The Rise of Jaz – A Harrington Family Christmas, was nominated for a RuBY award and her novel, Almost Perfect – A Dystopian Love Story, was nominated for an ARRA award.

The Life of Jo is the fourth book in the Harrington series. You can find out all you need to know about Tamara, her books and any upcoming events at www.tamaramartinauthor.com.

www.ingramcontent.com/pod-product-compliance
Lightning Source LLC
Chambersburg PA
CBHW020659110726
47901CB00001B/246